JAN   2015

BET YOUR LIFE

BET YOUR LIFE

BET YOUR LIFE

JANE CASEY

ST. MARTIN'S GRIFFIN
New York

BET YOUR LIFE. Copyright © 2014 by Jane Casey. All rights reserved. Printed in the United States of America. For information, address St. Martin's Press, 175 Fifth Avenue, New York, N.Y. 10010.

www.stmartins.com

The Library of Congress Cataloging-in-Publication Data is available upon request.

ISBN 978-1-250-04066-4 (hardcover)
ISBN 978-1-4668-3626-6 (e-book)

St. Martin's Griffin books may be purchased for educational, business, or promotional use. For information on bulk purchases, please contact the Macmillan Corporate and Premium Sales Department at 1-800-221-7945, extension 5442, or write to specialmarkets@macmillan.com.

Originally published in Great Britain by Corgi Books, an imprint of Random House Children's Publishers UK, a Random House Company

First U.S. Edition: February 2015

10 9 8 7 6 5 4 3 2 1

For Emma Young, queen of the one-liner

It was like a nightmare.

The girl opened her eyes and looked at the ceiling. Just the ceiling. That was all she could see.

She lay completely still, because she couldn't do anything else. She couldn't sit up. She couldn't move her feet. She couldn't wiggle her fingers or her toes. She was completely paralyzed. Helpless.

Maybe it *was* a nightmare.

Or maybe she was in hospital. If there'd been an accident, and she'd been hurt, she could actually be paralyzed. Stuck like this forever. Locked in her own body. Communicating by blinking.

A tear slid down the side of her face, running into her hair. She didn't want to be paralyzed for life. And she couldn't remember an accident.

She couldn't remember anything.

Except . . . she remembered dancing, her hands over her

head, her body moving as the music filled her brain. She remembered the sudden silence when she'd locked herself in the bathroom, her heart still pounding as if she was running when she'd been standing completely still. She remembered seeing her own face reflected in the mirror, flushed and smudgy with smeared makeup. She remembered walking down the hall, or trying to, and bouncing off the walls.

And someone laughing at her.

Someone helping her.

Someone making her lie down on a bed. To rest. To recover. To sleep.

She had been sleeping. Maybe she just hadn't woken up properly yet.

The girl closed her eyes again, and thought about waking up. She willed herself to move. Nothing had ever been as difficult. She imagined sitting up, swinging her legs off the bed, walking to the door.

It was as impossible as flying to the moon.

She would raise her hand, she decided. That was enough of a challenge. Her brain sent the message to her right hand and she waited. And waited. And waited.

Not a twitch.

She couldn't even lift one finger.

She opened her eyes again.

The ceiling didn't look like a hospital ceiling. The room was dark but there was some light from the window. Even though she couldn't see much, she could see enough to know it was a bedroom in a house.

Not her bedroom. Not her house.

I want to go home.

She tried to say it, but all that came out of her mouth was a low moan.

And *something* moved in the corner of the room.

She would have screamed if she'd been able to. She would have jumped off the bed and run away.

All she could do was make the stupid moaning noise again.

"It's all right." His voice was deep and reassuring. "It's fine."

What's fine? Where am I? What's happened to me? Why can't I move?

None of those questions actually made it out of her mouth. This time, the sound she made was more of a whimper.

The bed dipped under his weight as he lay down beside her and ran a finger down her cheek.

"Go back to sleep, princess. It's not time to wake up yet."

Another tear slipped out of the corner of her eye and he caught it on his fingertip before it could reach her hair. He put his finger in his mouth and tasted it.

"Sweet."

She couldn't respond. His hand came down over her eyes and she closed them, obedient.

It wasn't time to wake up, that was all. She'd be fine when she *did* wake up.

"You won't remember any of this," he murmured tenderly. "Which is a shame."

Everything was receding. The fear was still there, but it was so far away. And her body was drifting off too, spinning away from her into star-dappled space. She let it go. She let everything go.

"*You* won't remember," he said again, and this time he sounded as if he was laughing. "But don't worry. I will."

It was the last thing she heard before she slipped away.

1

Most people go out for the night and expect to have fun. I hadn't counted on it, and I'd been right.

That was a very tiny consolation.

Surrounded by people laughing and joking and enjoying life, I felt like the saddest, loneliest person on earth. As if that wasn't enough to deal with, it was the coldest night of the year so far, and I had no coat. I wrapped my arms around myself and tried to stop my teeth from chattering as my breath misted in front of my face. Luckily, there was something to distract me. Just like everyone around me, I tilted my head back and stared at the sky. It was pure black, with more pinprick stars scattered across it than I had ever seen in light-polluted London. The sky was spectacular enough on its own, but when the first fireworks streaked up and flowered into brief glory, I almost forgot I was freezing.

Almost.

I had started out the night with a coat, obviously, because

a Halloween fireworks party meant a lot of standing around on Port Sentinel's muddy recreation ground, waiting for the fun to start. I'd worn my favorite coat of all time, my new but old coat, found in the backroom clutter of the charity shop where I worked part-time. Fine Feathers was wall-to-wall designer cast-offs, thanks to the rich, fashion-conscious residents of Port Sentinel, but this coat had no label, just a couple of threads that showed where one had been. Narrow across the shoulders and waist, it swirled out before it ended just below my knees. It was made from ultra-black woven tweed and had tiny black roses embroidered around the *inside* of the hem, as if it wanted to keep them a secret. It made me walk taller and I adored it. And when I had gone to retrieve it from the cloakroom after a good two hours of not-totally-ironic dancing at the disco in the recreation center, it had disappeared. Now the heat of dancing had completely worn off and my thin cotton dress was keeping out precisely none of the cold. I had tights on, and boots, but I was still shaking with cold.

A skinny black cat elbowed me in the ribs as she sashayed past, waving her tail, her ears set at a jaunty angle. I tried to work out if I knew her but she disappeared into the crowd before I could see her face, and there were a lot of cats at the party. I'd been in Port Sentinel for four months and it didn't surprise me that the local girls had gone for tight-fitting costumes, preferably with plenty of cleavage on display. Any excuse, quite frankly. Top choice: ghost, featuring pale-blue lipstick and ashy foundation, because ghosts apparently wore almost nothing—sheer dresses rather than the traditional white sheet. Second: vampire. Leather and red lipstick appealed to a certain kind of girl and, more importantly, a certain kind of boy. There were a lot of bitten necks on display along with the fireworks. Third: witches in short black dresses, high boots and fishnet tights. Port Sentinel was full of witches, in my experience, but they usually didn't bother with the costume. Finally, there were the pirates, a nod to Port Sentinel's smuggling past. These pirates wore tiny skirts, half-buttoned shirts, knee boots, and cheeky grins along with their eye patches. And all of them, but all of them, had got their coats before they came to stand outside.

It was notable—and typical—that if any of the boys were wearing a costume, they had made a token effort at best. I wasn't really in a position to criticize. I hadn't spent a huge amount of time on my own outfit. I'd only decided to go at the last minute, having resisted every effort my cousin Petra had made to persuade me.

"You don't understand. *Everybody* goes. It's always the Saturday closest to Halloween, which in this case is the first of November, and it's really the start of half-term. Everyone who's away at boarding school comes back, and all the holiday-home kids turn up. It's like summer all over again," she had said, sounding wistful. Almost fourteen, she was still too young to go to the over-sixteens disco, though she'd promised me she'd be there for the fireworks.

"Saying it's like summer is not the way to sell it to me," I'd pointed out.

"You know what I mean. It's not like nearly dying and everything," Petra said impatiently. "There's a buzz. It's fun. You see people you haven't seen for ages."

"That sounds great." I didn't manage to sound enthusiastic, because I wasn't. I was determined to keep my distance from anything that might remind me of the summer. The *everything*

7

Petra mentioned in passing had been a whole world of pain. Nearly dying had been the easy part.

Mind-reading as usual, my cousin Hugo looked up from his book and smirked. "Don't worry. He won't be there. Halloween parties and fireworks are not his thing."

He. Hugo meant his friend, my ex, Will Henderson. Will, who had been sent away to boarding school at the start of September, mainly because he'd been going out with me. I longed to see him and I hoped to avoid him. It was the sort of confused thinking that made my head hurt.

"I wouldn't have thought Halloween parties would have been your thing, either," I said.

The smirk had widened to a wicked grin. "I wouldn't miss it for anything."

Now that I was surrounded by so many scantily clad girls, I understood the appeal.

It occurred to me that I hadn't seen Hugo for a while, or Petra at all. I stopped watching the fireworks bloom and fade so that I could scan the crowd. Everyone was packed tightly together and I wasn't tall enough to see very far, what with all the rugby players and surfers who were standing shoulder to broad shoulder in front of me. I saw plenty of people I recognized, but no one I would call a friend. That wasn't altogether surprising. In any Port Sentinel gathering, I was likely to find more enemies than friends. It was no wonder I was looking forward to the following day, when one of my best friends from London was coming for a visit. I had missed Ella more than I'd even realized.

In the meantime, Hugo. I moved to my left, trying not to step on any toes, and worked my way toward the front. A skeleton swore in my ear as I moved past her. Her face was a glowing skull that floated against the dark night and I couldn't tell who she really was, but I was absolutely sure I should keep my distance from her. Skirting a kissing couple, looking back over my shoulder, I skidded on the slick mud and almost fell. I put a hand out to stop myself and grabbed the nearest thing, which turned out to be Ryan Denton's arm.

Oh no.

"Hey, Jess. How's it going?" Because of the fireworks exploding above our heads he said it loudly enough that the guys standing nearest to us heard, and turned, and I saw the same look spread across their faces: amusement and anticipation. I could have done without turning into a running joke, but I hadn't been given much of a choice about it.

"Sorry," I said. "I was just falling over. Thanks for lending me your arm."

"Any time. Hey!" I'd already started to walk away, but he caught hold of my wrist and pulled me back. "Don't go. Watch the fireworks with me."

"I'm looking for someone."

His eyebrows drew together. "Who?"

"Just Hugo."

"Oh." A smile, like the sun coming out from behind clouds. Cousin, not competition. "It'll be easier to find him when the fireworks are over."

He was right. Everyone was packed together on the recreation ground, kept a safe distance away from the pyrotechnics behind a semicircle of barriers. Once the display was over I would be able to move around without colliding with people.

"OK. Good idea."

"Come here," he said, and drew me toward him. A small gold dot shot into the sky and transformed itself into a huge shimmering orb that hung for a few seconds before fading. The light slanted across Ryan's face, highlighting the line of his cheek, the edge of his jaw, the full curve of his lower lip. It struck sparks in his sea-blue eyes. God, he was cute.

So off-limits it was untrue, but cute.

While I'd been gazing at him and his perfect mouth, he'd been checking out my costume. "I like the ringlets. What are you supposed to be?"

I looked down at the dress my aunt had dug out from the very back of her wardrobe. It was pale pink, short, and covered in tiny flowers, and she said she'd worn it in the nineties with a striped top underneath, woolly tights, big boots, and a man's cardigan. I was wearing cowboy boots (to cope with the mud) and a frilly apron. I'd have given quite a lot for a thick woolly cardigan at that moment, whether grunge was back in fashion or not. "Isn't it obvious? I'm Little Bo-Peep."

"No sheep, though."

I couldn't prevent myself from smiling. "Well, exactly."

"Oh yeah." He grinned back. "Not what I'd call a typical Halloween costume. It's not exactly spooky."

"I know." It wasn't all that surprising I'd resisted the chance to dress up as a ghoul or a ghost. I'd had a gutful of death during the previous summer. Mocking it didn't seem like a wise thing to do.

As for Ryan's costume, he looked exactly the same as usual. Hot.

"And what did you come as?" I asked, hoping he wasn't good at mind-reading.

"My identical twin."

"How is that spooky?"

He leaned down so that his face was inches from mine. "My identical twin is *evil*. He's capable of anything."

"Good to know."

"My identical twin thinks you look stunning tonight."

"Also good to know." *Playing it cool . . .*

"So do I."

I felt myself blushing, not because he was flirting with me but because I could see Ryan's friends grinning ever more widely. The flirting happened a lot, and I still found it hard to cope with.

"I thought you'd be looking for Will."

I jumped, surprised he'd mentioned Will's name. Once they'd been friends, then sworn enemies from the age of nine. Then I'd come to town and ended up as the prize in the latest competition, which Will had won. Ryan wasn't giving up, though. "No, I'm not looking for him."

"He's coming back this week, isn't he? Not spending half-term at his fancy new school."

"He's back," I said. "But I don't have any plans to see him."

Ryan raised his eyebrows. "Not planning to pick up where you left off?"

"That is where we left off. We broke up. Just before Will left." And I wasn't going to think about that painful little scene for a minute more than I had to. "What about you? Is Natasha coming back this week?"

It was his turn to look unsettled. "No. No way. She's on lockdown. No taking breaks from rehab."

Natasha, my arch-enemy and Ryan's psycho ex-girlfriend,

had been found out in a big way at the end of the summer, when I'd uncovered the truth about the part she played in my cousin Freya's death. Natasha's mother had shipped her off to an ultra-strict boarding school to get her under control. I wished her good luck, but I was pretty sure she wasn't going to change. She was as evil as they came, I thought.

"It's not rehab, though."

"In all but name."

I shrugged. "You'd know more about it than I do."

"Not really. I haven't been in touch with her."

"She's been in touch with you, I bet."

"She might have been. Jealous?" He sounded hopeful.

"Not even a little bit. Wow." I leaned out to look past him as the sky turned crimson, then jade-green, then ice-white. "That really is amazing."

Ryan glanced over his shoulder. "They always spend a fortune on the fireworks."

"I'd heard it was a big deal. How much longer is it going to be?"

"A few minutes."

My heart sank. My teeth were actually chattering. I wasn't sure I could make it to the end.

"Are you all right?" Ryan asked.

"F-freezing. I lost my coat."

"Come here. I'll keep you warm."

I should have said no, but I was too cold to argue. I moved a step closer to him and he turned me round to face away from him. He unzipped his down-filled jacket and drew me back so I was leaning against him, then wrapped the jacket around both of us and held me, his chin on my head. I felt the heat from his body spreading to mine, and it was as comforting as sitting by a log fire. The fireworks were winding up for a big finish, which helped me to ignore the stares we were getting. I knew it looked as if he'd succeeded in wearing me down, but I didn't care. Damage to my reputation was survivable. Hypothermia was, potentially, not.

They kept the best for last: a flurry of hundreds of gold stars that hung against the sky for what felt like forever, then faded to black. I sighed and then applauded along with everyone else, genuinely impressed.

The crowd started to come apart, drifting away in twos and threes to seek further entertainment, or a quiet corner for some alone time together, or the next party. Ryan still had his arms around my shoulders and didn't seem inclined to let go.

"I need to look for Hugo," I said, twisting so I could see his face.

"In a minute." He ran a hand into my hair and held onto it at the back of my neck.

"Hey," I said half-heartedly. "Let go."

"It's traditional to round off the fireworks with a kiss."

I leaned away from him as far as I could, which was not very. "I keep hearing about Port Sentinel's traditions but I've never heard that one."

"You're still new in town. Give it a year and you should be up to speed." He leaned toward me and I did a quick calculation: was it more embarrassing to make a fuss or to allow it to happen?

"Jess!"

Saved. I wriggled free as soon as Ryan's grip loosened. Hugo was coming toward us.

"Where have you been?"

"I was going to ask you the same thing." Hugo had an odd expression on his face, I noted, and could guess why. My cousin was not a Ryan fan. You didn't have to be particularly sensitive to spot that, and Ryan was actually quite good at reading other people's reactions. He let go of me completely and nodded to Hugo.

"Glad you found each other."

"Ryan!" The shout came from across the recreation ground, where a figure stood, arms outstretched. A knot of people was milling around him but he was very definitely the center of attention. He was instantly recognizable, even to me, as Harry Knowles. His hair stood straight up from his head, adding an extra six or so inches to his already quite impressive height. "Are you coming or not?"

"In a minute," Ryan yelled back.

"Don't miss out, man. It's going to be big." He picked up a small witch and threw her over his shoulder, spinning around as she shrieked with laughter.

"I'll be there." Turning to me, Ryan said, "There's a party at Harry's house tonight. Come along if you can."

"I don't know Harry." I meant personally. Everyone in Port Sentinel knew who Harry was: the wild son of a genius city trader who had made his first million of the day before breakfast, every day, until the day he'd burned out. He'd quit, taken his money, and fled to Devon. Even in a town full of rich kids, Harry was renowned for being loaded, and spoiled rotten. He was a founding member of Ryan's group of friends, who were essentially the prettiest and richest teenagers around. And all this could have been mine as well, if I'd been prepared to indulge Ryan and go out with him.

"You don't need to know Harry. You know me." Ryan grinned down at me, ignoring Hugo. "Anyway, if you change your mind, let me know. Harry's folks are in Venezuela for half-term. He's aiming for a party a night."

"I'll keep it in mind."

Ryan's eyes narrowed a fraction, registering that I hadn't said yes. "It would be fun. You don't want to miss out."

"Definitely not. Thanks for asking me."

"Good luck with finding your coat," Ryan said, and then, as I was just about to reply, dropped a kiss on my mouth. My lips were parted and it was startlingly intimate, even if it was quick. I stared after him as he walked away, my mouth tingling. When Hugo spoke, I jumped. I had completely forgotten he was there.

"What were you doing with him?"

"Nothing. Keeping warm." I rubbed my arms, trying to generate some heat. "Have you seen my coat?"

He unwound his scarf and handed it to me. "Never mind about your coat."

"I do mind. Obviously. But thanks." I wrapped the scarf around my neck, watching him curiously. "Where were you during the show, anyway?"

For Hugo, he was oddly slow to respond. "Looking for you. Then looking *at* you."

"How fascinating for you. I'm surprised I was enough to distract you from the fireworks. You can stare at me anytime."

"*I* can. Will can't."

I was knotting the scarf but I stopped dead. "What did you say?"

"Will can't." Two syllables. Perfect enunciation. Nothing confusing about it. Except . . .

"He was here?" My voice was very small.

"Yeah."

"And he saw me."

"With Ryan."

"Where is he?"

"He just left."

"Just now?"

"A minute ago." After Ryan had kissed me. He didn't have to say it. I knew.

"Which way did he go? Hugo!" I grabbed his arm and held onto it. "Tell me."

"When he got to the gate he turned left, so into town, I assume." He dragged himself free. "I wouldn't bother, Jess. Leave it for now. You can explain the next time you see him."

He was talking to cold, thin air. I was already sprinting for the gate. I dodged through the stragglers who were leaving, the mud clinging to my boots as I ran. I cut between two cars and snagged my tights on the front wing of one of them, where an accident had left it buckled and bent. I lost valuable seconds freeing myself, but once I hit the road I was able to go faster and I flew down the hill in the direction Hugo had indicated, keeping to the center of the streets because the pavements were wonky and narrow, and I would definitely, certainly trip. I liked my front teeth enough to want to keep them intact, but I wasn't going to slow down until I had to.

There was no sign of Will down any side street or round

any corner—just little groups of costumed revellers and the occasional pumpkin grinning in a window or on a doorstep, eyes flickering as the candle inside guttered. I took a chance on him heading for the city center and did likewise, hoping I'd find him there, or near where I lived. His house backed on to my family's home, Sandhayes, so if I headed in that general direction I had a chance of finding him.

What I would say when and if I did find him was another question.

It was a long way to the center of town from the recreation ground and I started to feel it in my legs just around the time a wicked stitch skewered my side. I slowed and then stopped, my breathing ragged, one hand gripping my waist where the pain was worst. The chill in the air was nothing to the cold horror that was sending shivers over my skin.

Will had been there.

Will had seen me with Ryan.

Will had seen Ryan kiss me.

Will would have the wrong idea.

Will might even care.

The very thought jolted me back into action. I moved forward at a pace that was a long way from a sprint, limping and wincing, so wrapped up in my own misery that I turned down a narrow lane and saw a flashing blue light irradiating the side of some buildings in the distance and didn't even think that it might be something to concern me. I was closer to it when I started to hear the radio squawking, and another joining it, and a low throaty roar that was an engine turning over. I hurried round the corner into St. Laurence Square, a tiny paved space in the heart of town in front of an old church. There was an oak tree in the center with a bench circling its trunk. In the summer it was a nice place to sit. Now, on a cold dark autumn night, the tree was shedding leaves with every breath of wind. An ambulance was parked beside it. Beside that, there were two police cars. Beside that, another car I recognized. It had a blue light on the top that swung and swirled and caught me in the eyes, but not before I'd noticed the figure on the ground, under a blanket, and the spreading pool of blood around his head. He was young, my age or so, and his face was battered beyond recognition. I stared for a long, horrified moment—short dark hair, and he'd be tall if he was standing—before a paramedic knelt down beside him and blocked my view. I went forward on wobbling legs, really, truly terrified that, somehow, it was Will who was lying on the paving slabs. As I edged sideways to see him, the boy on the ground moaned, and I felt a sting of relief as I realized it wasn't Will. I felt guilty for being glad.

Two policemen in uniform were crouching by a drain, trying to reach something that had been dropped in it, while another unrolled blue-and-white tape to cordon off the crime scene. I stood, unobserved for the moment. I couldn't take my eyes off the boy on the ground.

"It's all right," one of the paramedics said, holding his head steady while the other one prepared to put a neck brace on him. "Don't worry, mate. We'll look after you."

The boy groaned again and lifted a hand, as if he meant to push them away. His wrist was ringed with a red mark that was bleeding a little where the skin had been rubbed away. One of the paramedics gently pushed his arm back down by his side. The effort seemed to have exhausted the boy and he lay completely still while they treated him. If I hadn't seen him move and heard him moan, I'd have thought he was dead. His skin was bleached white where it wasn't marked with purple bruises or streaked with darkening blood.

The paramedics were talking in low voices, scrawling notes on the backs of their gloves as they assessed him. They were obviously worried about his condition and in a hurry to get him into the ambulance. I made myself concentrate on his face and realized, with a shiver, that under the blood, despite the swelling around his eyes and mouth, I recognized him. I had met him before.

The next minute I jumped out of my skin as someone grabbed my arm and held onto it, tightly enough to hurt.

2

"What are you doing here?"

The voice didn't sound friendly, which wasn't a surprise, since it belonged to Dan Henderson, Port Sentinel's police inspector.

Will's dad.

Not my biggest fan.

"I was just—" *Looking for Will.* The truth, but I couldn't say it. It would be like throwing petrol on a bonfire. "Can you let go of me, please?"

"Not until you tell me why you're here."

"I was walking home from the fireworks. I took a short cut this way."

"On your own?" Dan frowned at me. His hand was still on my arm but his grip loosened a little. "What happened to your friends?"

"I don't know." *Mind your own business.*

"Did you see anyone you know at the fireworks?"

"Lots of people." I knew where this was going.

"Did you see Will?"

I shook my head.

"Sure?"

"Of course I'm sure." I tried to pull my arm back and he held onto it for a second longer, his thumb stroking my skin, very lightly. Dan wasn't stupid. He was standing between me and everyone else who was there so they couldn't have seen it. I felt like throwing up.

"You're going to be a good girl, aren't you, Jess? You're going to leave him alone."

"We've had this conversation before," I said, and used my other hand to peel his fingers off me. "I don't think we need to have it again."

"As long as you understand I won't tolerate any sneaking around." His eyes were bright with malice. He was enjoying this. "You know I'd find out. You know what would happen, and you know how that would make Will feel. If you really care about him—"

"What if I *don't* really care? What if I keep my distance from him because the whole thing bores me to tears?" I glared at him. "You're the one who's made this into a big deal. Just because you've spent years pining for my mother, you seem to think the two of us are head over heels in love. Newsflash: we're not. There are plenty of boys who don't come with so much drama."

"I thought that was part of the attraction."

"Not for me."

The corner of his mouth lifted and it was a cruel reminder of something Will did, a trick he had of almost smiling when he was just about to kiss me. A tiny shudder went through me.

"Cold?"

"A bit." I stepped back, wanting some more air between us. "What happened to him?"

"What happened to who?"

"That guy on the ground—"

"Is going to hospital."

"Did someone hit him?"

"So it seems."

"Why?"

He gritted his teeth. "I don't know. We'll look into it. I can't spend any more time on you tonight, Jess. Get going. Go on. Go home. Quick as you like." He was crowding me, his arms stretched out, herding me toward the narrow lane I'd walked down.

I was walking backward as slowly as I dared, leaning to see round Dan's bulk. He was wearing a big high-visibility jacket, neon yellow with POLICE on the front and back, as if he could be anything else. The light from the ambulance headlights flared on it as the paramedics turned their vehicle, now fully loaded, and headed away. "Is he going to be OK?"

"I don't know. I'm not a doctor." Massive disapproval from Dan; he hated me asking questions. His eyes were dark gray, and even in the orange glare of the streetlights I could see they were as hard as flint. "I could do without it, tonight of all nights. We've got enough trouble with Halloween mischief without having to deal with a mystery. And we don't even know who he is."

"I do," I said. "His name is Sebastian Dawson."

"Jim Dawson's son? From West Hill Road?" Dan reached into his coat for a notebook and started scribbling.

"I think so. I know him from school. I think he lives around West Hill Road, though, now that you mention it. But didn't he have ID on him? Or a phone?"

I thought he was going to answer me, but instead he sighed. "I'll say it again. Go. Home. Or do you want me to drive you?"

The last time I'd been in a car with Dan Henderson alone, I'd been seriously worried for my safety. It was among the top five experiences I wanted never to repeat. "No need. I'm going."

I turned and walked off, feeling his eyes on me as I headed down the street. Chips of broken glass crunched under my boots and I tacked sideways to avoid the worst of it. I was almost out of range when he called after me.

"Jess."

I turned.

"You remind me of your mother in that dress."

Yuck. "It's Tilly's, actually."

"It looks good on you. But you should have a coat."

I didn't answer him, but I thought my response loudly enough that he could probably have heard it if he'd been listening.

No shit, Sherlock.

I trudged on toward home, still looking for Will but knowing he was long gone. Laughter and singing hung on the night air as Halloween parties started to get underway in earnest. The fireworks were just the curtain-raiser. I didn't regret turning down Ryan's invitation to Harry Knowles's house, but I did wish I had somewhere to be, among friends. As I walked down a narrow street with darkened houses on either side, a loud scream made me flinch. A girl reeled out of an alley on my right, her eyes staring. Her dress clung to her body because it was soaked in blood. Her hair hung in rat-tails around her blood-streaked face and she reached out to me with hands that were like claws, whispering, "*Please . . .*"

I would have screamed myself, but terror made me mute. I stood still, unable to move. The girl dropped her hands to her sides. Her voice was flat when she spoke.

"If I'd known it was you, I wouldn't have bothered."

Imogen Hinch, Immy to her friends, of whom I was not one. I recognized her at the same time as I realized the blood was fake. I felt my heart begin to slow down from all-out gallop to a more sustainable canter. Shock made me angry and I snapped, "What was *that*?"

"Just a bit of fun." She reached up a languid hand and rearranged her hair. "Not that I would expect you to recognize it."

"What's fun about pretending you've been attacked?"

"It makes people scream." Another girl emerged from the darkness, tall and gangling in a black onesie with bones printed on it. Her face was painted chalk-white and she had drawn black circles around her eyes, a black triangle on her nose and vertical lines across her lips. It was the skull-face from earlier, I realized, and now it made perfect sense that she'd threatened me. Claudia Carmichael was still loyal to Natasha Watkins, her best friend, the once-upon-a-time princess of the social scene. She was viewing what she'd filmed on her phone. "You were rubbish. Not even funny."

"Sorry to disappoint you, Claudia."

"Well, we're not surprised. You spoil everything." She came and stood beside Immy, the two of them effectively blocking my path.

"This again," I said softly. "You still blame me. I didn't make anyone behave the way they did. I wasn't even here when it happened. And Natasha—"

"Don't talk about her. She didn't deserve what you did. Or the consequences."

"All I did was find out the truth. She thought she'd got away with what she did. She bullied Freya and set her friends on her and Freya died. I just made sure Natasha had to take responsibility for it. Most people think she got off lightly," I said.

"Most people don't matter." Claudia leaned in. "You don't matter. And Natasha will be back."

"Bigger and badder than ever." I sighed. "OK. Fine. I'll look forward to it. Now can I go?"

"I wish you would," Immy said. She watched a group of girls walk past on the other side of the street. They were giggly and a little bit drunk, and Immy's face was sullen as she stared at them. "They would have been perfect."

"Too bad." I made as if to walk off, but Claudia put out her hand to stop me.

"Natasha asks about you and Ryan, you know, every time we speak. What should I tell her?"

"Tell her to get over it."

"Are you with him or not?" Claudia demanded. "I saw you at the fireworks."

"Everyone saw you at the fireworks." Immy smoothed her hair again. "Next time, get a room."

"It's not like that."

"I saw exactly what it's like. Natasha is going to freak out." From the way Immy said it, she was looking forward to telling her.

"I'm not interested in him." Their faces didn't change. Why was I wasting my time?

Because I was annoyed beyond belief that no one could accept that I didn't fancy Ryan. Because it would make my life a little bit easier if Natasha wasn't trying to take revenge on me for something I hadn't even done. Because I was sick and tired of being a punch line.

"Look, Ryan's just not my type."

"Are you saying he's not good enough for you?" Claudia demanded.

But he's good enough for Natasha . . . I avoided the trap without too much difficulty. "No, I'm not. I'm saying I don't want to go out with him. And I've said it to him too. He just doesn't like that I turned him down."

"Why was that?" Immy's eyes narrowed. "Did you have a better offer?"

I had to be tired, because suddenly I was blinking tears away. "No. Look, I don't want trouble. I just want to go home."

"Home as in London?" Claudia suggested.

"Home as in up the hill. That's where I live now. And you'd better get used to it because I'm not leaving." *For the moment.* I was relieved that there wasn't a wobble in my voice this time. I sounded as if I was in control. I sounded tough. "Are you going to get out of my way or what?"

They didn't move off the pavement, but I was able to squeeze past Claudia without her attempting to stop me. I walked away at a steady pace, not hurrying, even though I felt the back of my neck tingle until I was out of range.

"Don't get cold," Immy called after me, which I ignored.

One of them said something to the other in a low voice, too quietly for me to catch, but I definitely heard the cackle that followed. I was meant to.

And I had two suspects for the theft of my coat.

As I walked up the steep road to Sandhayes, I distracted myself by wondering what had happened to Seb Dawson. He was the only person I'd encountered who seemed to be having a worse time than me. At least I was finishing up my evening in the ramshackle, sprawling Victorian villa that was my family home rather than the hospital.

The house was dark when I got back, except for the candles in the pair of leering pumpkins in the porch. I had forgotten to get keys from Hugo, I realized, and my own had been in my coat pocket. I stretched up to run my hand along the lintel, hoping no one had borrowed the spare key and finding, for a few heart-stopping seconds, nothing but dust, until my panicky pawing dislodged it. It bounced on the ground and spun away into the shadows. I rolled my eyes. It was just not my night. I borrowed a candle from one of the pumpkins and hunted around the porch until I saw the metal gleam. At least I'd found one of the things I'd been looking for.

In the hall, Hugo's coat wasn't on its hook and neither was Petra's. I was glad they were still having fun somewhere. Hopefully together. It wasn't a night to be alone.

I shivered my way down to the kitchen, where a small lamp was still on. The room was full of shadows and I stopped for a second, feeling as if there was someone else there. But that was pure paranoia. Or even wishful thinking, I thought, skirting the chair where Will usually sat. It was askew, as if he had been here tonight. And if he *had* been here, I had missed him. And now he might never come back.

I cut off that line of thinking before I collapsed into a tiny heap on the floor. My aunt's big fringed paisley shawl hung on the back of one of the chairs and I wrapped it around me, feeling as if I would never be warm again. I put on the overhead light and hummed to myself as I made tea, pretending to be brisk and cheerful when I was actually hollowed out from heartbreak. The pretense was a crowd-pleasing trick I'd learned in September, when my mother had threatened to take me back to London. She had been worried about the not-speaking, not-eating, not-sleeping version of me—all that was left when Will went away. And she'd been there herself, in her time. She knew how it felt. Her own solution had been to run away. Mine was to stay and tough it out. Pretend everything was fine, until it actually was. And I had thought it was working. I'd thought I was getting over him.

I hadn't even seen him, but knowing he was back made my hands shake.

I flicked off the lights and carried the steaming mug of tea back through the silent house, up the stairs to the attic, feeling my mood lift just a little as I climbed higher and higher. No matter what, I always felt a little thrill of pleasure when I walked into my bedroom. I had inherited it—sloping ceiling, window seat, bookshelves and all—from my dead cousin Freya. In the months since I'd been living in Port Sentinel, I had gradually changed things, moving the desk and swapping some of

Freya's art for band posters. Her books had mostly made way for mine, though I still kept them stacked in neat piles. I was aware that Freya was still a part of the family, much missed, and I didn't want to lose her, either. I'd never known her but I felt as if I had.

The other thing that I had inherited from Freya, I thought, settling on the window seat to drink my tea, was a big problem in the shape of Will Henderson. Freya had liked him too. More than liked him. And it had done her no good whatsoever.

I'd left the light off, not needing anything except moonlight to see the way. The dormer window gave me a perfect view down the garden, and as the leaves had started to fall I could see more of Will's house. A light was on in an upstairs room, shining steadily in the darkness. I didn't know if it was Will's room or not; I'd never been upstairs in his house. Upstairs was where his mother lay suffering. Dying, in point of fact, though no one knew how long it would be before that happened. Not long, by all accounts. I shook my head slowly. I couldn't just find someone without issues. I had to pick the guy whose heart was breaking over something he couldn't change.

Even as I watched, the light went out. I pulled the shawl down over my knees and sipped my tea, feeling miserable. From the moment I'd met Will I'd known he was trouble, and I'd been moderately successful at keeping my distance—until the warm summer afternoon when he kissed me for the first time. I'd fallen, hard and fast, totally in love. I knew it was going to be complicated, given that his father and my mother had history with a capital H. But for the first couple of weeks, it was as close to perfect as you could get.

We kept it a secret, or thought we had—sneaking out to meet at the end of the garden where the tangle of trees and shrubs meant we weren't overlooked. Will was a regular visitor to Sandhayes, a friend of Hugo's since forever. Because of his mother's illness, my aunt Tilly liked to look after him. He came for meals, sitting across the table from me, setting my blood on fire every time he glanced in my direction with those silver-gray eyes that were anything but cold. He had kissed me in the dusty back room of the charity shop where I worked, while I protested (not very much) about having to get back to the till. He'd kissed me in the garden with leaves glowing green overhead and birds singing love songs in the branches above us. And he'd kissed me in the very room where I was sitting. I put my head down on my knees and sighed. I didn't want to think about it, but somehow I couldn't stop myself from playing it back.

I hear quick footsteps on the stairs, and Will calling to Hugo, telling him to go ahead without him. Hugo's voice is raised in complaint and Will tells him to stop shouting because he'll only be a minute. I go to the door, and when I open it he's there. As he walks in he puts his finger on my mouth to stop me from saying anything. He kicks the door shut behind him with his heel, then pushes me against the wall. His breathing is fast and my heart is racing. His mouth is on mine, his hands tangled in my hair. I am deaf and blind to everything except him. When he breaks off and stands back, still breathing hard, I am dazed. His eyes are locked on mine, telling me beyond any doubt how he feels about me, and what he would do if we had longer than a single stolen minute. I reach for him and he kisses me again, twice, quickly, and then he leaves me without looking at me, without saying a word. I hear him running down the stairs, flight after flight, all the way to the hall. I'm still standing in the same place, one hand to my mouth, when I hear the front door bang.

My lips feel bruised for hours afterward. Days.

I have never been happier in my entire life.

I came back to the present with another sigh, and turned to look at the door where Will had kicked it. A black scuffmark was my constant reminder of what I had had, and what I had lost. As if I needed a reminder, frankly. I remembered every kiss. My body remembered every touch. Two months, and I still ached for him.

So, basically, one minute, everything was amazing. The next, it was over. It was like dropping a crystal vase on a hard floor. Instant, total devastation.

And I was the one who'd made it happen. I'd broken up with him for the best of reasons.

It didn't make it any easier to bear.

I unfolded myself, stiff from sitting for so long in one position, and got ready for bed, still without putting on a light. It felt right to be in the dark. Once I was tucked up, snug in flannel pajamas and socks and with an extra blanket on top of the duvet, I started to feel warmer. Not better. Just warmer.

I lay for a while thinking about Sebastian Dawson, more to distract myself from worrying about Will than for any other reason. Seb was the living definition of tall, dark, and handsome. Blue eyes, black hair, cheekbones that could cut glass.

He was almost too good-looking, I had always thought. And he had plenty of arrogance to go with it. We went to the same school but he'd never bothered to speak to me. To be strictly accurate, I'd never bothered to speak to him, either. I wondered if I'd really seen what I thought I had seen—the marks on his wrist and the bruises like shadows on his skin. Dan was right: I should keep out of it. But I thought about it all the same, until I glanced at the clock on my bedside table and realized how late it was.

I turned over, got comfortable, and completely failed to go to sleep.

3

"W hat happened to you last night?" Hugo demanded, his mouth full.

"I was about to ask you the same thing." I shuffled across the kitchen like a zombie questing for brains, arms outstretched. Tiredness meant I was running off my primordial brain. It could only cope with the basic necessities of life. At the moment, what I needed was heat, food, and caffeine. The ancient Aga had made the kitchen tropical when the rest of the house was definitely Arctic Circle territory. And by a lucky coincidence, it was also where I could get a bacon sandwich and a cup of tea.

"A cure for all that ails you." My uncle Jack grinned as he slid two rashers onto a plate and pushed it toward me. He was wearing an oversized apron that could have wrapped twice around his lanky frame. "Did you have a good time, Jess?"

"The fireworks were pretty." *And that is all I can say for the evening . . .* "I didn't know it was such a big deal."

"Always," Jack said. "It's going to be a big week. Lots of people in town for half-term. There's something on every night. Then the big display on Bonfire Night."

"What happens then?"

"Boats."

It took me a second to realize that Hugo's little brother, Tom, had answered me. I waited for him to go on, but he'd relapsed into his usual silence and was shoveling cereal into his mouth with the grace and finesse of a digger. I turned to Jack. "What about boats?"

"Everyone who has a boat sails into the bay after dark, and at a given time they all light a torch."

"He means the old-fashioned kind. A flaming brand," Hugo said. "Stupidly dangerous things."

"They make them by wrapping wooden batons in rags and dipping them in tar. You've probably seen them down on the quay."

"Oh, that's what those are!" I had seen them stacked up, the ends sticky and black. "But there are hundreds of them."

"There'll be hundreds of boats too. It's pretty spectacular," Jack said. "And everyone on shore starts their bonfires in response. There's a total blackout in town—even the streetlamps are switched off, so the only light is from the bonfires. The whole bay and the hills around it are lit up. They've been doing it for centuries."

"It sounds like something Ella would love. I really want her to see Port Sentinel at its best."

"I prefer spring." Jack scraped at the frying pan.

"I can't wait that long."

"Missing her?" he asked.

"Just a bit."

"You've done well with settling in, Jess. Anyone would think you'd lived in Port Sentinel forever."

"I'm not so sure."

"Well, we're happy to have you." Jack was concentrating on the cooking, but I knew he meant it. "And Ella, if it comes to that. What time is she arriving?"

"I think her train gets in at three."

"Damn. I can't go and get her, I'm afraid. I've got a meeting." Jack looked past me. "Hugo—"

"Nope."

"Please."

"I have a life too. Just because I have a driving license and a car, I don't see why I should be a free taxi service."

"First of all," I said, "I'm not sure that thing qualifies as a car. Secondly, Ella is lovely. You'll be glad you helped."

Hugo snorted. "You insult Miss Lemon and expect me to drive you anyway? I don't think so."

Miss Lemon was a yellow Fiat and the current love of Hugo's life. I dug my phone out of my pocket and found a holiday picture of Ella in sunglasses and a strappy top, all glossy dark hair and a big smile. Holding it up, I said, "Want to change your mind?"

"Show me?" He snatched it and peered at the picture. "What did you say her name was?"

"El"—I paused—"la. Two syllables. Not difficult."

"Boyfriend?"

"Not presently."

"Personality disorders?"

"You're in luck. She doesn't mind them."

"Funny." Hugo shrugged. "I'm not doing anything else."

"Excellent." Now as long as he didn't freak Ella out completely, we'd be fine.

I sat down between Hugo and Tom, who had propped a book against the milk jug. He was leaning forward so he could scoop cereal into his mouth without even looking, his head practically in his bowl. Hugo, long-limbed like his father, stretched to grab a carton of milk off the counter and dumped it in front of me.

"Don't even bother trying to get the jug. He'll fight you for it."

"Thanks." I poured treacle-colored tea into my cup. I needed something more like rocket fuel.

Hugo stole half the bacon from my plate to make another sandwich for himself. "So did you find him?"

I didn't need to ask who he meant. "No, and that was my food."

"You must have just missed him by a couple of minutes. Shame." He took a massive mouthful and said, through it, "Dad'll do you another one."

My appetite had taken a nosedive. I flapped a hand at him. "Never mind."

"You've got to eat."

"I *am* eating." I nibbled some toast, which was dry and had all the gourmet appeal of loft insulation. "Did he say anything? About me?"

Before Hugo could answer, my mother raced into the kitchen. I glared at him, hoping he'd get the message that I didn't want him to say anything in front of her. He chewed his sandwich and stared back inscrutably.

"Morning." Mum grabbed a banana and started peeling it. "I'm late. How was last night? What time did you get back, Jess? I hope it wasn't too late."

"Around eleven." I appreciated the effort at being a disciplinarian, but I could have got back at four and Mum would have been none the wiser. Dad had always been the one who enforced rules in our family, until he became preoccupied with his midlife crisis, their divorce, and his stream of increasingly youthful girlfriends. I was used to bringing myself up, pretty much.

"Do I look all right? Professional, I mean. But arty." Mum worked in a gallery on the main street in Port Sentinel. She took it very seriously and, as far as I knew, had yet to make a single sale.

I scanned her. Long dark hair in a ponytail, gray jumper, narrow black trousers, boots. "You need something else. A necklace or something."

"I don't have time." She smudged lip gloss on with her finger. "I'm late. The gallery opens in ten minutes. Or at least, it's supposed to. I've got the keys. I'm supposed to be in charge. Nick should never have trusted me to be there." She was on the verge of tears. "I'd drive but there's nowhere to leave the car."

"Hugo can take you," Jack said.

"It's the thin end of the wedge," he said darkly. "I knew it would be a mistake to say yes once." He stood up, though. Despite the cynicism, Hugo was a soft touch. To me, he said, "Did you hear what happened to Seb Dawson?"

"Yeah." I decided not to tell him how I knew. "Is he OK?"

Hugo shrugged. "Do you care? I don't."

"You can't say that." I had a sudden vivid memory of Seb's blood on the pavement and felt sick.

"He's an idiot."

"He's one of Ryan's friends." I said it without thinking and Hugo's eyebrows shot up.

"So if he's one of Ryan's friends you're worried about him, is that it?"

"No. Obviously not."

"Hugo, I've got to go," Mum said. "Do you mind?"

"Let's do it." He followed her out of the kitchen, putting his head back in with a parting shot. "By the way, Jess, Petra found your coat."

My joy at getting my coat back was short-lived. What Hugo hadn't said was that Petra had found it in a muddy ditch. It was saturated, and reeked of stagnant water, and every inch of it was filthy. Petra had hung it over the bath and it was still seeping, hours later.

"I'm sorry." She was sitting on the floor of the bathroom, staring up at it with huge, woebegone eyes.

I opened the window before I sat down beside her to let out the ditch smell. "Why are you sorry? You rescued it."

"I'm not sure it's going to recover."

"Me neither," I sighed. "Annoying."

"It's more than annoying. Who do you think did it? One of Natasha's friends?"

"Doesn't matter," I said easily. "Someone's idea of a joke, probably. I'll get the coat cleaned once it's dried out. And if it doesn't survive, I'll buy another one."

"You'll never get one like it."

"I'll find something. Have you seen Fine Feathers recently? We've got more stock than space."

"Yeah, but that was a one-off. You could try on every coat in the shop and not find one that fitted you as well as this coat. It was made for you."

"It's a tragedy," I agreed.

"Aren't you upset?"

I was livid, but I shrugged. "It's stupid. Pathetic. At least I got the coat back, though. And that's thanks to you."

She had carried it all the way from the recreation ground, heavy and dripping though it was. I'd almost have been tempted to leave it in the ditch, myself.

"It was nothing."

"I don't think that."

She gave me a faint smile, but she still looked troubled. I sat down on the floor beside her and put my arm around her shoulders.

"What's wrong?"

"Beth's brother."

I frowned, trying to remember if I'd known that Petra's best friend even had a brother. "What about him? Did he say something to you? Do you want me to have a word with him?"

"No. Nothing like that. He's in hospital."

"What happened?"

"I don't know. Beth called me this morning. She was so upset, I couldn't really understand what she was saying. She said he'd been run over."

"Wait. What's Beth's brother called?"

"Sebastian."

"Seb Dawson?"

"Yeah."

I leaned back against the wall. "I would never have guessed that in a million years. They don't look anything like one another." Beth was small and wore thick glasses that overwhelmed her face. She had the sweetest smile, but it was nothing like her brother's wide grin.

"Different mothers. Sebastian's mum is French."

Port Sentinel seemed to specialize in complicated families. Wealthy people weren't any better at being happy than ordinary ones, it transpired.

"That sort of makes sense. Seb looks French."

"And Beth doesn't. Seb used to live with his mum, until he was sixteen. She moved to the south of France and Seb moved back in with his dad. Beth and her mum hadn't even met him until then because Seb's mum had wanted him to stay away from his dad's new family. Imagine how awkward that must have been."

"Horrendous," I agreed.

"Beth said Seb's mum is coming over." The tears brimmed in Petra's eyes. "It must be serious, mustn't it? If she's coming all the way from France?"

"Well, she's his mum. I'd want my mum if I was in hospital."

Petra's voice was a whisper. "Beth asked me what it was like. After Freya."

After Freya died, she meant. I squeezed her shoulders, wishing I could think of something comforting to say. Grief sucked. That didn't quite cut it.

"Which hospital is he in?"

"The big one in Exeter."

Which meant it was serious. "They'll look after him," I said, hoping it was consoling.

"They said . . . last night—" Petra gulped. "They said his head was split open. They said his *brains* were all over the pavement."

"Who said that?"

"Everyone."

"Well, *everyone* obviously didn't see him. I did. And there were no brains on the pavement, I promise you."

"You saw him?"

"On my way home. They were just putting him in the ambulance."

"How did he look?"

"A bit battered," I admitted. No point in going into the grisly details, even if they weren't anything like as bad as what she'd heard already. "He'll be OK, Petra."

"I hope so."

"Try not to worry. There's nothing you can do except wait. And be there for Beth when she needs you."

Petra nodded and blew her nose. "I'm all right."

"Come and help me sort out Ella's room. I've got to make the bed and I think it needs dusting. The last time I was in there a giant cobweb attacked me. The spider must have been the size of my head."

"Which room is it? The one at the top?"

"The one with the sea view." We grinned at each other. The sea view was a longstanding family joke. When the house was built, Port Sentinel had been more or less undeveloped and the whole bay had been visible. Now, a tiny gap between houses was all that was left. It amounted to two inches of water that you could only really pick out on a bright sunny day, when it glittered. Still, it counted, and it was the only bedroom apart from mine on the top floor. I thought Ella would love it.

I was wrestling with the duvet and Petra was running a duster over the windowsill when Tilly came in. She had a vase of branches from the garden that looked like the work of a super-expensive florist. Typical Tilly to be able to make something out of nothing, but then she was a real, proper artist, painting portraits of animals that sold for mouthwatering amounts. I'd inherited my father's logical mind rather than the Leonard flair for art, and it was that more than anything else that made me feel like an outsider, three months on from arriving in Port Sentinel.

"I thought your friend might like these."

"She'll love them," I said truthfully.

"Petra, Beth is downstairs. I didn't like to ask, but is everything OK?"

"Nope." Petra dropped the duster and ran, leaving me to fill in the details for Tilly.

Her forehead wrinkled. "Oh, the poor darling. I must go and make something for them. Stew, or something they can reheat. Vegetarian lasagne." She wandered out of the room, on a mission. "Moussaka . . ." floated back from the landing.

Tilly just loved having someone to mother, I thought, which brought me back to Will. It was no wonder she had practically adopted him. I knew she missed him too. I had never spoken to her or Mum about him, despite gentle questions from both of them separately and together. It was too painful to talk about it, and too complicated. It was my fault that Will had been sent away, when all was said and done. I couldn't have said whether the guilt was worse than the pain of missing him. All I knew was that I'd better keep my misery to myself.

Which was a cheery thing to think about when you were fighting the most evil duvet imaginable. For roughly the hundredth time I discovered I'd put the wrong corner in the wrong bit of the cover so it didn't fit. I ripped it out and threw it on the floor, then jumped up and down on it.

OK, so it wasn't the most mature thing I'd ever done, but it made me feel better, briefly. And call it coincidence if you like, but when I picked the duvet up and forced it into the cover again, it ended up fitting perfectly, first time.

I'd finished tidying up there and was in my own room, lying on the bed reading, when there was a tap on the door. Petra peered in. "Jess? Is it OK for us to come in? Beth wants to talk to you."

"Of course." I put the book down and sat on the edge of the bed. I assumed she wanted to know what I'd seen. Mentally, I started to edit it. Less blood and bruising. No mention of Dan being creepy. I'd just downplay everything and try to sound reassuring.

Beth trailed in after my cousin, her little face puckered with woe. I marveled again at the fact that there was absolutely no resemblance between her and her half-brother. Even if she lost the glasses, she would still be sweet rather than stunning, her coloring mousy, her demeanor *Don't look at me.* Seb was more *Why aren't you looking at me?* She was a couple of inches shorter than Petra and very much a child in the way she dressed. Today's top had a pink cat on it and her hair was in two long plaits.

"How are you doing, Beth?"

"I'm fine." Her voice was a whisper.

"How is Seb?"

"In intensive care. Mum brought me home. She said there was no point in us hanging around." Beth sat down on the edge of a chair. "I'm so worried about him."

"I'm sure he'll be fine." Not that I knew one way or the other, but I wasn't going to say that. "Intensive care just means he's getting the best possible treatment."

"He's still unconscious. They might have to operate if the pressure gets too high in his brain."

"I'm so sorry, Beth."

"I mean, he's not always the easiest person to live with, but he doesn't deserve this." She pulled her sleeves down over her hands and added, very quietly, so I almost missed it, "Or maybe he does."

Petra cleared her throat. "Beth wanted to ask you a favor."

"What is it?" I looked from Beth to Petra, waiting for one of them to tell me. It was Petra who spoke again.

"She knows about what you did—finding out about Freya. She wants you to do the same for Seb. Tell her what really happened."

"Me? But the police—"

"The police say it was a car accident." Beth shook her head. "How is that even possible? Petra said you saw him."

"Just for a minute. And it was dark." I was frowning. There was absolutely no way that Seb had got his injuries from being hit by a car.

Beth was thinking the same way. "Did you see the bruises? The marks on his arms? I can't believe they think I'm that stupid."

"There was glass on the road. It could have come from a car. Sometimes people get injured in odd ways, and—"

She cut me off. "Did you know he was only wearing underwear when he got to the hospital? No socks, even. Just his boxers."

"Where were his clothes?"

Beth shrugged. "No one knows."

"That was some car accident," Petra said, and I was inclined to agree.

"What do your parents think, Beth?"

"Mum says I shouldn't worry about it. Seb has never got on with her since he moved in with us, so she's not upset about him being injured, really. She's worried about Dad. He's like a zombie. They said at the hospital it was shock. Inspector Henderson was talking to him about Seb and he was just staring into space, not answering. It was so embarrassing."

I hated to disappoint the two girls. "Look, I know I found out what happened to Freya, but that was just luck. I mean, I managed to trick people into telling me how she died, basically, because I look like she did and they didn't know me. That's not going to happen again."

Beth was looking stubborn. "Petra told me what a difference it made to the family to find out the truth."

"Yeah, and I'm glad I did it, but that doesn't mean I'm going to set myself up as Port Sentinel's answer to Nancy Drew. Even if I wanted to, I wouldn't know where to start. I don't know Seb. I've barely had a conversation with him. I don't know his friends, for the most part, and I definitely don't know his enemies."

"You know Ryan," Petra pointed out. "And you're good at finding things out. You could ask around."

"I could get myself in a lot of trouble." I shook my head. "No. No way. The whole Freya situation turned into a massive drama and I can't cope with another one."

Beth closed her eyes for a moment and two tears ran down from behind her glasses. "Please. Look, I'm worried about Seb. I'm worried that he's done something awful and that's why he's been attacked. I'm worried that even if he doesn't die, whoever beat him up will try again."

"You don't think someone was trying to kill him . . ." I saw the look on her face. "You *do* think someone was trying to kill him. But why?"

"I don't know." She shivered. "Doesn't it make you a little bit suspicious that no one wants to talk about it? Like the grownups know there's something to cover up? Mum told me not to ask any questions and Inspector Henderson told me not to worry about it."

"Dan Henderson doesn't want any negative publicity for the town," I said. "You know that. Tourism is everything. He covers up every little thing that might make us look bad."

"Yes, but my parents don't care about that. Dad cares about Seb. Mum cares about our family's reputation. It's got to have something to do with him. He did something awful and this is his punishment."

"You sound so sure . . ." I said slowly. "What do you know, Beth? What haven't you told me?"

She wriggled. "I don't know if this matters or not, but a couple of months ago his phone was ringing and ringing when he was in the shower and I picked it up to switch it off, but I didn't really know what I was doing and I must have connected the call instead. It was a girl and she was crying. She said she'd never forgive him for what he'd done." Beth's face was so white it looked green. "I could hardly hear her, she was so upset. And I made my voice really gruff and said, 'Who is this?' but she just hung up. Her number wasn't stored in the phone and I didn't recognize her voice."

"Did you ask Seb about it?"

"He'd have killed me for touching his phone," she said. "But I did try to listen to his next conversations, just to see if she called him again."

"And?"

"I don't think she ever did. It was just him talking to his mates."

"Apart from her, do you know anyone else who dislikes him?"

"Not really, but that doesn't mean much. He doesn't let me spend much time with him. I can try to find out."

"Great," I said faintly, wondering when exactly I'd agreed to help. It was just that Beth seemed so convinced that I would come to the rescue.

And I wanted to know too. I was curious. It would annoy Dan Henderson. It gave me something to do with my week off school, to take my mind off Will being back in town. All good reasons to do what they were asking.

Almost immediately, Petra came up with a reminder of why I shouldn't get involved. "It might help to talk to his friends. Ryan might know what he's been doing lately."

"Is there anyone else I could ask?" I didn't even bother trying to hide my dismay.

"Harry Knowles is one of his best friends," Beth said. "And I think he hangs around with Guy Tindall."

Neither of whom I knew. I'd have to call Ryan. And he would *definitely* take it the wrong way.

"Is there any chance you could get hold of Seb's mobile phone for me? If the police don't have it."

"Inspector Henderson gave it back to Dad this morning. He said they'd recovered it from the scene of the accident and they didn't need it for their investigation into the car crash that never happened. The last time I saw it, Dad had it in his jacket pocket. I'll have to wait until I can get hold of it without Mum or Dad noticing."

"OK." It wasn't as if I was desperately keen to get my hands on it. "Even if you do get it, we'd need to know the password."

"I know that. Six nine six nine." She looked unimpressed. "He said it was easy to remember."

"Classy," I commented.

"I don't get it," Petra said, and Beth grinned.

"You've been reading all the wrong books, Pets. I'll lend you my Jilly Coopers."

Not so young and innocent after all, I thought, with an internal grin that quickly faded. I wasn't sure that I was doing the right thing. It wasn't that I went looking for trouble. Trouble had a knack of finding me.

And I had a feeling that it was about to come knocking again.

4

I sat in Miss Lemon, staring out resignedly as Hugo swore and thumped the steering wheel. Never was a car better named. He turned the key in the ignition again, his lips pressed together as the engine coughed and spluttered.

"Sounds promising," I said.

"Shut it. I'm only doing this to be nice."

"Don't flood it."

"You don't even know what that means."

He was right, but I didn't admit it. "How much did you pay for Miss Lemon again?"

"On a cost-per-use basis, an unacceptable amount." He shook the steering wheel. "Don't think I won't trade you in, Lemon. I'm giving you one more chance, and if you don't start, it's the knacker's yard."

"It's sweet that you think she can understand you," I said, then laughed as the engine roared into life. "No way."

Hugo grinned at me. "Works every time."

"I'm not complaining. But let's go." I tapped the clock on the dashboard. "I'm assuming this works. If it's right, we're late."

"Oh no. I'm going to have to drive really, really fast," Hugo said happily, and tore out of the gate in a shower of loose gravel. I just about managed to text Ella a promise that we really *were* on our way before I gave myself up to complete terror, bracing one hand on the dashboard and the other on the door handle. I was past caring that Hugo laughed at me every time I squealed in fear. After the return journey, I promised myself, I was never going to get into a car driven by Hugo again. Ever.

We were only about three minutes late for the train but the car park was full. Hugo stopped to let me out by the station entrance.

"I'll try to find somewhere legal to leave Miss Lemon. If I can't, I'll come back in five."

"We'll meet you outside."

I dodged through the crowds outside the station, looking around in case Ella had come out to find us, but there was no sign of her. It was a small station. It couldn't be that hard to track her down. In fact, the hard part was not falling on my face on the way. As soon as I got inside the station itself, I tripped over a suitcase and then bounced off a man wearing a giant backpack; I don't think he was even aware of it. At last I spotted Ella standing in a corner near the ticket barrier. She was looking very London, with skinny jeans, a little curvy blazer, and high-heeled boots. I suddenly felt like a total scruff in comparison. I was back in my old green parka since my coat was on the critical list, my boots were muddy, my jeans had a rip in the knee, and she'd never seen me with short hair. I'd basically gone native, and for a moment I wondered if she would mind.

Then again, Ella was one of my oldest friends.

"Hello, stranger."

"Jess!" She threw her arms around me. "Oh. My. God. I can't believe it! Look at your *hair*!"

"Thank for coming." I hugged her, breathing in Chanel Mademoiselle. "I warned you."

"It really suits you." She leaned back so she could look. "I mean, it's a huge change and your hair was amazing when it was long, but I think it's good to have a new look now and then. Experiment. And you'd never have had the nerve to do it without good reason, so it was really *lucky*."

It was friend logic—not what most people think of as logic, but very comforting all the same. I pulled at the ends of my hair, trying to make it longer.

"I'm getting used to it. It takes much less time to wash."

"You see? Practical benefits too." She grinned at me and I hugged her again.

"I've missed you."

"You mean you haven't replaced me? Or Lauren?"

"How would that even be possible? How is Lauren, anyway?"

"She's fine. She's definitely coming down with me next time. She's dying to see you. And Port Sentinel." Ella was looking around like a visitor to a safari park. "This is . . . different."

"Different is the word." I looked at her doubtfully. "I hope you'll like it."

"Jess, I'm going to have a blast." She linked arms with me. "Now, where are all these hot men you keep promising me?"

"Not here just at this moment."

"I wouldn't say that," Ella purred, looking past me. "Who's that guy? The one who's staring at us?"

I turned to see and laughed. "That's just Hugo. He must have managed to get a parking space."

"That's your cousin."

"Yeah."

Ella was blushing. She leaned closer to me so she could whisper. "Why didn't you tell me he was really cute?"

I stared at him. He was now leaning against the wall, arms folded, glowering at a woman who was trying to get past him with a giant wheelie suitcase. If I was being kind, he was lean. Truthfully, he was lanky. Straight dark eyebrows. Untidy dark hair. The mocking smile when he wasn't being hostile. "Cute?"

"Yeah. Totally."

"Fortunately for me, because he *is* my cousin, I don't see it." I pulled her toward him. "Come on. I'll introduce you."

I'd been missing Ella ever since I left London and I'd been looking forward to her visit for weeks, but it took about two minutes for me to feel as if I was surplus to requirements. She was totally smitten with Hugo, at first sight, and I didn't know if he'd noticed or not but he was being *very* nice. I wouldn't have expected him to carry her bag to the car, for instance, or hold the door open for her. Or insist on taking us for a tour of Port Sentinel before we returned to the house.

I sat in the back and Ella turned round in her seat to talk to me now and then, but mostly she concentrated on what Hugo was saying about the sights. After twenty minutes or so, I became restive.

"Is there much more of this, Hugo?"

"Every visitor to Port Sentinel needs to see the view from Wrecker's Point."

"I've never seen the view from Wrecker's Point, and I've been living here for months."

"Then you've been missing out."

So we took in the view from Wrecker's Point, a cliff just outside town where the rocks stuck out in a long jagged line that had snagged countless ships in its time. Nowadays there was a buoy marking the safe channel beyond it, and an official tourist trail on the cliffs, with information boards and benches and an ice-cream van. It was busy there too, the bright sunshine making everyone feel as if summer wasn't totally done and dusted. It wasn't all that warm, in fact, but we got ice creams anyway, because it was Ella's holiday and that was what you did on holiday. We walked along the cliff path, reading about stormy nights and drowning sailors. There was nothing like a bit of tragedy to add to your innocent touristy enjoyment. No one else seemed to find it incongruous, even Hugo, who was usually ready to mock any kind of hypocrisy. He was strolling along beside Ella, not even complaining about the children rushing up and down the path or the elderly walkers who were causing major delays in front of us.

I walked a few paces behind them, glad to be left to my own thoughts. I absolutely knew for certain that it was not the sort of place you would ever find Will, but I couldn't stop looking over my shoulder to see if he was around. Every dark head made me catch my breath. *Ridiculous.*

A voice right behind me made me jump. "Ex-*cuse* me."

When I turned, I saw Ruth Pritchard, one of the cleverest girls in my class. She was small, with long dark curly hair and hostile eyes. She had very white teeth and reminded me of a ferret. On a good day she was unpleasant. Today looked like a bad day. Her face was pale, her eyes puffy and red. She was looking at the ground, not at me.

"Sorry, Ruth," I said, moving to one side to let her pass. It was as if I hadn't spoken. She steamed past me, right up behind Ella and Hugo, where she repeated her line. Ella jumped a mile. Hugo gave her a sardonic look and stepped aside with a flourish. Again, Ruth ignored it and carried on. Her head was down. She was wearing black from head to toe, her legs spindly in thick tights. In the sunshine she looked strangely out of place, like a black beetle forced out into daylight against its will. Ella looked back to where I was standing watching, and rolled her eyes. I grinned, but didn't close the gap between us. I was fairly sure she and Hugo didn't mind.

We walked all the way to the end of the trail, where Ruth was sitting on a bench, staring out to sea. Her shoulders were hunched as if she was trying to hide. I felt no urge to ask her if she was all right, shamefully. She just wasn't that nice. When I'd started at school, the only thing that had concerned her about me was whether I was clever. I did all right academically, but she was far better than me. She had been very glad that I wasn't a threat to her position at the top of the class.

At Ella's request, we stopped to take some pictures. Hugo managed to look away or pull a strange face in every one she took of him, and I couldn't work out if it was deliberate or not. Knowing him, he was trying to avoid being featured on Ella's Facebook page. And knowing her, that was exactly what she had in mind for the pictures.

"My face is beginning to ache," I said as Ella angled her phone to try to get all three of us in the same shot.

"Stop complaining."

"Is it going to be like this all week? Only I'm going to need to start training."

"Hugo, why are you squinting?" Ella wailed.

"That's just my face. Look, I'm not going to ruin any more of your pictures." He sounded genuinely bored now. "I'll see you two back at the car. Don't hurry. Try to get a shot of Jess looking human, if you can."

"Jess was not the problem," I said, watching him walk away. "Jess is not even the point of these pictures."

He was too far away to hear, but Ella shushed me anyway.

"I just want a record of what happens this week, so I can remember every bit. Also, I promised Lauren."

"Fine," I said, resigned. "But I wouldn't focus too much on Hugo. I don't think he's going to be your best souvenir."

Ella put down her phone. "He doesn't like me?"

"Oh no, I'm sure he does. But he's tricky."

"Tricky."

"Hard to read."

"I don't mind that."

"He's a cynic. And an intellectual snob."

"My type."

"Your last boyfriend couldn't read."

"He could," Ella said calmly. "He just chose not to."

"Seriously, there are lots of really attractive boys around Port Sentinel. I don't want you to think Hugo is the best that's on offer."

Ella busied herself with putting her phone away. "You make it sound like I'm here to cruise for boys. I came to see you."

"I know."

"I've missed you. And you are crap at e-mails."

"I wrote to you a lot," I said, wounded.

"Yeah, but about your job and redecorating your room. Not about the important stuff. Not about family. Or that guy."

"That guy."

"The one you were seeing in the summer."

I felt the tension radiate through my jaw as I clenched my teeth. I made myself relax. "There was nothing to tell you. It ended."

"And you shut down." Ella pulled her sunglasses down from the top of her head. "Don't think we didn't notice."

"I didn't want to talk about it," I admitted. *I don't want to talk about it.* "Look, I had a bad breakup. *Another* bad breakup. Hey, at least he didn't cheat on me."

"You see, I didn't know that. You haven't told us what happened."

"Another time."

"Jess!"

"It would take too long to go through it now." The wind had picked up and my eyes were watering. Because of the wind that was blowing in my eyes. No other reason. "We should get back to Hugo."

"He's a big boy. He'll survive."

"He might be missing you."

"Oh, ha ha." She put her bag on her shoulder. "Now I can cross Wrecker's Point off my list of things to see."

"What else is on there?"

"Wouldn't you like to know?" She grinned. "But Hugo has made me very keen indeed to meet the rest of your long-lost family."

The Leonards as a family always reminded me of a flock of starlings. Before they could settle down to anything, they had to flit about exhausting themselves. Hugo disappeared as soon as we got back to Sandhayes. Petra and Tom were both out, Petra with Beth and Tom playing football. I helped Ella to unpack and showed her the sights of the house and garden, which took most of the rest of the day as it was really an excuse for a good old gossip about everyone I'd left behind in London. It wasn't until evening—and the rain—came and dinner was ready that all three of my cousins came in to roost, arriving in the kitchen as Tilly and Jack put the last dishes on the table. Mum slipped in after them, pale and tired from her day in the gallery.

"Ella, how lovely to see you."

"Hi, Mrs. Tennant." Ella waved shyly from her place at the end of the table, beside me. She had a single sister, so the sheer level of noise generated by Hugo, Petra, and Tom bickering with their parents was enough to make her mute. It had taken me ages to get used to it.

"Did you have a nice time today?"

Ella nodded. "We went to Wrecker's Point."

"Oh, lovely. I took some pictures there a while ago. It's very dramatic when the wind is from the west."

"Not much wind today," I said. "Just sunny. But cold."

"Wimp." Hugo helped himself to water. "It was fine."

"Were you there too?" Mum asked, her eyes round with surprise. "I wouldn't have thought—"

Ella was blushing and Hugo had a scowl on his face. The one thing that was sure to put him off was attention from his family.

"It was so busy," I said loudly, drowning out Mum's soft voice. "So many tourists in town. You don't count, Ella, obviously."

"Spoken like a true local," Tilly said with a grin. "Were you busy today, Molly?"

"Ye-es. I mean, we had lots of visitors." Mum looked worried, which was her usual expression when it came to the gallery. "I didn't sell anything. Nick sold a pair of pictures to a nice German couple. The little landscapes."

Tilly nodded. "I saw them last week. Very commercial."

"They weren't very expensive." Mum chewed her lip. "I can't imagine that Nick's breaking even at the moment. And I don't really know why he employed me."

I did. It was as a favor to evil Dan Henderson, who was more than keen to keep my mother in Port Sentinel. If Mum didn't know that, I wasn't going to tell her. I wanted to stay too. But I would have given a lot to know what Dan had on Nick that made him give Mum a job that was barely worthy of the name. Especially when she was so *bad* at it.

Mum was still talking. "There isn't enough work for the two of us—we keep tripping over each other. I'm useless at selling. I really think I should quit."

With the exception of Ella, I think every single person around the table said, "No!" at the same time.

"You can't quit," I said. "We need some money to live on."

"You'd never get another job here at this time of year. We're coming into the off-season. No one is hiring." Jack, the voice of reason. He was a builder and the offseason was his busy time, as all the hotels and guesthouses rushed to get work done while the tourists were elsewhere. Port Sentinel would be battening down the hatches for winter all too soon.

"You're still learning the ropes. Nick is a good businessman," Tilly said. "If he didn't need you, he wouldn't employ you."

"Don't go back to London, please," Petra said, her eyes already brimming. "If you leave the gallery, you'll leave here too. I know it."

"And you have your photography to think about." Hugo looked around the table, where everyone had fallen silent from sheer surprise. "I don't know why you're all staring at me. I care about Aunt Molly's career. She's good. She should get to pursue it."

Spoken like a true Leonard. If he'd thought she wasn't any good, he'd have said that too.

Mum was pink, embarrassed by all the attention. "I wasn't looking for compliments. But I do feel guilty about how little I contribute."

"Have you talked to Nick about it?" I asked.

"I can't." She looked terrified. "He doesn't really talk to me. I say things and he just looks at me and then goes into his office."

"He sounds great," Ella said.

"Not the most sociable of men." Tilly leaned her chin on her hand. "Probably because he's so attractive—when he first came down here every single woman within ten miles tried to chat him up."

"Most of the married women tried too," Jack said slyly.

Tilly glared at her husband. "*I* didn't."

"No, but you were pleased when he came to your exhibition and admired your work."

"He's got good taste." She smiled at Mum. "And he likes you. I know it. He likes your photographs and he likes having you in the gallery. You must stop worrying so much."

"Why break the habit of a lifetime?" I asked, and then squeaked as Mum threw a roll at me.

"Add Nick to the list of Port Sentinel's must-sees," Ella whispered to me. "I like an older man."

"Noted."

I didn't think Mum had heard our conversation but she got the gist, or at least an innocent version of it. "You should come and see the gallery, Ella. The building is fascinating. Most of it is an old barn that was behind three of the houses on Fore Street. The gallery's entrance is in one of them, but the barn behind has been completely converted. The original building dates from 1607."

"Wowzers," Ella said obligingly.

"It *is* pretty stunning," I said, and winked at her when Mum turned back to join in the general mayhem of conversation. It was as good a reason as any to go and admire Mum's boss, strictly from a distance. And from the way she was sneaking covert looks in Hugo's direction, I thought Ella would be happy enough to admire Nick from afar, no matter what she said about older men.

Dinner over, we all drifted into the big sitting room off the hall. After the kitchen, it was the warmest room in the house. Petra and Tom sat on the floor in front of the television watching *Doctor Who* with acute concentration. Hugo sprawled on a small sofa with a book propped on his chest. Ella and I lay on the floor in front of the fire, talking, while Mum edited pictures on her laptop, frowning and muttering to herself.

Tilly came and stood in the doorway, surveying us. The rain was tapping at the windows.

"Are the cats in?"

"Aristotle is on my bed," Hugo volunteered.

"And Di?"

"I saw her in the garden earlier," I said.

Tilly groaned. "Stupid cat. I'd better go and get her in."

"I'll go." I jumped up.

"Really? It's raining." As if to prove her point, the wind blew a scattering of drops against the window.

"I don't mind." I wanted to leave Ella on her own so Hugo could join her, or blow his chances once and for all by ignoring her. He'd been distant all evening. This was his opportunity to make amends or make an exit from Ella's plans for the week, did he but know it.

I hadn't said any of this to Ella, but she passed on the opportunity to join me in the kitchen; I left her staring into the fire, looking quite ravishing in a big woolly jumper, with her hair loose around her shoulders.

Now or never, Hugo.

I opened the back door and peered out into the garden. Except for the rectangle of light at my feet, spilling out from the kitchen behind me, it was entirely dark. I couldn't see Tilly's studio at the end of the garden, or even the path that led to it. The rain was falling more softly now, but persistently. It gurgled in the gutters and pattered on fallen leaves. I strained to hear a rustle in the bushes or paws on gravel.

"Diogenes," I called into the darkness, not too loudly. I could have wished the Leonards were less inventive about their cat names. "You idiot cat, where are you?" I cranked the volume up just a little. "Diogenes!"

One minute I was alone. The next, a figure stepped into the light, Diogenes cradled against his chest. The cat was staring up at him adoringly, her face pillowed on his shoulder. His face was half in shadow, but I would have known those hands anywhere, and the easy way he moved. I caught my breath, wondering how I could ever have mistaken anyone else for him. Will came toward me and then stopped short, out of reach.

"Looking for this?"

All my life.

I didn't say it. I didn't say anything. I stood back and held the door open and he walked in. He didn't touch me, or even look at me as he walked by. There was no reason why I should feel close to fainting as his sleeve brushed mine, shedding water that soaked through the wool of my jumper. It was cold.

A reminder, as if I needed one, that getting too close to Will was a bad idea.

5

When I turned round, Will had already put the cat down on the floor. She was rubbing herself against his legs, her eyes half closed with pleasure.

"Wearing your catnip aftershave again?"

"How did you know?" He reached down and stroked Di. "It's nice to see her. Nice to be missed."

"Oh, you were missed." The words seemed too significant once I'd said them and I started filling the kettle, just to have something to do. "Tea?"

"Yeah." He leaned on the countertop, watching me, in all my makeup-free scruffiness. I had dragged my hair into a knot on top of my head but I knew it was untidy. I also knew I couldn't do anything about it without looking vain. Of course I was wearing my oldest jeans and a hoodie that was too big for me; it was as if I'd known he was coming and had taken steps to look as unattractive as possible. I glanced at him and noticed he'd taken off his coat. It was hanging on the back of a chair, dripping. He was wearing a fisherman's sweater with the sleeves pushed up a little. His arms were still tanned from the summer. Naturally, obviously, he looked stunning, but he also looked different somehow, and I couldn't allow myself to stare at him for long enough to work out why.

"How are you?" he asked. Well, it was as good a way of starting a conversation as any.

"Fine," I said, a little too brightly. "You?"

He shrugged. "Fine."

"How's your mum?" *Straight in there with the tough questions, Jess. Nice one.*

"She's doing all right. Much the same."

"How's the new school?" Safer territory.

"Making me work hard."

"But do you like it?" I asked.

"It has its good points. It's not here, for starters." I flinched and Will saw it. He added, casually, "It's just nice to be somewhere no one cares who my dad is."

"Are they nice? The other students?"

"Mainly." He relented. "I've met some nice people."

I heard *people* and thought *girls*. There was no way to ask. But I looked at him, with his hair a little ruffled and the fading tan that made his eyes look very light, and thought there was no way he wouldn't attract attention from any female with a pulse.

Speaking of which, I really needed to start paying attention to what he was saying rather than how he looked. I'd just missed a question. "Sorry?"

"I asked how you were finding it. *Your* new school, I mean."

"It's fine." Sentinel College was a good school; a state school but one generously funded and resourced by wealthy parents.

I had wondered why they didn't just send their little darlings to boarding schools elsewhere, but Hugo set me straight: when you'd been expelled three or four times and had come very close to getting a criminal conviction for drugs, your parents tended to want to a) stop wasting money on your education and b) keep you nearby. Guilt funded a lot in Port Sentinel, I was learning.

"Fine," Will repeated, grinning. "Doing a good job on improving your vocabulary, anyway."

He looked relaxed, I realized. The strain that had put shadows under his eyes had left him. I concentrated on pouring boiling water into the mugs. "Oh, come on, what do you want me to say? It's not amazing. There are some nice people in my year. I quite like some of the teachers. I'm doing all right. Keeping up with my homework. Making friends."

"Better than your old school?"

"In some ways," I said carefully.

"So you'd say you're settling in well."

"When did I say that? With the whole Freya thing—"

"You started off with a reputation and you haven't been able to shake it. You'd better do something to distract them. Give them something else to talk about."

"Like what?" I didn't know what he was getting at.

He didn't answer me straight away, and when he did speak, his eyes were focused on the counter in front of him. "I got back last night. I saw you at the fireworks."

I held myself very still, waiting. "Hugo told me."

"I saw you with Ryan."

"I didn't think you'd be there." Great. Now it sounded as if that was why I'd been happy to rub up against Ryan, with about as much dignity as Diogenes had shown earlier.

"I thought it was a good place to catch up with people. Find out what I'd missed while I was gone." A flick of a look from eyes that were suddenly as dark as smoke. "And I was right."

"What's that supposed to mean?"

"Absolutely nothing."

"Because you sound as if you're jumping to conclusions."

"Just saying what I saw."

"What you saw was Ryan making sure I didn't die of hypothermia. Someone stole my coat."

"Stole it."

"Took it. Dumped it in a ditch."

"Why?"

"How should I know? I don't even know who it was."

He was looking straight at me now, and I couldn't tell from his expression what he was thinking. "I thought you said you were making friends?"

"You know there are a lot of people in Port Sentinel who have a grudge against me because of what happened in the summer," I said flatly. "Here's the news: people can be mean-spirited."

"Did you report it?"

"To the cops? No. Of course not." I laughed. "It was from Fine Feathers. It cost about three quid. Anyway, I got it back."

"From the ditch."

"It's hanging over the bath upstairs if you want to check. Probably still oozing scummy water. I should just throw it out. It needs a miracle worker, not a dry cleaner." I crossed my arms tightly, holding onto myself, holding myself together. "All these questions. Anyone would think you didn't believe me."

Will was frowning, and he had gone back to studying the counter. "It's none of my business."

"I'm not trying to hide anything from you. You can ask whatever you like."

One eyebrow lifted a millimeter. "Anything?"

"Within reason," I said, feeling the color wash into my cheeks.

"How many questions do I get?"

"One."

"But I want to ask two."

"Well, I suppose you can ask. But I might not answer."

"You have nothing to hide, remember?"

I lifted my chin. "Go on. Ask."

"What's going on between you and Ryan?"

"Nothing." Will looked skeptical and I sighed. "He likes me. He wants to go out with me. I keep saying no. That's why he keeps asking—he hates being turned down. And I don't really know what to do about it."

He took a second to reply. "Is he bothering you?"

"No. Not at all. It's just a little frustrating that I can't stop people talking about it. I like him, but as a friend. Not even a friend, really, because you can't be friends with someone who keeps trying to stick their tongue down your throat."

"I can imagine that gets awkward." Will's tone was Sahara-dry.

"Awkward is not the word." Just as it was more than a little awkward to be talking about it with the one person I would have liked to be kissing. I didn't dare look at him. "Anyway. He's been kind to me and he's tried to persuade everyone to get to know me before they make up their minds about me. So I'm grateful to him and I can cope with the flirting. And what you saw last night was just friendly. He was helping me out."

"You must think I'm blind," Will said, quite calmly. "I saw him kiss you."

"When he was saying good-bye? It was a joke, really. As I said—friendly."

His mouth twisted just a little before he lifted his mug and hid it from my view. I remembered that he was Dan Henderson's son, and although they had little in common apart from their looks, they both had a temper. Dan's just ran nearer to the surface than Will's. But underground fires could smolder for years before they burned themselves out.

"It's really not a big deal." I meant because it had just been a typical bit of opportunism from Ryan, but Will misunderstood.

"Not if it happens all the time."

"No, that's not what I said."

"It's fine. To borrow your word. None of my business." He grinned at me and I blinked, confused. I hadn't imagined that he was angry about Ryan pawing me, had I? Because I *wanted* him to be? This version of Will was so far from angry that he was yawning, and stretching. "Sorry. I could sleep for the whole of half-term. The last few weeks have been busy. Lots of late nights."

And I was back to imagining the pretty girls who kept him up late.

"Well, you should get some rest tonight. There's nothing much going on."

"Except Harry's party."

"Harry?"

"Knowles. He's planning to have a party every night this week."

"I know. Ryan told me. But I didn't think *you'd* know."

"I have my ear to the ground. I know everything that's going on around here, I think."

Will drained his mug and came round to the sink to rinse it. I scooted sideways to get out of his way, fighting down the urge to touch him as he stood facing away from me. I wanted to run my hand across his broad shoulders and down his back. I wanted him to turn round and press his body against mine. I wanted to remind myself what it was like to kiss him, even though I thought I remembered it pretty well.

"And are you going?"

"To the party?" Will shook his head. "But I do want to go out. The house is too quiet. That's why I came over."

It was on the tip of my tongue to say I wasn't dressed for going out, but I had only got as far as opening my mouth to reply when he continued, "I wanted to see if Hugo felt like coming along."

He had come to see Hugo, not me. He had stayed in the kitchen and talked to me out of politeness, because I'd assumed he was there for me and he was too kind to tell me the truth. I felt like sinking to the floor under the weight of humiliation. Through a smile that felt stiff on my face, I said, "Well, you can ask Hugo, but I don't know if he'll be interested. He's in the sitting room, probably chatting up my best friend."

"Which one?"

"Ella."

"I remember," he said, in a way that made me feel he really did. "If he's that keen, she can come along too."

And he still didn't ask if I wanted to join them, I noticed.

"Thanks for the tea," he said, and headed for the door.

I went after him, but I stopped short of touching him. "Will."

He turned and looked down at me, and I'd have said his expression was tender rather than anything more hostile.

"You said you had two questions."

"I did."

"You only really asked one."

"I'm going to save the other one, I think. I will ask you. But not now."

"Because what my life needs is more suspense."

"Everyone needs something to make their hearts beat faster," Will said, and gave me a smile that made my heart race, as I thought he probably knew it would.

I stood in the kitchen after he'd gone. I couldn't follow him. I couldn't be in the same room as him and listen to him making arrangements to go out without me. I didn't want everyone to watch me and how I was around him or, worse, *not* watch me because it was too embarrassing all round. In the end I slipped through the hall, past the door to the sitting room, which was thankfully closed. I ran up the many stairs to my room, where I got into bed to read. It was cold in my lovely attic room with all its windows, and bed was the best solution.

It would also make it easy to decline a belated invitation to join them, I thought. Who gets out of bed to go out drinking? Not me.

As it turned out, it didn't matter. No one asked me to.

Ella tapped on my door about an hour later and poked her head in. "Are you all right?"

"Never better," I lied. "What's going on?"

"Nothing much. I'm heading to bed too."

"Not out?"

She smiled. "Not this time. Although Hugo did try to persuade me to go."

"And you said no."

"Playing hard to get."

"Good idea. Keenness is anathema to Hugo. He hates enthusiasm."

"How sweet," Ella said, and I thought she was properly smitten if she imagined Hugo was sweet.

"Is Hugo going?"

"Gone."

"Where were they heading?"

"They didn't know. They said they'd find something to do."

"On a Sunday night? Good luck."

Ella came into the room properly and shut the door behind her, then sat on the edge of my bed. "So."

"So?"

"I met Will."

"I thought you might have, given that you were in the same room and everything." I put my book down. "Well?"

"He's—" Ella shook her head. "Oh, girl. I see the problem."

"Do you?"

"I think so." She held up her hands and counted off on her fingers. "Gorgeous. Nice voice. *Beautiful* eyes. Good manners. Sense of humor. Obviously clever—I mean, Hugo said he wants to study medicine so he must be intelligent. What am I forgetting? Oh, he's really impressively fit. Marks out of ten? I'd give him a solid nine."

"Why did he lose a mark?"

"You can see a mile off that he has *ishoos*." Ella rolled her eyes. "Life's too short for that kind of thing."

"It's a little harsh to punish him for something he can't help."

"Oh, I only took off a half-mark for that. The other half was for breaking your heart."

I gave a little sigh. "Well, that wasn't his fault. That was all mine."

"You see, I'm going to need the full story."

"The full story is that I broke up with him." I couldn't look at her. I didn't want to see the surprise on her face. "I broke my own heart and maybe chipped a bit off his. Take it from me, you should give him ten out of ten."

"Why did you break up? Did he cheat on you?"

"No. Nothing like that."

"Well, I don't get it. If he's super-perfect and he wanted to be with you and you are completely damaged by breaking up with him, why did you do it?"

"It's complicated."

"I'm pretty good at listening."

"Will's dad told him he'd send him away to boarding school to stop us from being together. Don't even ask me to explain why he'd care." I couldn't go into the whole *Dan-loved-my-mother-once-and-maybe-still-does* thing there and then. "I thought I'd save him the trouble. If we broke up, Will could stay and be with his mother. You know she's dying."

"Hugo said." Ella's face was grave.

"No one knows how long she's got left. I couldn't be selfish about it. How I felt didn't really matter."

"Did you tell Will why you were breaking up with him?"

"No. He'd never have gone along with it. He hates his dad. He wouldn't want to do anything that Dan wants him to do." I shivered. "And it was that too—you know, I thought he was attracted to me because his dad hated us being together, not because he really liked me."

"I'm sure that's not true."

"I'm not." I blinked some tears away. "I was just trying to do the right thing."

"And you got yourself into a mess." Ella sighed. "Maybe he's not the one for you, even if he is a ten out of ten. I don't think you could cope."

"Thanks, Ella."

"What? I'm just trying to make you feel better."

"This is what they call tough love."

"This is what they call reminding you you're better than this. You don't need to cry over Will. You'll find someone else."

I tried to smile. "Maybe."

She went to the door but stopped before she went through it. "You know, I really like Port Sentinel, from what I've seen of it so far, but I'm not sure it's the right place for you."

"Why do you say that?"

"You used to be happy."

She closed the door softly behind her and I lay back against my pillow, staring at the ceiling. The tears I couldn't seem to stop slid down the sides of my face and lost themselves in my hair. I really hoped there was a limit to how many tears one person could cry. And I really hoped that, one of these days, I'd reach it.

6

In the morning, Petra and I scored a lift to Exeter with Beth and her mother in their big, luxurious Audi. I left Ella working on holiday homework, or trying to while Hugo sat on the other side of the table, pretending to work too but actually making her laugh. It was very Ella to insist on getting her work done on day one of her holiday.

"I started it on the train. It won't take long. If I don't do it, I'll just have it hanging over me until I go back and I won't be able to enjoy anything."

"If you're sure," I said, doubtful. "It doesn't seem like a lot of fun. And you could go shopping in Exeter."

"I can go shopping any time I like in London."

Hugo yawned. "Anyway, shopping is boring."

"Tired?" I asked.

"A little."

"How was last night? Did you go to the pub?"

"Briefly." Hugo yawned again. "It was amusing. But not amusing enough to stay for very long."

"Did you go somewhere afterward?"

"Will met a few people he knew from his new school. We hung around with them for a while."

Approximately one million questions popped into my mind, chief among them whether the people Will knew included any girls. I made myself smile at Hugo as if nothing he'd said bothered me at all. "Sounds fun."

"I'm paying for it now. I'm tired today."

"I'm glad I had an early night," Ella said virtuously. "You should try it some time."

"And you should try coming out instead of being a boring stay-at-home social outcast like Jess."

I blinked. "Don't hold back, will you?"

"I'm just saying, you tend to be a bit of a hermit."

"Says the boy who hasn't left his room willingly in the last three months, even for meals."

"I just need a good enough reason. You missed out, both of you."

"Well, I wasn't invited," I said. "So I couldn't have gone even if I'd wanted to."

Hugo stared at me for what felt like a long time, then nodded, as if he'd worked something out.

"What?" I asked, defensive.

"Nothing at all." Hugo looked around, checking to see if Petra was within earshot. "Look, Jess, do you mind going to the hospital with Petra? I know Beth needs her support but it's tough on her. It reminds her of Freya."

"I hadn't thought of that." Petra had been twelve when her big sister died—old enough to know exactly what was going on. Old enough to understand that she wasn't coming back, ever.

"They did the postmortem on Freya at the hospital in Exeter." Typical Hugo to make a statement that was precisely factual but hit with the impact of a grenade. "I don't know if Petra remembers that, or if it would mean much to her, but I don't want her there on her own with the Dawsons. It could be upsetting."

"Go," Ella said to me. "I really will be fine here."

I went.

I sat in the front of the car with Mrs. Dawson, who was dark-haired with high cheekbones and the same sweet smile as Beth. She was model-thin and wearing Port Sentinel casual chic—very expensive knee boots, skinny designer jeans, a swathe of caramel cashmere, and a lot of jewelry. She was a vague, distracted driver today and perhaps always—the passenger door had a really handsome dent in it and one of her sidelights had shattered. Fear kept me wide-eyed on the winding roads from Port Sentinel to Exeter. I was almost glad of it because otherwise I would have found it hard to stay awake. Mrs. Dawson seemed to have an inexhaustible supply of boring stories about people I didn't know—friends of theirs who had houses in France and were being ripped off by local builders, or the people who'd invited them to St. Lucia, or the woman with a daughter the same age as Beth who was "a very gifted ice skater, Jess. I mean, really talented. She puts us to shame, doesn't she, darling?"

The sun was streaming in, heating up the interior, which

smelled chemically clean. The sharp, artificial odor made me feel dizzy and slightly high.

"Do you mind if I open the window?"

"What?" Mrs. Dawson glanced at me as if she'd forgotten I was there. "Oh. Yes, of course. It does stink in here. They always use that stuff when they valet the car even if I tell them not to."

The smell was so strong she must have had the car valeted that morning, and I wondered briefly about her priorities. I'd have thought the stepson in intensive care was more important than getting the car polished, but what did I know?

In the back seat Beth talked to Petra, the two of them barely glancing at Mrs. Dawson when she broke into their conversation. The burden of keeping Mrs. Dawson happy fell on me, and I spent the forty-five-minute drive saying *yes*, and *no*, and *really*, and *how interesting*, and *watch out*, and not much else.

We were almost in Exeter when she asked, abruptly, "Do you know my stepson?"

"We're in school together."

She swerved round a slow-moving Ford Fiesta. "This situation is typical of him. Causing trouble is what he does best."

It seemed a little harsh to blame him for what had happened, but I nodded.

"Jim's had heart trouble. My husband, I mean. Seb's father. He doesn't need this kind of stress." Her mouth was a line.

"He must be very worried about Seb."

"More than Sebastian deserves, certainly."

I didn't know what to say. Mrs. Dawson looked in her rear-view mirror and her face softened. "All right, darling?"

"*Yes*, Mum. I'm fine." Beth sounded irritated to be

interrupted. At least she hadn't heard her mother complaining about Seb, I thought. Happy families it wasn't.

At the hospital, Beth led the way to intensive care through a labyrinth of corridors and waiting areas. I stayed close to Petra, who was very quiet indeed.

"Here we are." Beth stopped, triumphant, in front of a locked door. "You need to press the bell to be admitted."

"Wait for me, Beth." Her mother had fallen behind. She was carrying an overnight bag for her husband and some magazines she'd bought in the hospital shop. "Girls, I don't think you two will be allowed to go in. It's family only."

"That's fine," I said. Petra was so pale I was worried she was about to faint. "We wouldn't want to get in the way. We can sit here." There was a convenient row of seats by the door.

"Oh," Beth said, disappointed. "Can't they come too?"

"Really not." Mrs. Dawson pressed the intercom button. "We'll try not to stay too long."

The door opened for them and the two of them disappeared. Petra came and perched beside me, looking very slightly better. "I didn't want to have to see Seb."

"Don't worry about it. I'm not disappointed. I'm sure Beth won't be, either."

"This is so terrible. Poor Seb. His poor parents."

"Mrs. Dawson doesn't seem too bothered."

"You heard what Beth said. She doesn't get on with Seb. He blames her for splitting up his parents."

"Is that so?"

Petra nodded. "She totally did. Even Beth admits it. But

apparently Seb's mother is a real high-maintenance type and Mr. Dawson is much happier with Beth's mum."

Who didn't strike me as *low* maintenance, but everything was relative.

"What do you make of Seb?"

"Me?" Petra looked surprised, then thoughtful. "I don't know. I fancied him for a while when I started going round to Beth's house. He was always there and he'd say flirty things sometimes, just to make me blush. Then I got annoyed about it. He was too determined to get a reaction. It felt like he was being mean, even though he was really smiley and chatty. He'd come up behind me and lean over me and whisper things in my ear and it was annoying. Beth said he always ignored her if there was no one else there. If his parents' friends were there he'd be all over her, showing off what a good big brother he is. I mean, I'd rather have a brother like Hugo. He never makes any effort but you know he cares about you, deep down."

"He definitely does." I put my arm around Petra and let her lean against me. One of the best things about moving to Port Sentinel had been taking over the role of Petra's big sister. I was supposed to know what to do in every situation, and what to wear, and how to apply liquid eyeliner (which I could do— though privately I felt life was far too short for liquid eyeliner). I really liked that she depended on me. I'd made a promise to myself—and to Freya if she was still interested—that I'd never let her down. And that included not backing out of a promise to find out what had happened to Seb Dawson, if that was really what she wanted me to do.

If I was feeling good about myself, it was short-lived. The doors to intensive care opened and Beth bounded out, followed by a tall, heavy-set man in a crumpled checked shirt. He had bags under his eyes and his hair was untidy. He still had the Port Sentinel sheen of wealth, though: a chunky signet ring on his left little finger, and a watch that had about as much metal in it as Hugo's car.

"Here they are."

"Girls." He shook hands with me first, then Petra. "It's good of you to come."

"I'm so sorry about Sebastian, Mr. Dawson. How's he doing?" I asked.

"The same." He rubbed his eyes. "They say they have to wait to see what happens over the next few hours and days. They can't tell yet about his brain. Whether it will be affected, I mean."

Petra's cold little hand found its way into mine.

"I'm sure he's getting very good care here," I said, using my talking-to-parents voice.

"The best. The absolute best." Mr. Dawson's eyes welled up. "You're so good to come," he said again. "Beth's told me how much Seb means to you, Jess."

"She has?" I switched on a smile. "Of course. But he means a lot to so many people."

"Yes, but I feel you should be allowed to see him. They said it was family only, but I think you would count as family if we were able to ask Seb."

Sorry, WHAT?

Beth was pulling frantic faces at me behind her father's back.

"Oh. I mean, absolutely," I said, kicking for touch. "I didn't want to make a big fuss about getting in to see him. It's all about what's best for him, isn't it?"

"Well, I think seeing his girlfriend would count as a good thing. Even if he's not responding, we don't know how much he can understand. If you can talk to him, it might really help his recovery." Mr. Dawson shook his head. "I'm so sorry, Jess. We had no idea Sebastian had a girlfriend at the moment or we'd have made sure you were here yesterday. It must have been horrible for you."

"Oh, no. Not really. I mean, I was upset, obviously, but I understood."

Girlfriend.

I was going to KILL Beth.

"We just didn't know about you," Mr. Dawson said again.

"Well, it's a relatively recent thing. I don't know if he would even describe me as his girlfriend, officially."

"He totally would," Beth chipped in.

"I'm not so sure," I said, glaring at her.

She ignored me. "He's always going on about Jess."

"Not to us." Mr. Dawson smiled at me. "Don't let that upset you, though, Jess. He's not always the best at letting us know what's going in his private life. I mean, I suppose that's not unusual for a teenage boy. I wish he'd confide in me more, but . . ." He trailed off as his bottom lip began to quiver.

Oh, please don't cry. I jumped up. "Do you think there's any way I could see him?"

"Come with me." Mr. Dawson put his arm around me and guided me to the double doors. Beth sat down next to Petra with the air of one who has done what she came to do. While Mr. Dawson spoke into the intercom, I glowered at her. She smiled back.

"How could you?" I mouthed, following her dad through

the double doors. She shrugged and waved, and the doors locked behind me.

"He's just down here." Mr. Dawson's arm was still around me. "Now, don't be alarmed when you see him. He looks pretty rough around the edges compared to the way he is normally, but a lot of that is just bruising so he should look more like himself in a few days."

"OK," I said faintly. "I understand."

"We're just so upset. The idea of someone hitting him and then driving off without even waiting to see if he was all right . . ." Mr. Dawson shook his head. "I don't know how anyone could be so callous."

A nurse stood to one side and I saw the bed, and Seb. His head was bandaged, as were his wrists. I wouldn't have recognized him now that the bruises had made his face swell. His skin was red and shiny, his eyes almost invisible. Dark stitches tracked across his chin and up to the corner of his mouth. I didn't have to fake the gasp I gave, because he looked dreadful. He looked as if he was more than half dead. They had left him bare-chested, with sensors attached to his skin, feeding information to the various machines that beeped and hummed around the head of the bed. I could see that the skin on his body was scratched and bruised too. Three long parallel scrapes ran down his chest, and his arms looked as if he'd rolled through brambles.

Mrs. Dawson was sitting nearby. She was reading a fashion magazine with all the emotion of someone waiting to see the dentist. She glanced up. "Jess, you were naughty not to say anything about Seb. All that way with me chatting about everything that came into my head and we could have been talking about how the two of you got together."

The absolute horror of that thought made me feel faint. "Oh, please, Mrs. Dawson, it's not a big story. We just got to know each other in school. And then, you know . . ." Let them think I was super-inarticulate if they liked. That was as far as I was prepared to go. With Seb lying there, unconscious, I felt worse and worse about lying to his parents. I wasn't going to draft him into a romantic scene that hadn't happened at all.

"Don't be afraid, dear. Take his hand." Mr. Dawson pushed me forward and I sank into the chair closest to Seb.

"I'm not sure . . . I mean, I don't know . . ."

"Talk to him. Tell him you're here." Mr. Dawson was leaning on the end of the bed, watching his son for signs of life.

"I'm sorry," I said desperately. "I just can't think what to say."

"We should leave the two of you alone," Mrs. Dawson said. "You don't want Seb's daddy listening in, do you?"

Oh, vomit. "It's stupid, I know."

"It's normal." Mr. Dawson looked disappointed, though. Seb was as still as a carved effigy on a tomb. "Normal is what we want for Sebastian."

"Come on." Mrs. Dawson stood up. "Leave them alone. I want to get a coffee and you need a shave."

She bustled him away, leaving me feeling like the absolute worst person who ever drew breath. Taking advantage of the Dawsons hadn't been my idea, but I felt just as guilty about it as Beth should have.

Still, I was there. And unattended. The nurses' station was close by so I didn't have total privacy, but I could have a look around for the phone. There was a small locker in the corner but it was empty. Maybe Mrs. Dawson had already taken the phone home with Seb's other things. Not that he'd had much to take home—no clothes, I remembered.

Mr. Dawson's jacket hung on the back of my chair. I patted the pockets quickly, finding a fat wallet and some keys and—I allowed myself a little crow of triumph—a phone. I pulled it out and checked the screen.

Not Seb's phone. Not unless he was in the habit of using a picture of his stepmother as his wallpaper. It didn't seem likely, knowing what I did about their relationship. I put it back where I'd found it and sat, disconsolate, watching Seb's chest rise and fall. The three scrapes looked more and more like gouges left by long nails. He had a bruise on his chest—a round one that looked as if someone had punched him.

"What happened to you?" I said softly. "Where did you go? Why doesn't anyone want to admit the official story is a lie?"

No answer. I hadn't really expected one.

The Dawsons came back eventually. I got my hand on top of Seb's in time for Mr. Dawson to see me patting it, and he beamed at me.

"It does me so much good to see the love my son's inspired."

I cringed. "Well. He is very special."

"He is. He really is." Mr. Dawson looked down at him. "I want you to come back, Jess. Come and see us again when Seb's mother is here. She's flying in tonight."

"Showing her usual sense of urgency," Mrs. Dawson said.

"It took Séverine a while to arrange things in France. She couldn't just leave straight away. She has a lot of pets."

Mrs. Dawson licked her finger and flicked to the next page of her magazine with a snap.

"I should go," I said, standing up. "Petra's been waiting for ages."

"I'll drive you back." Mrs. Dawson stood up too.

"We can get the train."

"It's no trouble." She was almost as desperate to leave as I was, I thought.

"You might as well go." Mr. Dawson put his arms around his wife. "I don't mind staying on my own."

"I wish you'd come home with me. Have a proper rest." For the first time, Mrs. Dawson looked genuinely upset. She might not have cared much about her stepson but it was obvious that she adored her husband, and worried about him.

"I can't leave him here on his own. When Séverine gets here I'll have a break. I might check into a hotel."

"Not the same one as her," Mrs. Dawson said, her voice tight with tension.

"Whatever." He sounded exhausted. He slid a hand into his shirt pocket and pulled out a phone, then frowned. "That's not mine. I keep forgetting I've got Seb's."

He started to put it away but Mrs. Dawson held out her hand. "Give it to me. I'll take it home."

"He'll want it when he wakes up."

Mrs. Dawson looked down at the still figure in the bed. Her voice was gentle when she replied. "So we should look after it for him. It might get lost, or stolen. Let me take it home and mind it."

"All right." He gave it to her and I watched it disappear into

Mrs. Dawson's bag, out of sight and well out of my reach. Beth would have to try to get hold of it. It was the least she could do. *Girlfriend*, indeed . . .

Mr. Dawson was patting his pockets. "I wonder what I did with mine."

"Your jacket," I said without thinking. Then, quickly, "I mean, try your jacket. That's where I usually keep mine."

"Good idea." He came over and lifted his jacket, searching through it until he found the phone.

"Thank you for coming, Jess."

"No problem whatsoever." I looked at Seb one last time, in the role of the dutiful girlfriend. He looked so vulnerable, lying there. So damaged. I'd been in two minds about getting involved—reluctant, to say the least, to take on the role of detective again. But it was beyond wrong that he was lying there in a coma and no one was even trying to find the person who'd hurt him.

I left the Dawsons to say goodbye to one another and walked out. I didn't have to pretend to be upset. Mr. Dawson's misery made me feel immensely sad. It was another reason to dislike Dan Henderson, I thought. The Dawsons deserved justice.

Outside the double doors, Petra and Beth were giggling. It was the kind of laughter that involves a lot of snorting. I was glad to see it, but I still frowned at Beth.

"You are in a lot of trouble."

"No need to thank me."

"Beth," I said, a warning note in my voice, "don't even think about elaborating on whatever story you told your parents. When Seb wakes up, he's going to be very surprised to hear about his girlfriend. Let's just keep it simple and vague and hope that he's too confused to work out what you did."

"Actually, you would make a really lovely girlfriend for him. I've always wanted him to have a nice girlfriend," she said wistfully. "We could go shopping together."

I tried and failed to hold onto my anger. "Oh, Beth, what are you like?"

She blinked, all innocence behind the glasses. "Just think about it."

I only had time to shake my head before Mrs. Dawson came out of the intensive-care unit and put an end to the conversation. She shuddered. "Come on, girls. Let's get out of here."

On the way home, I chose the lesser of two evils and kept my eyes closed, pretending to be asleep so I didn't have to talk about Seb, and our fake relationship. It had the added advantage that I couldn't see the countless accidents we almost had on the way. I could hear Mrs. Dawson swearing under her breath, though, and it was both entertaining and an education.

I walked into Sandhayes, Petra following, the two of us weak with relief to have survived two journeys in Mrs. Dawson's car.

"How did it go?" Hugo was running down the stairs, Ella not far behind him. She was blushing. Hugo looked the same as ever. I tried to work out what that meant and came up blank.

"It was fine."

"Did you get what you wanted?" Ella asked.

"Sort of. I didn't get Seb's phone, but I did get a new boyfriend."

The two of them looked baffled as Petra snorted beside me. I grinned too. It was so unusual to see Hugo look totally nonplussed, I felt it had almost been worth it.

7

S o this is where you work?"

"Now and then."

Ella peered through the window, her hands cupped around her eyes to try to make out the dim interior. "It looks interesting."

"It looks like the worst charity shop in the world. And that might actually be true."

"Oh, come on. The stuff in the window looks great."

"From what you can see through the filthy glass," I said, rubbing at a smudge with my finger. "This is the last busy week for tourists before Christmas, so of course the shop is shut. Sylvia decided to go on a Mediterranean cruise and I can't be trusted to open the shop on my own."

"You sound really fed up. At least you don't have to work."

"Yes, but I like it. And it would give me something to do."

Ella shivered as the wind picked up. "I'm sorry if I'm not entertaining enough."

"Not what I meant," I protested. "It's not exactly hard work. Just a couple of hours a day, and only weekends during term time. But it gives me something to do with my brain. I like making the shop better. I'm proud of it."

"So you should be." She had another look. "How much is that bag?"

"Which one?" I leaned in to see. "Oh, that's Mulberry, but it's last season. I think it's twenty."

"Pounds?" Her voice was a squeak.

"Yeah. Too much?"

She dug in her pocket for her wallet. "Not what I was thinking. Here. Take this. Next time you open up, that bag is mine."

"I'll make sure no one else gets it."

"I can't believe I'm here and it's not open." Ella was actually pressing her face against the window now, desperately craning to see if she could spot anything else worth having. "You need an online shop. Although it would be seriously dangerous. Look at those shoes. Add to basket, please." She gave a long sigh that fogged up the window in front of her.

"You don't even know if they'd fit you—and can you get off the window, please? I'm going to wash it when I get the chance, but until then I'd like people to be able to see through the glass and your face is greasing it up."

"How dare you." She stepped back, though. "Jeez. You weren't joking about being proud of this place."

Some rubbish had blown into the shop's doorway, making it look even more derelict than usual. I picked up the bits of paper and candy wrappers. There wasn't a bin nearby, so I shoved them into the pocket of my parka. "It's my pet project."

"I thought that was investigating crimes." Ella fell into step beside me as we carried on down Fore Street. We were making slow progress because we'd been stopping at almost every shop. Ella was examining Port Sentinel's retail opportunities with extreme attention to detail.

"That's just something that keeps happening to me. Or near me, really. I don't go looking for crimes to investigate."

Ella pointed at the other side of the street. "Is that the gallery?"

"That's the one." We crossed the road to the neat glass door and I peered in. "No sign of Nick but I can see Mum. Want to go in anyway?"

"Very much so."

Mum was sitting behind a big desk in the corner of the gallery, leaning her chin on her hand and doodling. She looked up, beaming, when I opened the door and the bell jangled.

"People! People I know and like. Come in, come in."

"We won't stay too long," I promised.

"OK. Probably wise." She leaned back and peered into the back gallery. "Nick's in there with some customers."

"Isn't that your job?"

"Supposedly."

"Well, why doesn't he let you do it?"

Instantly, Mum looked terrified. "Oh, I don't mind. He's better at it than I am."

"How are you ever supposed to learn how to do it if he won't give you a chance?"

"Jess, stop." She looked at me and narrowed her eyes. "What's different? Is that makeup?"

"I thought I'd make a bit of an effort, since Ella is here," I said, blushing. "It's just some mascara."

"I can't remember the last time I saw you wearing mascara." Mum grinned. "You look good. You look like yourself."

Meaning that recently, most of the time, I had not looked like myself. I got the picture.

Ella was wandering around the gallery, eyeing a particularly vivid shipwreck painting. "What is it about this place and violence?"

"Everyone loves a good shipwreck. In fact, the only thing better than a shipwreck is"—I turned her round to see the matching painting on the other wall—"*two* shipwrecks."

"Where would you even put them? All that water. Your bathroom?" Ella shuddered. "Not keen. What's out here?"

"The barn," Mum said. "And my boss."

"We'll be quiet, I promise."

We edged past a bronze statue of a deer with a four-figure price tag, and through the doorway to the back of the gallery.

"Wow." Ella tilted her head back to take in the roof, which was half glass and wholly spectacular. Beams arched across the ceiling like the spars of a ship. The walls below were painted a dove-gray that set off the paintings and photographs to perfection. A glass flight of stairs in one corner ran up to a gallery where Nick had his office. I loved the mixture of ultra-modern design and the old, bumpy walls of the barn.

"Wow," Ella whispered again. This time, she was looking at Nick, who was tall and dark and broad-shouldered, and had the rapt attention of a couple who seemed to be buying everything in the place. "Spectacular."

Her voice was low and reverent, but Nick turned to glower at us.

"Let's go," I said, pulling Ella back.

"Wait. I want to see your mum's pictures."

I pointed at a collection of black-and-white prints hanging at the end of the gallery—landscapes, mostly, but also a close-up of Aristotle that made him look unbearably cute. "Those."

"Can I have a closer look?"

"Another time," I said, wary of annoying Nick any more. This time, Ella came to heel and the two of us slipped back into the front gallery.

"How's he doing?" Mum asked.

"Selling. A lot," I said. Working in Fine Feathers had made me a good judge of customers. These people were easy money.

Nick spent another half-hour with the couple, and at the end of it they'd spent upward of twenty thousand pounds. He walked them out to their car and Mum watched him go, her expression doleful.

"It should have been me."

"It *could* have been you," I said, "if you'd just stepped up."

"Twenty grand. I can't believe it."

"Nor can I." Ella cast a long, appreciative look at Nick. "He is a stunner. Those dark eyes. It's funny, because I always like blue eyes, but his are pretty much black."

"I know," Mum said, stapling a copy of the invoice and sliding it into a file. "It makes it hard to know what he's thinking."

Nick came back and shut the door carefully. I was expecting him to look pleased, but his expression was unreadable.

"Not a bad morning's work."

"You should have let Mum handle it." I blurted it out, ignoring the shocked gasp from Mum's direction. "There's no point in giving her a job if you don't let her do it."

"Were you waiting for an invitation, Molly?"

Mum looked down at the desk and rearranged the papers in front of her. I could tell she was trying not to cry. I felt terrible. If I could have taken back what I'd said, I would have done it, there and then. To fill the awful silence I mumbled, "She didn't want to look as if you were desperate to make the sale."

Nick glanced at Mum, then returned to me. "When are you going to come and work here instead of wasting your time in that dingy little shop?"

"I like Fine Feathers. Anyway, Mum's doing a great job."

"Jess"—Mum sounded tired—"it's all right."

"No, but you *are*."

"She totally is," Ella said, gazing at Nick, hypnotized. He did look like something from a catalog. A catalog of ultra-hot forty-and-looking-good-on-it men, specifically.

Nick set off toward his office without answering. Over his shoulder, he said, "Molly, come and see me in half an hour."

Mum's face had gone white. I started after Nick and she hissed at me to stop, to stay where I was. "I can handle this."

"Handle what?"

"I imagine I am going to get the sack. I'm no good at it, Jess. And he knows it." Mum started tidying the desk in front of her, shuffling pages together. "There's nothing you can do. I'll just have to find another job."

"But didn't Jack say there weren't any?" Ella asked.

"He did, and he was right." I bit my lip.

"Nick doesn't have to employ me, Jess. If I can't find a job, Tilly will probably let us stay until the end of the school year. Then we'll have to go back to London."

"Which would have certain advantages," Ella pointed out. "You could come back to school. Pick up where you left off."

For some reason, that didn't sound terribly appealing. I liked my new life, heartbreak aside.

It was a shame I hadn't realized that until it was too late.

The rest of the tour of Port Sentinel didn't really happen. Ella and I were feeling subdued after what had happened in the gallery, so we made our way to Mario's, a coffee shop on the seafront. It was a perfect time capsule, decorated in the 1950s and never refurbished. The red leatherette seats in our booth were ripped, with yellow foam poking out through the holes, and the round white light that hung over our heads was chipped, but it had character. We hadn't been there for five minutes before Hugo made an appearance, sloping in with Petra behind him.

"What a surprise. Do you mind if we join you?"

"Of course not." Ella scooted sideways to make room and he folded himself into the seat beside her.

Petra sat down beside me, hunched in her jacket. "I don't know why Hugo said it was a surprise. We just asked Aunt Molly where you'd gone and she sent us here."

"Shut up, Petra," Hugo said calmly.

"He's playing it cool," I whispered to Petra, loudly enough for both Ella and Hugo to hear. Ella blushed and Hugo gave me a look that could char paper.

"I'm going to die of caffeine withdrawal if we don't get a waitress over here soon," he said.

"We've already ordered," Ella said.

Petra's nose was running and she kept sniffing.

"What's up?" I asked quietly.

"I was just going to ask you that."

"Mum has work trouble. She thinks Nick is going to sack her." Even saying it made me feel sick. "Your turn."

"I just can't stop thinking about Seb. I mean, what if he dies?"

The waitress was leaning over the table, setting Ella's hot chocolate down in front of her. As Petra spoke, her hand jerked and the cup overturned. A tide of brown, steaming liquid spread across the table. I grabbed a handful of paper napkins from the dispenser and tried to mop it up before it ran over the edge. The waitress had pulled a cloth out of the waistband of her apron and was dabbing at the other side of the hot chocolate lake. She looked as if she was going to burst into tears.

"I'm sorry. I'm so sorry."

"No harm done," Ella said nicely. "At least you missed me."

"I'll get you another one straight away." Her hands were shaking, I noticed.

"And a coffee for me, Lily. Black." Hugo was playing no active part in rescue operations, which was typical. He was leaning back with his arms folded, staying well clear of the sticky mess.

"Anything else?"

"A Coke for me," Petra said. "But there's no hurry."

Lily nodded, biting her lip. At Mario's the waitresses wore their hair up with little white caps perched on top. It was a properly old-fashioned look, and it suited her, even if it didn't really go with her nose stud. The hoo-ha with the hot chocolate had distracted me, but now that I looked at her properly, I realized that I knew her from school. She finished wiping the table and hurried away to the counter.

"Lily Mancini. Mario's daughter?"

"Granddaughter," Hugo corrected me. "She works here at weekends and during the holidays."

"Nothing like a family business to keep you busy. Still, I'm sure they'll forgive her for spilling a drink on us."

I watched her fiddling with the enormous coffee machine. In school she was all dark eyeliner and attitude. At work, she was scrubbed clean, and the only things that hinted at rebellion were her piercings. She had three in her left ear and five in her right, mostly through the cartilage at the top. I had only been able to endure getting one there, it hurt so much. I admired her commitment. Without the heavy makeup I could see how pretty she was, with a cute snub nose and a beautiful mouth. She had classic Italian coloring—dark hair, brown eyes, and skin that tanned easily. I'd always seen her looking sulky, but currently she looked more worried than touchy.

"It's just typical that it was my drink," Ella said sadly. "I attract disaster."

"No one died." Hugo dropped an arm around her shoulders, ultra-casually, and gave her a quick, comforting squeeze. Under the table, Petra's foot connected with my anklebone and I bit the inside of my cheek, trying not to react.

It was one of the other waitresses who brought the drinks in the end. I looked around and saw Lily standing by the kitchen door, talking to the manager who, on closer inspection, had to be her mother. Lily had one hand to her head and looked upset. Her mother nodded and walked away as Lily took the cap out of her hair. Going off duty early, with a bad headache.

I felt sorry for her, and glad that we hadn't made a fuss about the hot chocolate, when it had just been an accident.

"So have you found anything out?" Petra's eyes were fixed on me as if she was waiting for me to perform some sort of trick.

"Since this morning? I haven't had much of a chance. I've been a bit busy with Ella." I glanced across the table, but Ella and Hugo were deep in conversation and weren't paying attention to us. "I was sort of counting on starting with Seb's phone. Has Beth had any luck with getting hold of it?"

Petra shook her head.

I considered my next move. It involved the customers sitting at a table in the window, and it was almost certain to be a failure. I levered myself up to stand on the seat and climbed out of the booth, more or less over Petra.

"Where are you going?" she asked.

"Nothing ventured, nothing gained."

Mario's was full of people from school. I was aware of them watching me as I walked across the café—out of the corner of their eyes or with frank, open interest. Port Sentinel was that sort of place. Everyone would be hoping for a scene, and I just hoped they weren't going to get one.

I don't think either Claudia or Immy were aware I was in the café in the first place, and even if they'd noticed me, they would never have expected me to come and speak to them, let alone pull up a chair. They were sitting with Darcy Gray, who had been Freya's best friend, and owed me, big time. She was wearing bright patterned trousers and brogues and a white shirt buttoned up to the neck: very much the fashion student, which was exactly what she wanted to be. Dress for success was her life plan in a nutshell. I made eye contact with her as I sat down. *Help*.

They had the remains of their lunch in front of them and I hoped they wouldn't just get up and leave. The first thing Claudia and Immy did was turn and stare at me with matching expressions of shock and disapproval. Darcy just looked surprised, and more than a little intrigued.

"Mind if I sit here?"

"Yes. Go away." That was Immy, waspish as usual.

I narrowed my eyes. "Just trying to work out what's different about you. Your hair. It's—is it *pink*?"

She glowered. "Drop dead."

"I'm guessing fake blood's not that easy to wash off."

"She's right. Your hair *is* pink," Darcy said.

"I know, OK?" Immy turned back to me. "I notice you're still here. You're not welcome to stay."

"Sorry," I said, meaning it. I really needed to be more diplomatic. "I think pink hair actually suits you. Maybe you'll start a trend."

"Look, what do you want?" Immy asked, but she looked marginally less hostile.

"Have you heard about Seb Dawson?"

The three of them looked at one another for a moment.

"He's in hospital," Darcy said.

Claudia raised her eyebrows. "How does it concern you? Or us, for that matter?"

"He's not very well. His sister's asked me to find out what happened to him."

"He got run over." Immy was scrabbling through her handbag, hunting for a mirror. She held it up, eyeing her hair. "It's not pink. It's just got a bit of a strawberry blonde tint."

"He did not get run over. Not with those injuries. I know you don't like me, and that's fine, but his little sister is breaking her heart over him and you lot are friendly with Seb. Can you tell me anything that might help?"

"Of course," Darcy said enthusiastically.

"What sort of thing do you want to know?" Claudia got a look from Immy for that, and rolled her eyes. "So what? I used to babysit for Beth. I'm not doing it for her."

Her being me.

"It would mean so much to Beth if you could tell me anything about Seb. Do you know what he was supposed to be doing on Saturday?"

"I know where I saw him," Claudia said slowly. "At the party in Guy's house before the disco."

"What party?" I asked.

"Guy had everyone round for drinks because the disco is always dry. They're too good at spotting booze at the door." I'd noticed. They'd been checking everyone's bags for drinks.

"I wasn't there," Darcy said. "It took me forever to get my hair right. I missed it."

"We had a few drinks at Guy's place. Then we all went to the rec together."

"Was Seb there?"

"N-no." Claudia looked at Immy. "Was he?"

"I didn't see him after Guy's." She frowned. "I think he left early."

"I didn't see him at the fireworks," Darcy said. "And I was

looking." She caught a glower from Claudia. "What? He dresses really well, that's all."

"Did you see him with anyone at Guy's?" I asked Immy. "Was he talking to anyone in particular?"

"Not really. He got there late. I saw him in the kitchen getting a beer out of the fridge, talking to Guy. Then I didn't see him again, I don't think."

"I saw him with Guy and Ryan and a few other people," Claudia said. "All the boys. I don't know what they were talking about. Boy stuff."

So of course the girls hadn't tried to do anything as radical as join in. It occurred to me that one reason why Ryan liked me was that I was prepared to speak to him and his friends without having an attack of the vapors.

"Do you know if Seb had done anything to upset anyone lately?"

Immy laughed. "Seb? That's all he does."

"What do you mean?"

"He's a joker," Claudia said, running her thumbnail along the edge of the table so she could look at it rather than me.

"What does that mean?"

"He gets his kicks from making fun of other people. He's not a nice guy," Darcy said.

"What kind of making fun?"

"You name it. He makes up nicknames for people." She looked at Claudia, obviously uncomfortable. "Mean ones."

"If you hear people calling me Horsey, it was Seb's idea originally." It was not possible for Claudia to look more like a sad horse than she did at that moment. I didn't feel like laughing, though.

"Did you ask him not to call you that?"

"No. What would be the point? He'd just have known it upset me."

Immy leaned in, lowering her voice. "Olly Penrose asked him to stop calling him Olly Bignose. He put up posters around school—Olly's face with different noses stuck on it. He had Gonzo and a toucan, and an elephant's trunk . . ."

"It was really clever," Claudia said quietly. "But Olly was upset."

"Do you know if he came up with any new nicknames recently? Maybe he teased someone he shouldn't have."

"I can't think of anyone. I mean, the one thing about it is that he does it to everyone. It's almost like a sign of being popular to have a Seb Dawson nickname." Claudia didn't even look as if she'd convinced herself, though.

"He calls me Assy." Darcy sniffed. "SO original, I don't think."

"What about you, Immy? What does he call you?"

She bit her lip. "Nothing very clever, actually."

I could tell she wasn't going to say it, and Claudia shook her head when I looked to her. "OK. Fine. Well, what about his personal life? Was he seeing anyone?"

Claudia answered that one. "I don't think so. Not properly. He tends to turn up with someone new every time." A look passed between her and Immy and I wondered what I was missing.

"Was he with anyone at the party?"

"I didn't see."

Immy stirred the coffee in front of her, which was black and had stopped steaming a long time before. "If you must know, he was supposed to be going to the disco with me. Then he ignored me at the party and I was so not bothered."

"Why were you going with him when you don't even like him?" I was genuinely baffled.

"I don't know. He could be sweet. And he's so good-looking. I thought he actually liked me." She gave a little laugh. "I mean, that's how he gets away with it."

"Gets away with what?"

"Treating girls like dirt. And we fall for it, every time." Coffee slopped over the side of the cup as she whirled the spoon around in it, not even seeing what she was doing.

"Careful," I said, putting a hand on her arm. "You're spilling it."

She looked at the mess and pulled a face. "I need the toilet."

"I'll come with you." Darcy jumped up.

"Claudie?" Immy raised her eyebrows expectantly.

"I'll be there in two secs."

They got up without saying anything else to me and wobbled through the tables to the toilets, Immy unsteady on her high wedge trainers.

"She'll be throwing up," Claudia said. "It's the smell I can't stand."

"Does she do that often?"

"All the time." She sounded tense. "I wish she wouldn't."

"I don't see the attraction myself."

"You wouldn't." A deep sigh. "She'd been doing so well. Now she's in there constantly."

It was no big deal in Port Sentinel for a girl to throw up after every meal. The school toilets were pretty much a no-go area after lunch.

"If that's what she wants to do, it's her choice."

Claudia stared at me. "You don't get it, do you? It's not a choice. She's ill."

I felt stupid, and thoughtless. "Sorry. I shouldn't have said that."

"You're not like her so you don't understand. You wouldn't fall for someone telling you you'd be pretty if you could just lose the last ten pounds, or commenting on your thighs. You'd tell them to get stuffed and never think about it again."

"Did someone say those things to Immy?"

"Seb did. And now she's completely obsessed with her weight." Claudia leaned toward me. "Do you want to know why Seb was taking Immy to the disco? He told her it was to apologize for tricking her before. He calls her Dim-ogen, Dimmy for short. He completely fooled her into going to a party with him and doing all this stuff, just because he asked her to."

"What sort of stuff?" I asked. "Sex?"

She looked shocked. "No way. Immy's not like that. Stupid stuff. She didn't realize his mates were texting him, betting him he couldn't make her do all these random things."

"Like what?"

"He got her to bark like a dog—I still don't know how. He made her hold a pint of beer for him for an hour. Every time she went to put it down, he came up with some reason why she had to keep holding it. Everyone was in hysterics."

"Including you?"

"I wasn't there at first, and then I didn't know what was going on. No one would tell me because they knew I'd stop it. I happened to overhear someone suggesting another prank and I worked it out." She pressed her lips together. "I had to tell her everyone was laughing at her. She is a bit of an idiot but she's too sweet to be treated that way."

"That sounds seriously unpleasant."

Claudia gathered up her stuff and stood up. "You know, Seb Dawson had it coming. I'm sorry for Beth, but whatever happened to him, I bet he started it."

I went back to the others as Claudia headed for the bathroom and her date with Immy's lunch.

"What was all that about?" Hugo asked.

"Research." I told them the highlights of what I'd found out.

"He's so awful," Ella said. "How does he get away with it?"

"Girls will forgive anything," I said. "I think Immy wanted to believe he really regretted being mean to her. She thought she'd changed him, but apparently not. And he is ridiculously handsome. Charming if he wants to be. I can see how you might let yourself be fooled."

Hugo tapped the table. "Less of that, please. You have enough man trouble without including Seb Dawson."

"Seb In-a-Coma Dawson is not exactly in a position to woo me. Calm down." I leaned back against the fake leather, thinking. "So the next thing I should do is talk to Guy, I suppose. He might know why Seb left his party. We know he never made it to the disco, so we really need to know where he went instead."

"Guy will be at Harry Knowles's house tonight, I guarantee you. They've been mates forever," Hugo said.

"Then I'll go there."

"You can't. You don't have an invitation."

"But if I just turn up—"

"Harry doesn't let just anyone in to his parties. You have to be with someone he knows unless you're actually on the list."

"There's a list?"

"You'd have a list too if you had Harry's reputation. After the third time the house was trashed, his dad told him he'd have to stay at school for the holidays unless he made sure it didn't happen again."

"Why don't his parents just take him with them when they travel?"

"He's terrified of flying." Hugo saw my eyebrows go up. "It's true. You can't get him on a plane. They have to leave him behind and they can't stop him having his friends over. All two hundred of them. Music, drinking, and bad behavior, every night this week."

"Sounds like fun." Ella grinned as Hugo turned, surprised. "Not really. But I'd like to see a proper Port Sentinel house party before I go."

"You can come with me," I said.

"Let's recap. You're not invited." Hugo was looking distinctly put out, probably at the thought of Ella going anywhere without him. They were sitting so close together, they touched at the knee, hip and shoulder.

"Well, I'll have to get in somehow. I'll find a way."

"Good luck." Hugo's voice was skeptical.

I smiled at him sweetly. "I won't need luck, Hugo."

"Why's that?"

"My invitation just walked through the door." I waved as Ryan detached himself from his friends and headed straight for me, like a girl-seeking missile. Seb Dawson, master of manipulation, had absolutely nothing on me.

8

Life is full of compromises. I'd sworn I wouldn't, ever, but I met Ryan halfway across the café and asked him out on a date before I could think better of it.

"You want to go out with me." He turned to his mates, who were sitting down in the corner, and yelled, just slightly louder than he needed to if he wanted to be heard over the noise of the café, "She wants to go out with me."

They cheered as he held his hands in the air, celebrating. I yanked on his sleeve to get his attention.

"You said you'd take me to Harry Knowles's party the other night. I want to take you up on the offer. If you're going, that is."

"I am now." He frowned at me, though. "What's going on? Why the sudden interest in Harry?"

"I felt I was missing out. Everyone's been talking about his parties. I wanted to see for myself."

"Curiouser and curiouser."

"What's that supposed to mean?"

"It means that you don't usually pay attention to what other people talk about."

Damn. I always forgot that Ryan was not one of your dumb blonds. "I know, but it's all part of the settling-in process. I need to live like a local." I lowered my voice. "And my friend Ella really wants to see a Port Sentinel party while she's here."

He looked over my shoulder. "Is that her?"

"Yep."

"Pretty girl." His eyes came back to me. "Not as pretty as you, but pretty. I'm sure I can find someone to take her."

"They'll have to fight Hugo for the privilege. Not that they should be scared, or anything."

"I reckon Hugo could handle himself in a scrap." Ryan grinned. "Runs in the family, from what I hear."

"If you mean me, I haven't fought with anyone."

"Not strictly true. I don't know if you remember my crazy ex-girlfriend . . ."

"Oh, her. I don't count that."

"She would not be pleased to hear you say that. Seriously, though, you've done your share of damage. You haven't done much more than look at me and I'm a broken man."

"Looking surprisingly well on it," I commented. "Broken is not the word I'd use."

He looked interested. "What word would you use?"

Walked into that one . . . I couldn't think of anything except "fit," which I obviously couldn't say, so I ended up blushing, which was actually worse.

The bell jangled as the door opened and Ryan turned to see the two boys who were walking in. "Ah. The man himself."

I'd already recognized Harry Knowles, though I didn't know his companion, who was short and cute, with sandy hair and little round glasses. He slid into a booth, leaving Harry to come over toward us. Behind big sunglasses, Harry's face was pale, but he was grinning.

"Dude. How's it going?"

"Not bad." Ryan put an arm around my shoulders. "Have you met Jess?"

"I can't say I've had the pleasure." The sunglasses went up on top of his head and Harry smiled at me. He looked tired but focused. His eyes never left my face, as if I was the most fascinating person in the room and all he'd ever wanted was to talk to me.

"Jess Tennant," I said. "I was just asking Ryan about your famous parties."

"Believe everything you've heard. Actually, believe that they're twice as extreme as you've heard."

"I do," I said truthfully. "I gather they're pretty amazing."

"You could say that." He snapped his fingers. "You know, you should come along tonight. Ryan's coming, aren't you, mate?"

"Wouldn't miss it. What's this about a theme, though?"

Harry's eyes glittered. "I got bored with the same-old same-old. I wanted a change. It's Deadly Decadence tonight, and if you don't make an effort, you're not getting in. The girls have to look beautiful. I mean, really stunning."

"You could go as you are," Ryan said to me, and Harry clapped, slowly.

"Smooth. But actually, I'd have to put my foot down. You

need to look the best you've ever looked in your life, Jess Tennant. That's what we're going for here. Exceptional."

"I'll bear that in mind." I was already quite sure my wardrobe wasn't going to cover it. Glancing over, I was relieved to see that Darcy had sat down beside Petra. I was going to need all the fashion advice I could get.

"I'll look forward to it." Harry looked at me again, for slightly longer than I might have expected, and then punched Ryan on the shoulder. "Mate. You don't change."

"What's that supposed to mean?" Ryan asked, but all he got was a grin as Harry slipped the sunglasses back down and went to sit with his friend.

"He is seriously charming," I said.

"When he wants to be." Ryan looked down at me. "What time do you want to get there? People usually start turning up after ten."

"That sounds about right."

"I'll come round to your house."

"OK."

"We can walk over there together. I'd drive, but . . ." He mimed drinking.

"Fine by me." I was amused that Ryan was taking charge. It was what came naturally to him. All the unrequited yearning had obviously been a strain.

"Do you want me to find someone for your friend?"

"Ella?" I looked round to see Hugo murmuring something in her ear as she giggled. Petra and Darcy were looking utterly bored. When Petra saw us looking, she mimed slitting her wrists. "Could you get Hugo on the list so he can take her?"

"I don't see why not."

"Thanks, Ryan." I really meant it.

"I'll see you later." He leaned down, and instinctively I turned my head, so that his kiss landed on the corner of my mouth, instead of right on it as he'd intended. He grinned at me anyway before turning away and I headed back to my table feeling heartless. Maybe I should stamp on a few kittens for an encore.

"How did that go?" Ella asked.

"As well as can be expected."

"Did you get him to invite you to the party?"

"Of course."

"And you met Harry Knowles himself."

"I did."

"Then why do you look grim?"

"Guilt," Hugo said. "She's just using him for social success."

"I am taking advantage," I admitted. "But it's for a good cause."

"I think you should stay out of it," Hugo said. "For the record."

"Let the record show that Hugo thinks I should stay out of it."

"But you're not going to."

I smiled at him pityingly. "What do you think?"

"I am going to need to know all about this," Darcy said. "But the main question is obviously what you're going to wear."

"I don't really have anything suitable."

Petra grinned. "You don't. But I know where we can find something perfect."

"I'm starting to wish I hadn't bothered to bring going-out clothes. If I had known you had the keys to this place all along . . ." Ella was wandering around Fine Feathers, picking things up and putting them down again. She looked as if she was in heaven.

"I didn't have the keys. I didn't even know Tilly did."

"Sylvia asked her to keep them in case the shop caught fire or got burgled. She always leaves them with her." Petra jumped up to sit on the counter, swinging her legs.

"Be careful up there," I warned. "If you go through the glass, you'll hurt yourself. More importantly, you'll ruin the display, and it took me ages to do."

"Can we put the lights on?" Ella asked. "It's gloomy in here."

"I don't want people to think the shop is open. And you get used to it after a while." Besides, the lighting actually didn't make that much difference. Two dim bulbs hung from the ceiling, and unless you were standing directly underneath them, you wouldn't have known they were even on.

"What you need," Darcy said authoritatively, "is a dress."

"I'm not wearing a dress. I was thinking jeans and a top."

"That's what you always wear and you need to be transformed." Darcy waggled her fingers, fairy-godmother-style. "You said it yourself. You need to get Seb's friends to talk to you, and the best way to do that is to look incredible. If they're anything like Seb, they'll be all about appearances. You've got to make an extra effort."

"Unlike my usual look, which is zero effort."

"You said it." Petra grinned at the expression on my face.

"I just don't think—" I started to say, but Ella interrupted.

"Jessica Tennant, if the girl says you need a dress, you need a dress. And I don't see the problem. Your legs are fine. You used to wear dresses in London."

"*Did* she?" Darcy asked, interested.

"Frequently."

Petra grinned. "She wore one the other night. But that was for her Bo-Peep costume and she made a huge fuss about it."

"Can you stop talking about me as if I'm not here? Ella, why don't you go and find Hugo?" The thought of a clothes-shopping trip—even an illicit one—had sent Hugo home in a hurry.

"Don't try to distract me. Why don't you want to look good, please?"

I wriggled. "It's not that I don't want to look good. I've just got in the habit of trying to avoid attention. And if I have to be Action Girl for any reason, I'd rather be in jeans."

"Why would you need to be Action Girl? You're just going to the party to meet Seb's friends and ask a few questions."

"You never know, though."

Darcy clapped her hands to get our attention. "OK, so you'll need to be prepared to swing into superhero mode. I like a challenge. You can still wear a dress."

"Not a short one," I said, wary.

"It'll be fine." Darcy sounded confident. "Now where do you keep the going-out stuff?"

I went over to a rack by the wall and pulled a little red dress off the rail. "This kind of thing?"

"Exactly."

"But not this."

"Probably not." Petra climbed down and came over to hold the dress up against me. It was short and sleeveless, with a belt, a high neckline, and a full skirt. I absolutely hated it. Ella stood beside her, the two of them tilting their heads to stare at me. They had exactly the same critical expression.

"It would fit," Ella said. "Perfectly."

"I think we can do better," Petra announced.

"Me too." Ella took it. "But let's put it in the changing room. Just in case."

Petra nodded. "Just in case."

Darcy rolled her eyes. "Yeah, why don't we waste our time? We've got a little under six hours to transform Jess. What's the point in trying on something no one likes?"

"I just thought we shouldn't rule it out," Ella said, holding onto the hanger. "You never know."

"You absolutely know." Darcy lifted up a fold of the skirt. "Ugh. Cheap material."

"Darcy," I said. "Tone it down."

"What? I'm just saying we don't have time to mess around." She looked super-innocent, but she'd been getting at Ella ever since she found out she was my best friend. Darcy and I had never got to be as close as Darcy and Freya had been, but that wasn't from lack of trying on her part. Now that Ella was here, she felt threatened. I wished I could explain the situation to Ella but there hadn't been a chance. Anyway, Ella was well able to stand her ground.

"We are in a charity shop, you know. We'll be lucky if we find anything that fits Jess, let alone the perfect dress." Defiantly, she hung the red dress on the rail in the changing room.

"It's not my first pick, but I still think it's worth keeping it in reserve."

Recognizing that she'd lost the battle, Darcy started rummaging through the rails. "What else is there?"

"Lots of stuff," Petra said, peace-making. "We'll find something perfect."

"Do I get any say in what I wear?" I asked.

The reply was swift, and came in unison. "No."

They did, however, allow me a veto, which I used twice: once for a sky-blue draped dress with a fitted strapless top and a poufy skirt that made me feel like a skater who'd wandered away from an ice-dancing competition. The other time was for a gold-sequined number that was too Vegas showgirl for me.

"Try it on," Ella suggested.

"Not even so you can laugh at me." I handed it back to her and pulled the changing-room curtain across so I could tackle the next hanger. "You try it on if you want to see how it looks."

"This always happens," Darcy said wisely. "You get cooperation for a bit and then she starts getting difficult."

Ella nodded. "And she can be *so* difficult."

"Just so you know, the curtain isn't soundproof." I poked my head through it. "I can hear what you're saying about me."

"All true." Ella pulled the curtain over so I had to duck back inside the cubicle or risk getting a face full of dusty material. "Get on with it. What about the black-and-white one?"

I pulled a face—the black-and-white one was not my favorite—but I did as I was told. *Difficult*, indeed. I preferred it when Ella and Darcy were sniping at one another instead of focusing on my shortcomings.

Two dresses later, I pulled the curtain back and stood in front of them. "This one."

"Oooh." Petra went one way, Ella the other, circling me with narrowed eyes. Darcy stood at a distance, her arms crossed, frowning.

"You're making me nervous." I turned to see myself in the mirror. The dress was black, of course, and short, but with a straight skirt that flared very slightly. The top was a fitted bustier with the most delicate lace overlay that ran on to make cap sleeves. It swooped low at the back. Very low, I thought, seeing a lot of bare skin in the mirror. "Maybe it's too much."

"No way. I love it." Ella bit her lip. "You can't wear a bra."

"It'll show," Petra agreed.

"Well, I don't know if it was Mr. Dolce or Mr. Gabbana who thought of that, but someone did. The bodice is boned so I don't need one."

"Excellent," Darcy purred. "Now you just need shoes."

"And you need to do something with your hair."

"And makeup. Proper makeup."

"OK." I held up my hands. "I know you three are enjoying this, but give me a break."

"No breaks. This is important. You want those boys to talk to you and you know what they like," Darcy said.

"They like girls like Immy Hinch."

"So you need to be like Immy Hinch. And Immy Hinch wears heels." Darcy started rooting through the shoes on a low shelf by the changing room. "What size are you? Five?"

"And a half." I sighed. "I hate wearing heels. And I have to walk there, may I remind you. And stand around while I'm there. *And* walk back."

"Poor, poor you." Ella patted my shoulder on her way to join in the search through the shoe shelf. "The things you do for the truth. Maybe Ryan will give you a piggyback."

"I bet that's not all he'll offer to give her in that dress."

"*Petra!*" I was outraged. "Get your mind out of the gutter, please."

"It's true. He's going to flip," Petra said happily, flinging a pair of strappy sandals at me.

"Not those. I can't have bare legs. I'll die of cold."

"Just try them so we can see if that's the right height," Darcy ordered.

I could see why someone had abandoned the shoes to a charity shop. Not only did you need a degree in engineering to know how the straps were supposed to go, they were vilely uncomfortable. It took me ages to get into them. I straightened up warily.

Ella stared. "Wow. They look fab."

"Amazing," Petra said.

"Perfect," Darcy agreed.

"Horrendous. Forget it." I wobbled toward them. "Look at me. This isn't fab. This is a chiropractor's appointment waiting to happen."

Ella winced. "You really need to practice to be good in heels."

"And I skipped it. Silly me." I almost overbalanced and clutched a rack of suits. "The last time I got all dressed up in weird clothes to fight crime, my feet nearly died. I had to go to hospital. I can't do this again."

Petra sat back on her heels. "If we can find shoes that you can walk in, will you wear them?"

"That's a big if." I sighed. "I don't want to be accused of being uncooperative again, but seriously, this is too much. Can't I pick the shoes?"

"Will you let me do your makeup?" Ella asked. "The way I want to do it?"

"Fine."

"OK then. No heels." Darcy shook her head sadly. "It could have been so beautiful."

"Only if I was able to stand still all night, like this." I held a pose while Ella scrabbled for her phone.

"Lauren will never forgive me if I miss this. Stay like that. One more second."

I did as I was told. With my head at an awkward angle, all I could see was my reflection in the changing-room mirror. The dress looked fine. It was my face that was the problem. Specifically, the look in my eyes.

Fear.

I really hoped this wasn't going to turn out to be my biggest mistake yet.

9

Petra was right about one thing—Ryan did like the dress. I heard him with Hugo in the hall and ran downstairs, glad that I had insisted on wearing my silver Converse instead of heels. The two boys glanced up as I turned the corner and came into view, and Ryan, who'd been talking, fell silent. I started to feel very self-conscious indeed as they both stared. And stared. And stared.

"What's wrong?"

"Absolutely nothing." It didn't take all that long for Ryan to get back to his usual self. "You look gorgeous."

"Looking good, feeling great." I jumped down off the last step. I did look all right, even I had to admit. My style advisers had decided against straightening my hair, so it was all loose curls that didn't quite reach my shoulders. Ella had gone to town on the eye makeup. She was far better at it than me. Left to my own devices, I'd have looked as if I'd punched myself in both eyes, but Ella had managed to make me look like a living anime character. To make sure I fitted in with the Deadly Decadence theme, Darcy had come up with dangly earrings: a chain of pearls ending in a tiny skull. They practically brushed my shoulders. I turned my head to set them swinging.

"Why are you so happy?" Hugo asked.

"Because she's going out with me. Duh." Ryan was grinning at me.

"Thanks, Mr. Ego. It's not just that. I thought I was going to have to go back to London permanently, but I don't." I was still buzzing with relief. Mum's terrifying meeting with Nick had turned out to be a sales pep talk that had gone way over her head, but at least she still had a job. It surprised me how much I had minded about having to leave. Heartbreak or not, I'd fallen for Port Sentinel.

"Good news," Ryan said.

Hugo, who had already heard all about it, looked bored. "Where's Ella?"

"She's coming. She's just doing her face."

"How long will that take?"

"Honestly? It could be half an hour."

"I like her without makeup."

I laughed. "You've never seen her without makeup."

"Are you serious?"

"I know it's hard to believe." I did love boys sometimes. They were so innocent about that kind of thing. It took Ella twenty minutes to look as if she was wearing no makeup, and it involved twelve separate products. "Anyway, it'll be worth the wait."

"Do we need to wait too?" Ryan was still looking at me, with a degree of concentration that I found unsettling. "Hugo can find his own way to Harry's house."

"I should probably see if Ella wants me to hang around," I said, edging toward the stairs.

Hugo sighed. "You know she'll say yes. Come on, Jess. Give me a chance to spend some time with her."

"Yeah, Jess, give him a chance." Ryan turned to Hugo. "If I were you I'd take the scenic route round to Harry's. Spin it out a bit. Take advantage of some time alone."

"Good thinking."

"Be honest, Hugo. Have you fallen for her?" I asked.

He looked embarrassed. "Not yet."

"Sure about that?"

"I'm not sure about anything at the moment. Except that the clock is ticking and you're missing out on valuable interrogation time."

Out of the corner of my eye I caught the look of surprise on Ryan's face. I glowered at Hugo. "Thanks for the reminder."

"Any time." He was giving me the same look back. He really didn't think this was a good idea. Which was no reason to give the game away in front of Ryan, I would have said, but Hugo wasn't the sort to let an opportunity like that go by.

I grabbed my jacket—well, Mum's jacket, a fitted leather one she'd had for years that I coveted beyond words. The only good thing about my coat being stolen was that I had a reason to borrow it. "Ready?"

"Definitely." Ryan followed me out to the porch, where he took the jacket out of my hands and held it for me to put on. I let him, amused by the old-school chivalry. It was cold out, and I was glad of both the jacket and his company as we started walking. The moon was almost full. It cast a silver-blue light that made everything ghostly pale.

"Which way is it?"

"We need to go down Eastville Road and hang a left on Sturbridge Lane. Then up Dartley Hill. I'm not going to lie to you, it's steep. Should take us fifteen minutes, I reckon."

"Good thing I wore trainers."

"You look good in them."

"That was a factor in the decision, obviously."

"Obviously." He sounded distracted and I walked along beside him in silence, leaving him to his thoughts. I had plenty of my own to deal with. It wasn't a comfortable sort of silence, though, and after a couple of minutes I broke it.

"Thanks for asking me to this."

"Let's be honest. You asked me."

"Not originally."

"I may have mentioned it at the fireworks, but we're here because you want to be." There was a pause before he added, "And I'd like to know why."

"Oh. I told you. I wanted to see a real Port Sentinel party."

He stopped, grabbing hold of my arm and spinning me round to face him. His eyes were cold.

"Just so we're clear, I'd like the truth. What did Hugo mean about interrogating people? What's going on?"

I wriggled. "You have to promise not to tell anyone."

"No promises in advance." He meant it too. His expression was forbidding. It came as something of a shock to me to realize that I liked this version of Ryan much more than the good-time guy who was always joking around.

"Right. OK. The truth."

"If you don't mind."

I explained about Petra and Beth, leaving out Beth's concerns about what her brother might have done to deserve a beating. "I didn't want to get involved, but they're counting on me. They think I can find out what happened."

"You should leave it to the cops."

"Who are not interested."

He frowned. "Seriously?"

"Very much not. Dan Henderson has a bad case of looking-the-other-way-itis."

"Not for the first time." Ryan chewed his lower lip, thinking. "I suppose it's fair enough. I'd have liked to know all this in advance, though."

"I should have said. I didn't know if you'd want to help."

He looked surprised, then irritated. "That's nice."

"Hugo thought I should stay out of it. You might have felt the same way."

"So you thought you'd lie about it instead. You didn't even give me the chance to say what I thought."

"When did I lie? You asked me to go with you before. I took you up on your invitation. What's the problem?"

"The problem is that you don't really want to be here, and you certainly don't want to be here with me."

"That's not true," I protested. The wind was blowing straight off the sea and I shivered. "I mean, I'd rather be indoors. Somewhere warm, preferably. But I'm really happy to be going to the party with you."

"Don't take me for an even bigger idiot than I've been already. You wouldn't be here if you didn't want to find out about Seb. I just made it easy for you."

I could hear the hurt in his voice. My guilty feelings came back with reinforcements. "I'm sorry. I didn't mean to upset you."

"Yeah. It's good to know you care." He started walking again, striding so I had to jog to keep up. "Never mind. Who are you planning to interrogate?"

"Anyone who might be able to help. You, even."

"Me? I don't think I know anything useful."

"You know Seb."

"A bit. We're not close."

"I've seen you talking to him in school."

"He's friends with my friends. He's on the soccer team. I see him around a lot but I don't *know* him."

"Do you know if anyone's pissed off with him?"

"Enough to beat him up?" Ryan shrugged. "Nope. But he's not the easiest person to get on with."

"What do you mean?"

"He likes to get under your skin. It's all for laughs, but he'll find the thing that really bothers you and keep going on about it. He gets a kick out of annoying people."

"I heard he makes up nicknames for people. And plays jokes on them."

"Who told you that?"

"Claudia and Immy."

Ryan nodded. "They'd know. They've both been on the receiving end."

"Why does he get away with it?"

"He's a laugh. It's funny when it's not you."

"Sounds hysterical."

"Yeah, he can be." Ryan frowned at me again. "Look, you're not part of this world. You don't understand what it's like. Everyone has a good time, all the time, and no one cares who gets hurt."

I shivered, cold in my borrowed jacket. "I definitely don't understand why you'd want to be a part of it. You're too clever for that, aren't you?"

"Nice of you to say so."

"You pretend to be something you're not."

He stopped, looking taken aback. It only lasted for a moment, and then he was back on the attack. "And you don't?"

"No, I don't."

"Bull. You act as if you're the toughest thing going, but it's all a front." He ran a finger down my cheek. "You can fool most people, but you can't fool me."

I grabbed his hand and pushed it back toward him. "We're not talking about me. We're talking about your friends and their petty, hurtful games."

"You're taking it too seriously."

"Someone else took it seriously," I said softly. "And Seb's the one who got hurt."

He started walking again, head down. "You're too quick to judge people, Jess."

"That's not fair."

"Life isn't black and white. People aren't all bad or all good. Sometimes they do stupid things and don't even realize it until it's too late."

"I know that."

"You're just as bad as Seb. You despise people like Claudia and Immy because you think you're better than them, but you don't know them." He looked at me again. "And you don't know me."

"Ryan . . ."

"Don't write me off because I'm popular."

I laughed. "I've written you off because you're a flirt. You only want me because I haven't been taken in by it."

"Is that what you think?" He turned away so I couldn't see his face.

"Why else would you be interested in me?"

When he answered me, his voice was so bitter it made me wince. "If that's really what you think, I'm not going to try to persuade you you're wrong."

"Am I?"

"Very."

I walked along beside him, miserable. Jess Tennant. Specialities: rushing to judgment and leaping to conclusions. Romantic history: disaster followed by catastrophe. I seemed to have discovered an amazing talent for upsetting people lately.

"I'm sorry. I didn't mean to hurt your feelings."

"I'll survive." He stopped again. "Jess, is that why you haven't even considered giving me a chance? Because you thought I was just looking for a challenge?"

"I suppose so." It was a big reason. Not the only one, but big enough that he could think it if he liked.

"Is there anyone else?"

"No."

"What about Will Henderson?"

"That's not going to happen," I said quickly. "Ever. That's over."

"You sound pretty definite about that."

"I am." No tears this time. It was a fact.

"Then will you think again about us?"

I wanted to say no. I wanted to just end it there and then—make a joke about being celibate and move on with our lives. But he was heartbreakingly handsome in the moonlight, and I was the one who had made him look so sad, and I liked him more and more, as a person. It wasn't out of the question that I might change my mind one day, and see him as more than a friend. I couldn't decide if it was worse to give him hope or to tell him to stop trying. All I knew was I didn't want to hurt him any more.

"I'm not making any promises," I said.

"But you're not saying no."

"I'm not saying no."

I'd expected triumph, but his expression was grave. "That'll do."

I checked my watch. "I think Hugo and Ella are going to get there before we do."

"No way." Ryan grabbed my hand. "Not if we run."

"Run? In this dress? Ryan, I can't!"

"I bet you can."

"How much do you bet?"

"A new dress"—he grinned at me—"of my choosing."

"I think that's worse." Before I could say anything else, he'd pulled me off balance and started running. His grip was unbreakable. I had to go with it. And as it turned out, he was right. I *could* run in my dress, and we did, down the road and up the hill to Harry Knowles's road, and I could not stop laughing all the way, until we turned a corner and saw the house.

I slowed down, panting. "Wow. It looks like a ship."

The house was aggressively modern and wedge-shaped, all glass and wood paneling. Every window was lit up, and I could see people inside dancing. The music was loud and the thump of the bass was like a heartbeat.

"Wait until you see the inside. Pretty amazing." Ryan was still holding my hand as if he had no intention of letting go, and he led me through the high gates that stood a little ajar, up a narrow path with white lights on either side of it, toward the front door. A silver Audi TT crouched on the gravel beside the path, parked at an angle, as if the driver had just abandoned it. The front bumper was dented and it had a long scratch along the wing.

"Nice job, Harry," Ryan said, pausing to look at it.

"Is that his car?"

"Yeah. I don't know what his dad was thinking, buying that for him."

It was the car I'd seen at the fireworks, the one that had snagged my tights. Parking didn't seem to be Harry's strong point. By the looks of it, driving wasn't one of his talents either. A very sensible black people carrier was parked by the wall. "Is that his as well?"

"That belongs to the door staff."

"The what?"

"Look."

A couple of actual, honest-to-God bouncers in black suits were standing just inside the door, in a small hallway. One of them had a clipboard.

"Ryan Denton, and this is my date." Ryan leaned over the top of the clipboard, scanning for his name. "That's me."

"Got any ID?"

"Somewhere." With his free hand, Ryan started patting his pockets.

"You can have your hand back, you know," I whispered.

"Don't worry. My ID is in here, I know it."

"No need for that. Come in, buddy." Harry Knowles, drink in hand, was grinning widely. He seemed completely wired and I couldn't tell if it was his personality or if he was actually high. He wrapped an arm around Ryan's neck. "How's it going?"

"Not bad. How are you holding up?"

"I've got stamina, baby. I can party all week, no problem." He leaned out so he could see past Ryan. "Hello, lovely. You look stunning."

"Good enough to get in?"

"Absolutely."

One of the bouncers was waiting for my jacket and I shrugged it off with a pang. The last time I'd trusted a coat to a cloakroom, things had gone badly.

Harry grabbed hold of Ryan's wrist and squeezed it until he dropped my hand. Then Harry took hold of me and spun me around to see the back of my dress. He whistled. "Wow. Ryan, have you seen this?"

"Yep." Ryan grabbed Harry's wrist in exactly the same way. "Leave her alone."

"I'm just looking. Admiring. That's a hell of a dress."

"You don't need to touch her to admire the dress." The mood was friendly but Ryan's words weren't, and one of the bouncers took a step closer to us.

"It's OK," I said, freeing myself. "Which way is the party?"

"Through here." Harry strolled down the hall and I followed.

Ryan took hold of my hand again and I let him, rather than having a fight.

"Have a look around. Make yourself at home. Drinks in the kitchen. Dancing everywhere. Bedrooms are technically off-limits but I won't make a big deal out of it if you sneak in. Except mine. Mine is properly not open to the public."

"Good to know," I said, thinking there was no way I was going anywhere near a bedroom in that house.

"Are there many people here?" Ryan asked.

"What do you think? Full house, almost. Come and see."

A single door led off the hall. It was heavy, huge, and covered in black leather. When Harry pushed it open, the noise and heat hit me and I actually stepped back a little.

"Wow."

"Good, isn't it?" Harry spread his arms wide. "My people."

I was taking in the architecture, which was awe-inspiring: a big double-height open-plan space with vast windows that gave a stunning view of the town and the bay beyond. A glass staircase ran up one side of the room to a gallery and then, I presumed, the bedrooms. A walkway went from the gallery to the other side of the room: more bedrooms and another flight of stairs swooping down to the ground floor, this time metal. Currently the walkway was full of people leaning over the rail and chatting, watching the dancers below. Either Harry's parents weren't big on furniture or the place had been cleared because it was almost empty, apart from two enormous sofas pushed back against the walls. It just meant there was all the more space for everyone who was anyone in Port Sentinel to dance, drink, and do things they shouldn't.

And decadent was the only word for some of the things that were going on in front of me.

The music was so loud it made it hard to think, and it was extremely hot. There were faces I knew in the crowd, but I had to look twice to be sure it was really them. The girls' eyes were heavy-lidded, their faces were flushed and they seemed languid as they draped themselves around the boys. People had made an effort to dress for the theme. A stunning redhead had diamanté scorpions crawling through her hair. Calliope Roland, who was tall, ice-blonde and model-thin, had painted her eyelids and nails absinthe green, and was carrying around a bottle of the spirit for anyone brave enough to try it.

I squeezed Ryan's hand and he leaned down so I could shout in his ear, "Isn't that Lucy Blair? I thought she was going out with Archie."

"She is."

"That's not Archie." I pointed to where Lucy was wrapped around a guy I'd never seen before.

Ryan shrugged. "Archie's away."

"So it's fine for her to cheat?"

"I didn't say that. But it's none of my business." *Or yours.* I got the subtext.

"I'm not going to apologize for being judgmental about cheating."

"You'll never change."

"Not about that."

Watching, I felt as if I was on show too. Heads turned, with expressions ranging from interest to outright hostility. Darcy waved at me from her position halfway up the stairs and lifted her glass, saluting my new look. Her dress was a plunging Vivienne Westwood number that knocked at least three inches off her waist. Earlier, I had heard all about the clutch bag she had tucked under one arm, and had seen pictures. It was McQueen, with silver spikes down both sides. She had a matching cuff on one wrist. Still, even if the party hadn't been themed she'd probably have ended up wearing something similar.

"Get yourselves a drink." The noise level was too high for Harry to have heard what we were saying, but he'd noticed we weren't exactly embracing the party mood. "Come on, Ryan. Don't let me down. We have to show Jess a good time."

"The kitchen's that way." Ryan pointed past me to a white corridor lined with black-and-white photos. It was pretty much packed with people.

I was closer so I went first, pushing through the crowd and trying not to step on anyone's toes, literally. It was so crowded Ryan had to let go of my hand at last. I wondered how long it would be before he grabbed it again, and whether I minded. Someone bumped into me. A girl I didn't know pushed me away, her face twisted in irritation. I tripped over something I couldn't see and pitched forward, not quite falling. I heard someone laugh as they turned away from me. Tough crowd.

As I ducked out from behind a huge guy dressed as a not very religious monk who had effectively been blocking the whole corridor, I saw something that stopped me where I stood.

Will was standing at the end of the corridor, leaning against the wall, deep in conversation with someone. A second after I spotted him, he glanced up and his eyes met mine, and he broke off whatever he was saying. The expression on his face was hard to interpret, but it looked a lot like disapproval.

The guy who'd been talking to him looked round to see what

had caught Will's attention. It was Harry's sandy-haired friend from the coffee shop. He frowned, but obviously couldn't place me. He turned back and asked Will a question, and got the briefest of answers. I felt heat rising in my cheeks. I'd have gone back the way I came, but there were too many people behind me and the only option was to keep going, say hello, and walk on.

That was the plan, anyway. In reality I got as far as waving and giving Will a tepid, "Hi."

"What are you doing here?"

I'd been moving past, but I stopped. "The same as you, I imagine. Having fun."

"With me." Ryan, arriving at the worst moment possible. He grabbed my wrist and pulled me round to face him. Then he put his other hand flat on my back where my dress dipped down, pulling me against him. *I own this.*

The other boy waved. "Ryan. How's it going?"

"Good, thanks. How've you been?"

While Ryan was distracted, I wriggled out of his grasp and faced Will.

"I didn't expect to find you here."

"I'm surprised to see you too." Will's voice was so cold, it felt as if winter had come early. "You look . . . decadent."

"And you look as if you didn't make much of an effort. Neither decadent nor deadly."

Wordlessly, he held open his shirt to show me the logo on his T-shirt.

"The Killers," I said. "Cute."

"Are you Jess?" The sandy-haired boy held out his hand, grinning engagingly. "I'm Guy."

"Guy Tindall," Ryan murmured in my ear. "Seb's friend."

"Will and I go to the same school."

"Really?" I looked at Will. "Is that why you're here?"

"Guy asked me to come along."

"It's good to have someone to talk to. These things can get a bit boring." Up close, Guy had freckles across his nose and a wicked gleam in his eyes. "After the first couple of nights it's all a bit same-old, same-old."

"It's my first time here."

"We should get that drink," Ryan said. He leaned down and kissed my neck, just under my ear. "What is that perfume, Jess? You smell incredible, as usual."

"Stop." I pushed him away, embarrassed. I couldn't help checking to see what Will made of it, and quailed at the expression in his eyes—or rather the lack of expression. He might as well have been carved from stone. "We should go. We're blocking the corridor. See you later."

Guy raised his glass. "Looking forward to it."

As we started to walk away, someone bumped into Ryan. He clashed shoulders with Will, who handed him off.

"Watch where you're going, mate."

"You watch it, *mate*." The two of them glowered at each other.

"Stop it, both of you." I was genuinely annoyed. "Not here. Not now."

"Actually, I think here and now would be perfect." Harry Knowles had appeared at my elbow, as if he sensed trouble, but he wasn't there to stop it. Quite the opposite. "I needed volunteers for the next bit of the party, and I think you two have just offered your services."

10

You have got to calm down." Ella was stroking my arm while Hugo stood nearby, a glass of water in his hand, presumably in case I felt thirsty while I was crying my eyes out. Darcy was sitting beside me, her head tilted to one side, all sympathy.

"This is completely my fault." I sniffed. "There's no way they would be fighting if it wasn't for me."

"They never got on," Hugo said dismissively. "Or at least they haven't for years. Don't think it's about you. They've got history."

"I know the history. Trust me, this is current affairs." I blew my nose on a bit of kitchen paper and tried to ignore the curious looks I was getting from the people who passed through the kitchen in search of booze, which was basically everyone. I was sitting on a stool at a black granite breakfast bar, wishing I could go home. In front of me there were hundreds of plastic cups filled with the cocktails Harry had made: pink for the girls, naturally, and blue for the boys. They both looked and smelled revolting.

"I still don't understand what happened," Ella said. "You bumped into Will, and he and Ryan had a fight."

"Not even a fight. A scrap. But Ryan had been winding Will up about being at the party with me, so it was all a bit tense. And then Harry—"

"Our host," Hugo interjected for Ella's benefit.

"—turned up and said they'd volunteered. And when Will asked for what, he said they had to fight." I had long since abandoned any attempt to keep my eye makeup pristine but I was a bit alarmed at the amount of black that was coming off on the kitchen paper. "How do I look, Ella?"

"Sad panda." She dabbed under my eyes, but from the look on her face it wasn't helping much. I waved her away.

"The two of them went off with him and I don't know where. And now everyone is betting on who's going to win, as if it's perfectly acceptable for the two of them to batter each other. As if it's entertainment."

"Well, boxing . . ." Hugo said.

"This isn't boxing. It's fighting, pure and simple." I started going through my bag, looking for my phone. "I bet Dan Henderson would turn out for this if I told him his son was involved."

"You can't." Ella put her hand over mine to stop me. "I don't know Will but I know boys, and he's not going to like his dad turning up to rescue him, even if he is on duty."

Darcy nodded. "Besides, Will could just leave if he didn't want to fight. He's not in prison."

"Oh, he wants to fight." I thought of the look on Will's face and shivered. "I don't know who I should be more scared about."

"Who's the favorite?" Ella asked.

"Ryan, by a mile," Hugo said. "That's just because everyone knows him and they think he'd be handy in a brawl."

"I think that's true," I said slowly, "but I think Will has more to prove."

"Less to lose." Guy Tindall came and leaned on the breakfast bar; the pendant lights reflected in the small steel-rimmed glasses that kept sliding down his nose. "This fight has the potential to be an absolute classic. My money's on Will, for what it's worth."

"Mine too," Darcy said, sounding a little too enthusiastic for my liking.

"Guy, you have to do something to stop them." My voice cracked on the word "stop."

"Can't, I'm afraid. But don't worry. It's not a big deal. It's not as if they're gladiators. They don't have to keep fighting until one of them dies."

"Who decides the winner?"

"Either it's a knockout, or one of them gives up, or Harry calls a halt, which will be if either of them draws blood. No blood on the upholstery is the rule."

I shook my head. "Neither of them is going to stop. Neither of them gives up on anything that matters to them."

Guy levered himself onto the stool beside me. "And you'd know about that."

"What do you mean?"

"I share a study with Will. He may have mentioned you once or twice this term."

"What did he say? Does he hate me?" The second question tumbled out before I could stop it.

"Of course not. Why would you even ask that?"

"No reason." In the bright lights of the kitchen I could see a shadow on Guy's jaw, and the more I looked at it, the more I was convinced it was a bruise. I looked down at his hands and saw that they were swollen, his knuckles purple with bruising and grazes. "Who have you been fighting?"

"What?" He looked taken aback for the first time. "Oh. Just a friend."

"Some friend. Who won?"

"I did, I suppose."

"You don't sound too sure," Hugo drawled.

"You can get the better of someone in a fight and still not get what you want." For a moment his face was unutterably bleak. The next second it had changed back, so I almost thought I'd imagined it. Guy stood up straight. "Like I said, these fights aren't a big deal. Just enjoy it."

"What is there to enjoy?" I asked Ella as he left the kitchen. "This is sick, isn't it?"

Ella didn't get a chance to answer. A voice said, "It's just what they do."

I turned to see Claudia standing beside me, with Immy behind her. Immy's hair was still pale pink, but now straightened, and as a look it was actually starting to work for me. They both looked concerned.

"Are you OK?" Claudia asked me.

"Not really. I can't believe this is a regular thing."

"Every night," Immy said. "Harry and his friends like betting. And fighting."

"But it's just stupid."

"It's how they settle things," Claudia said. "Whatever they're upset about."

"I didn't think you'd like this." Darcy took hold of one of my hands.

"You were right. Even if it wasn't Will and Ryan fighting . . ."

"You'd still think it was horrible." Ella took my other hand, which was awkward as I actually really needed to blow my nose again.

"It's starting," someone called from the corridor, and there was a rush for the door. Claudia reached over and patted my arm before she went, which both surprised me and actually made me feel slightly worse.

I looked at Darcy. "Do I have to go?"

"It's going to happen anyway, whether you're there or not."

"Come on." Hugo pushed me sideways so I fell off the stool. "Toughen up. If it's your fault they're fighting, you have a moral responsibility to watch. Besides, I don't want to miss it."

"Who do you think is going to win?" Ella asked him.

"I'm not wasting my money. It could go either way." He came round behind me and took hold of my elbows, then propelled me out of the kitchen with main force as I squirmed.

"You can watch. Why do I have to?"

"You're our ticket to the best seats in the house."

I didn't know what he meant, but as we pushed our way down the hall and into the living room, people stood aside to let us pass. I got to the front of the crowd remarkably easily. Everyone knew who was fighting, and everyone knew why. Like it or not, I was part of the show.

Harry was standing in the middle of the living room, where

no one was dancing now. People lined the walls, five or six deep, and stood on the stairs, and leaned over the side of the walkway above. Anything to get a good view. The music was off but the room was still noisy, conversations buzzing on all sides. Harry clapped his hands above his head and got something like silence. "Is everyone ready?"

A cheer. I wondered if I was going to faint. Then I wondered if that would do anything to stop the fight going ahead.

"Remember," Harry said, "you can change your mind about who's going to win until I say the betting is over. Then that's it. You're stuck with whoever you picked. Blue for Ryan, red for Will."

There was a rumble of conversation around the room. For the first time I noticed that most of the guests were holding strips of paper, some red, mostly blue.

"Harry's the bookie," Hugo murmured in my ear. "His mates give out the tickets and keep track of the bets. It's a fiver a time but you can double your money if you're right."

I wasn't the best at maths, but even I could see the numbers didn't work. "If Ryan wins, Harry's going to lose a lot of money."

"He doesn't care. It's nothing to him. He's got more money than you can imagine."

"OK. Let's do it." Harry was literally jumping up and down with excitement as the crowd cheered. Heads turned as a door opened upstairs and the two of them filed out. They stood together for a moment at the top of the glass stairs. They were much the same height. Ryan was a shade broader in the shoulders and across the chest, but they both looked ultra-fit, and strong, and determined. Ryan moved first, running down the stairs without acknowledging anyone who spoke to him or patted him on the shoulder. A couple of steps behind him, Will had his head down, in a world of his own. The two of them came and stood in the center of the living room, flanking Harry, and there was a flurry of activity with red tickets changing hands. Will had taken off his shirt. His T-shirt showed off his body, and people were reassessing their choice as they noticed he was actually built. I looked at them both hopelessly, and realized that I really wanted Will to win—not because I preferred him, but because he was so thoroughly underestimated most of the time. Ryan got plenty of attention, but Will was only known for being the copper's son. It didn't make him particularly popular, and he deserved more.

To my left, there was a mild commotion. Lucy Blair had fallen over and was lying on the floor, eyes closed, a wide smile on her face. Two of her friends knelt beside her, squeaking with horror.

"Can someone give her a hand?" Harry called.

The two bouncers pushed through the crowd and one of them checked Lucy's pulse. "She's fine."

"She's been having a bit too much fun, that's all," Harry said. There was general laughter at Lucy's expense. I didn't find it funny.

"Take her upstairs," Harry said. One of the bouncers scooped her up and started up the stairs. Lucy's friends scrambled to follow.

"Ladies, she needs to sleep it off. There's no need for you two to go." Harry smiled and the edge had left his voice when he added, "You'd miss the fun."

They faltered and stopped, then turned back. I watched as

they disappeared into the crowd. The two of them looked worried, but no one seemed to notice, or care.

"Shake hands, boys." Harry stood back to let Ryan and Will share the briefest of handshakes. Ryan turned back and scanned the crowd until he found my face. He held my gaze and for just a second his stern expression softened. It looked as if he was going to smile, but then Harry spoke again.

"No more bets please, ladies and gentlemen." He hopped up onto a coffee table, out of the way. "Ready?"

"Ready," Will and Ryan said in unison.

Harry threw his arms up in the air. "Fight!"

The roar from the crowd was deafening. Will's head came up and he scowled at Ryan. The two boys circled, eyes locked on one another, and I cringed as Ryan made the first move with a short, vicious jab. Will twisted so that it landed on his arm rather than his torso, and swung back with a right hook that connected solidly with Ryan's midsection. Ryan winced but barely faltered, and the noise level went even higher as he went on the attack. The two of them traded punches as if it was nothing, as if they couldn't even feel pain. I couldn't bear to watch. Nor could I bear to see the excitement on the faces all around me, the lust for blood.

"They're so well-matched." It was a guy I didn't know, talking to his friend. "I can't work out which of them has the edge."

"This could go on for a while."

I shut my eyes. I really hoped they were wrong. But neither would back down. And Harry was enjoying it far too much to let them stop. A roar made me look up in time to see Will's head snap back as Ryan socked him on the jaw. Will took a second to get his balance back, and Ryan waited, on his toes, even as the crowd shouted at him to finish Will off. It was like Ryan to fight fair, even when he was angry. I wished he had been fighting anyone but Will, so that I could have wanted him to win. He was good too: as soon as Will was ready to fight again, he punched him in the side, and Will doubled over, holding onto his ribs as he winced.

"I think Will's in trouble," Ella said, hanging onto my arm so tightly I knew I would have bruises to show for it.

"Don't count him out yet." Hugo had his hands in his pockets and looked about as ruffled as someone watching two flies crawl up a wall.

"How can you be so calm?" I asked him, and he grinned.

"Watch."

I looked back and saw Ryan swing wildly, missing Will, who grabbed his hand and pulled, using his momentum to flip him over. Ryan landed on his back with a thud that got a groan from the crowd, but somehow he managed to drag Will with him. The two of them rolled around, grappling with one another. Will ended up on top, hammering Ryan with blow after blow as he held his arms up to try to guard his face.

"He's going to hurt him," I wailed.

"That's the general idea of fighting." Hugo was looking thoughtful. "I wonder, though."

As he said it, Ryan heaved Will off him and jumped to his feet. Will scrambled up as well and the two of them went back to circling, disheveled now, their T-shirts torn and marked with sweat. As smoothly as a dancer, Ryan stepped forward, and in the same movement landed a blow, out of nowhere, just under Will's left eye. It spun him round and he went sprawling on the ground.

"That's it," said the guy behind me. "He's not getting up."

Slowly, painfully, he did, though, shaking his head as if trying to clear it. Ryan stood back, waiting, breathing hard.

"This'll be the end." Mr. Know-it-All again, though I agreed with him. Harry had just checked his watch. Both boys looked utterly exhausted. Will's cheekbone was grazed and starting to swell already. He threw a punch that Ryan dodged, and another.

"Slowing down." The guy behind me cupped his hands around his mouth and roared, "Finish it. Put him out of his misery."

As if he'd heard him, Ryan moved forward again with a left hook that Will avoided by what looked like sheer luck. If it was luck, he was lucky again a second later, as his right fist smashed into Ryan's mouth. Ryan staggered back, one hand to his face. He took it away and looked at his palm, which was suddenly, shockingly red. I couldn't see exactly where he was injured but he was certainly bleeding from his mouth, and badly. Will stood back, side on to him, still with his hands in fists, still watchful. Rightly, because Ryan looked up at him with pure rage in his eyes. Before he could attack again, Harry waved his hands above his head and jumped down. "That's it! Enough."

Around me the crowd were chanting the fighters' names.

"I've got to pick a winner," Harry said. He stood between them again and held onto their wrists like a real boxing referee. "And I choose . . ."

The room went almost silent.

"Both of them." He yanked their arms in the air as everyone roared their approval.

"Does that mean Harry has to pay out on all the bets?" I asked Hugo.

"Yeah. He won't miss the money."

People were flooding in to congratulate Will and Ryan, thumping them on the back. Ryan was laughing, exchanging high fives with his friends. He'd stripped off his T-shirt to staunch the flow of blood from his mouth, and his torso, lean and rippling with muscle, looked like a Greek statue come to life. Will put up with the attention too, grinning at a remark that someone made, bending to let a random girl in a low-cut dress kiss his cheek. I was absolutely not going to humiliate myself by fighting through the crowd to do the same, for either of them. Now that it was over, my fear had turned to anger—with both of them.

Eventually Will detached himself from his admirers and started to make a move. I had five or six things ready to say, but I wasn't going to get the chance. He wasn't walking toward me, as I had expected, but to the door.

"He's leaving?" Ella looked surprised.

"So it seems."

"He should stick around. Enjoy the attention."

Hugo laughed. "Will doesn't care about that kind of thing."

"Well, what about Jess? Doesn't he want to say anything to her? He just had a fight over her."

"If it *was* over her," Hugo said. "Like I said, this argument goes way back."

"And now he's gone." I watched him disappear through the door without so much as glancing in my direction. He hadn't looked at me once, in fact, the whole time. And I'd been standing at the front; it wasn't hard to spot me. Feeling deflated, and not a little tearful, I turned back and found myself being swept off the ground, thrown over someone's shoulder. I held on, afraid of falling, but equally afraid of my skirt riding up. It didn't take me long to work out who had grabbed me, since he was half naked and wholly sweaty.

"I would kiss you," Ryan said as he lowered me to the ground, "but my mouth hurts too much."

"Are you all right?"

"I'll live." He grinned at me, then stopped with a wince. Up close I could see a gash in his lip; it was still oozing blood.

"That looks painful. You need to put some ice on it. Or frozen peas."

"There's loads of ice in the kitchen," Ella said.

"Who wants to be nurse?" Ryan's eyes were on me.

"I think I'm going to go home," I said.

"Jess . . ."

"No, Ryan." I pulled myself free. "I hate what just happened. I hate what you did. Both of you. You should be ashamed of yourselves."

"Wait, Jess—"

"No." I felt the tears stinging my eyes again and I turned away from him. "I've got to go. Ella, will you be OK with Hugo?"

"I can come with you."

"No, don't. You haven't even been here that long and you've spent the whole time looking after me. Enjoy the party. Dance. Look at the view. Kiss Hugo."

"Shh! He'll hear you." She was laughing, though her eyes

were still troubled. She held onto my hand. "There'll be other parties, Jess. Let me come with you. Make sure you get home all right."

"It's fine. I know the way, which is more than you can say." I hugged her, glad she was there but needing to be on my own. "I just need to get my head straight."

"I'll see you later, then." She stood with Hugo, the two of them watching me with very different expressions as I headed for the door. Ella was all doubt and concern, Hugo as sardonic as ever—proof if ever proof were needed that opposites attract.

I retrieved my jacket, which was fortunately unscathed, and one of the bouncers helped me into it.

"That's my job." Ryan let the big door swing closed behind him. He sounded slightly out of breath, as if he'd had to hurry to catch up with me.

"You look as if you've got your hands full," I said. He was pulling his coat on while draining a glass of something clear. "Is that water?"

He shook his head even as he tilted the last of it down his throat. "Vodka, I think. I nicked it off someone. I wanted it for this." He shook the ice onto a paper napkin and wrapped it up, then held it to his mouth.

"You should have gone to the kitchen. You'd have found any number of girls willing to tend your wounds."

"I only wanted one."

I rolled my eyes and glanced at the bouncers, who were pretending they weren't listening. "I'm not really that sort of girl."

He shrugged. "Never mind. Have you got everything?"

"I think so. But you don't have to leave with me."

"I came here with you; I'm leaving with you. End of story."

He dabbed at his lip. "I don't think I was going to have much more fun than that anyway."

"Yeah, that fight was a real high point for your evening."

"It wasn't my idea."

"You went along with it."

"The alternatives were worse." He followed me out of the house and down the path. "Harry doesn't like it when people say no."

"Are you that desperate to stay in with the in-crowd? Really?" I shook my head. "I will never understand this place. Or all those ghouls in there, cheering and making money off the two of you."

"Making money off Harry," Ryan said. He was rubbing his right shoulder as we walked down the road. "I think I pulled a muscle."

"You'll be lucky if that's all you did."

"You're really angry, aren't you? Most girls would have loved that."

I gave him a look instead of answering and he responded with a lopsided version of the usual grin.

"You're hopeless," I said.

"Not if you meant what you said earlier about maybe giving me a chance."

"You never stop. Ever. Not for a second."

"Quitters only have themselves to blame for being losers."

"Did you get that line off a poster?"

I was waiting for Ryan to come back with a snappy response, so when he didn't answer me, I looked to see if he was all right. He was staring fixedly at a point a little further down the road as we walked toward it. I looked in the same direction, and saw nothing, and looked again . . . and at last I saw what Ryan had seen: a figure by the side of the road, in the darkness.

By the time I saw him properly, and knew him, we were close enough to speak.

"What are you doing here?" Ryan asked.

"Waiting for you." Will stepped out of the shadows, the bruise on his cheek visible even in the moonlight.

"Oh good," I said lamely. "We can all go home together." I might as well not have been there. Both of them ignored me as they stared at each other. If they'd been dogs, there would definitely have been growling.

Earlier on they'd started something.

Now it was time to finish it.

11

I stood to one side, trying to think of something—anything—that would put them off fighting. I came up with absolutely nothing I hadn't said already. It hadn't worked before and it wouldn't work now.

Will moved to stand in front of us. He was still ignoring me in favor of staring Ryan down. "So. What part of *one good punch* did you not understand?"

"I had to make it look real."

"I made it look real, and I didn't have to hit you to do it."

"You drew blood. That wasn't part of our deal."

"I think you cracked my rib." Will's face was still stony. Then, suddenly, he grinned. "Good work."

"Likewise." Ryan put out his hand, and for the second time that night they shook hands, though this time it was an altogether friendlier experience.

"Wait. Wait a second . . ." I was looking from one of them to the other. "That was *planned*?"

Ryan looked sheepish. "Not all of it. Just . . . when we knew we were going to have to fight. Will didn't want to."

"You didn't either," Will said.

"True. But if I'd known what you were going to do to me I might have hit you for real. I mean, you hit me in the mouth. I could have broken a tooth."

"I didn't hit you that hard. And you hit me first." Will leaned to the right a little and gave a hiss of pain. He straightened up. "All right. I'm not doing that again."

"Do you really mean to say you faked the whole thing?" I asked.

"Not everything." Will pointed at the bruising on his face. "You can't fake this. But we made it look worse than it was."

"Why didn't you just say you weren't going to do it?"

"Harry wasn't going to give up," Ryan said. "It's kind of a rite of passage—if you're a guy and you go to his parties, some time or other it's going to be you. I'd dodged it a few times. Now I've gotten it out of the way."

"He wanted me to fight from the moment I walked in," Will said.

"Why?"

"You know what people are like. There's an extra thrill when I do stuff I'm not supposed to, because of Dad." He looked at me for a moment and I felt a shiver down my spine when his eyes met mine. "I'm sorry you were upset."

"Upset? Upset doesn't cover it. I was so scared for both of you. I thought you might really get hurt. Then I was angry with you for fighting. Now I'm angry with you for lying to me."

"We couldn't explain," Ryan said, as if it was reasonable.

"We couldn't take the risk that someone would guess. You made it believable. And I don't think I've ever seen you cry before."

Will, of course, hadn't been looking at me at the time. "Jess was crying?" he asked, intrigued.

"Big time. Ugly crying." Ryan launched into a series of hacking sobs, then laughed at the expression on my face.

"Don't worry," I said tightly. "It's the last time I'll ever cry over either of you."

"Oh, come on, Jess." Will was grinning too. "You were angry that we fought and now you're angry that we didn't. That doesn't make any sense."

"Feminine logic," Ryan suggested, and I incinerated him with a glare.

"It's typical of you to say something like that. And then you wonder why I think you're shallow."

The smile disappeared off Ryan's face. Will bit his lip to stop himself from laughing. "She got you, friend."

I turned on him. "Don't think I'm not cross with you. I don't even want to look at you, let alone speak to you."

"Jess," he protested, "give me a chance."

"To do what? Tell me I'm an idiot for minding what happens to the two of you? I don't think so." It was frustrating that the tears were welling in my eyes when I had specifically said I was not going to cry over them again.

The two of them exchanged a guilty look. For longstanding enemies, they had a lot in common.

"I've had it with this conversation. I'm going home." I turned and stalked off down the road.

Ryan caught up with me first. "I said I'd see you home."

"I can't stop you following me, but I don't have to talk to you."

"OK. Fine." He walked along beside me, while Will came up on the other side. "We're not forgiven."

"I'm not surprised." To me, Will said, "I'm sorry. *We're* sorry."

"We are. We really are," Ryan said.

"I thought the two of you hated each other."

Will looked uncomfortable. "Hate's a strong word."

"We just hadn't spoken for a while," Ryan said.

"Like eight years."

"Something like that."

"Well, I'm honored to have been present when the double-act got back together."

"Quite a big evening, one way or another," Ryan said. To my dismay, he went on to say, "Did you find out anything useful?"

"I was a little busy." I hoped Will wasn't paying attention, which was futile.

"What's going on?"

Very reluctantly, I said, "I want to find out what happened to Seb. His little sister asked me if I could help, and she's friends with Petra, so I thought I'd ask some questions."

"Because that worked out so well the last time."

"It's not like the last time. I'm not personally involved in any way, and no one is dead. I'm just finding out what happened so she can stop worrying about why someone put him in the hospital."

Will looked pained. "Jess, if someone hurt him deliberately, they're not going to want you to tell the world what they did.

They've got every reason to try to put you off. And from what I heard, Seb was pretty badly injured."

"Yes, but the consensus is that he deserved it. And your dad doesn't want to know what happened. He's still selling the car-crash line. I don't think he's going to want to take it any further even if I do find out what happened."

"So why put yourself in harm's way?"

"Because there has to be a reason why he was attacked. Beth needs to know if he deserved it or not."

"And you can't stand not knowing now that you're sure there's a mystery."

"I'd like to know what there is to cover up. Is that wrong?"

"Stupid, maybe? But in character."

"Oh, thanks a lot." I could hear Ryan laughing beside me. "Because you would just walk away."

"I didn't say that."

"But you think I should play it safe."

"I'd prefer it."

"Too bad," I said.

Will nodded. "OK. So it *is* you."

"What's that supposed to mean?"

"I wasn't sure if you'd had a change of personality to go with your new look."

My face burned. "Nope. Still me."

"And you still won't listen to common sense."

"If that's what you call it."

"Remind me not to get in your way, Jess. Ever," Ryan said.

Will looked at him over the top of my head. "Yep. Not worth it."

"Absolutely."

"Let her have her own way."

"My thoughts exactly."

I gritted my teeth. "Are the two of you finished? Or is it going to be like this all the way home?"

"All the way home, I should think," Will said.

Ryan nodded. "All the way home."

"Well, at least you could make yourselves useful." I thought for a second. "You said it was a rite of passage to fight at Harry's parties."

"Not just Harry's," Ryan said. "It's always his idea, though. Any time that gang are all together, there's a fight."

"Like on Saturday night?"

Ryan shrugged. "Probably."

"There was a party at Guy's house before the disco."

"So I heard. I wasn't there, though."

I turned to Will. "Were you?"

"I was at home."

"Did Guy get into a fight?"

Will looked at me for a long moment. "What makes you ask that?"

"When I saw him up close, in the kitchen, I could see he was covered in bruises and they looked pretty recent."

"He was in a fight on Saturday night."

"With?"

"Don't jump to any conclusions." Will warned me.

"Say it."

"Seb Dawson. But it was before the disco and Seb walked away. Guy didn't leave him with a fractured skull."

"Is that what Guy told you?"

"It's what I heard at the fireworks."

"Me too," Ryan said. "Seb got punched in the nose. He had a massive strop about it. He stormed off—said he didn't want to fight anymore and he wasn't going to bother with the disco. He said he had somewhere better to be."

"He was mortified that Guy got the better of him," Will said. "Guy's not exactly tough. Seb was expecting to walk it."

"What were they fighting about?" I asked.

"I don't know."

"Come on, Will. It has to be something that really matters to Guy to make him fight like that. According to him, you've been sharing all your problems with him. Don't tell me he hasn't done the same with you."

Will frowned. "What did Guy tell you?"

I couldn't tell him. "Nothing. Your turn."

"Guy doesn't take life too seriously, but that doesn't mean he's shallow. He has a massive crush on someone—and before you ask, I don't know who. He's been after her for years, literally, and never got anywhere. He had more sense than to tell anyone about it, but Seb saw him with her and worked it out. About a month ago, while Guy was away at school, Seb pulled her and sent Guy pictures. He went crazy, as you might expect. Seb did it to annoy him and it worked." Will shrugged. "That's the kind of person he is."

"The more I hear about Seb, the more I think someone did the world a favor," I commented.

"There's no justice in half killing someone because they're a dick."

"So says the policeman's son." Ryan's tone was mocking and I glanced at Will, worried that the look on his face meant we were about to have Round Two of their fight, this time for real. It took him a second, but Will got control of himself.

"The point is, Guy didn't hurt Seb. Not seriously, anyway. He got the better of him in their fight and Seb went off in a huff, and as far as anyone knows, no one saw him again until he was scraped up off the pavement."

"And you have no idea who the girl is."

Will shook his head.

I turned to Ryan. "What about you?"

"No idea," he said regretfully. "I'd tell you if I knew."

"Can you try to find out? Both of you?"

"Why is it relevant?" Will asked. "I told you, he walked away."

"I don't know. I'm just trying to make a list of people Seb upset. It might actually be easier to make a list of the people he *didn't* annoy."

We had reached a corner and Will turned to walk downhill.

"Hey, where are you going?" I pointed in the other direction. "It's this way."

Will raised his eyebrows. "Yeah, you could go that way. If you wanted to walk a lot further than you need to."

"But that's the way we came." I turned to Ryan, puzzled. "I'm sure we came down there."

He looked sheepish. "Mm. We did."

"But—" As I said it, I remembered what he'd told Hugo. "The long way round?"

"Might have been."

"I really wish I had a working sense of direction," I said bitterly. "You tricked me."

"It was a nice night for a walk."

"If you like the cold." I started down the road Will had chosen, shaking my head. "You really are something else."

"Can't blame a guy for trying."

"I don't blame you, for what it's worth." Will was walking backward. "Who wouldn't? Especially when Jess is looking like that."

"You'll trip." I said it flatly. It was too late for him to give me a compliment. I hated the dress. I hated my makeup. I yearned for jeans. I wanted to be at home, right now, and I started walking faster as Will turned round and walked beside me, silent now, as was Ryan. The evening was so over.

We came to the corner of my road and Ryan stopped. "This is where we say good-bye."

"Are you going?" I asked.

"*I'm* not. He is."

"I'll walk you to the door," Will said.

"No need. I'll do it." Ryan put his arm around my shoulders. "I said I would."

"It's not far out of my way." Will's eyes were on me, waiting for me to say what I wanted. But what I wanted was to stay out of it.

"You should get home, friend," Ryan said.

"I'll be there soon enough."

"Sooner if you go straight there."

Ryan's grip on me was tight and getting tighter. I winced. "Look, Will, there's no need for you to make a detour. I'll see you tomorrow."

He looked stubborn. "It's already tomorrow."

"Later, then. Go and rest." I yawned—I didn't even have

to pretend to be tired. "I've had it, I'm afraid. I need to go to bed."

"Let's go." Ryan pushed me gently in the direction of Sandhayes.

"Wait," Will said, and I stopped, expecting anything but what he said. "Make sure the back door is locked. Tilly's always leaving it open. There've been a few burglaries around here lately and Dad said I should warn you about it."

"OK," I said. "Thanks."

"No problem." He nodded to Ryan and loped off without looking back. I watched him go, the usual ache around my heart. I was still trying to work out if seeing him was worse than not seeing him. Equally painful, I thought, but different. And not getting better.

I trudged the last few meters with my head down, not even minding that Ryan's arm was still around my shoulders—barely noticing, in fact. We reached the porch and I ducked out from under his arm to get my keys, which had survived immersion in the ditch in the pocket of my poor coat. I pulled them out with a jangle and he put his hand on mine, holding it so I couldn't open the door.

"Jess . . ."

"What is it?"

"Just—" He sighed. "Just reminding you I'm here."

I looked up at him, feeling guilty. "I'm sorry. Was I ignoring you?"

He grinned. "I'm not used to it."

"You can't have everything your own way, you know. That would be too easy."

"Easy would be fine, actually. Easy is OK." He reached out

and stroked my cheek with his thumb. "Now is when I would usually try to kiss you, but—"

"Your mouth hurts too much," I finished for him.

"Also, you always avoid it."

"You usually try to kiss me in public. It's embarrassing."

"Oh, so here would be fine." He started to pull me toward him. I backed away. "Or maybe not."

"I'm sorry," I said, and meant it. "I'm a bit messed up."

"As it turns out, that's my type."

"I'm pretty sure I'm less psychotic than your usual type, if we're talking about Natasha."

"Maybe a little less psychotic." He twisted away as I went to thump him. "No more violence. I've had enough for one evening."

"Me too. But thank you for tonight anyway."

He looked guilty, which was actually pretty adorable. "Sorry for making you walk the long way round."

"Are you really sorry?"

"Nope." He looked down at me, and his expression changed to something serious for a moment. "I'm going to make you a promise."

"Go on."

"I'm not going to try to kiss you again."

"OK . . ." I said slowly. It was what I had wanted, but now that he'd said it, I felt as if I'd lost something I cared about.

"Next time we kiss, it'll be because you want to kiss me. Not the other way round."

"Is that so?"

"I'm pretty sure of it."

"Goodnight, Ryan," I said.

"Goodnight, Jess."

He was still standing there watching me when I closed the door. He looked like every girl's dream, even with his cut lip, and I dragged myself to the kitchen to check the back door, feeling like an idiot. He was perfect in every way, and I liked him. But I didn't *like* him. At least, I thought I didn't. But I hadn't thought about Will for at least five minutes, because of Ryan. Maybe Ryan was what I needed to get over him. I could think of worse ways to recover.

I stripped off my jacket and walked into the kitchen, smiling to myself, then gave a squeak as a hand clamped over my mouth. I fell back, off balance, and was caught, and held. And I knew who it was, even before he spoke.

"Don't scream."

I shook my head. Will let go of me slowly, and I turned round. "What's with the breaking and entering?"

"The door was open."

"I was just going to close it. Someone told me I should."

"Someone wanted you to come to the kitchen."

"Why?"

Will looked amused. "You can't expect me to go home. Not when you're wearing that dress."

My stomach flipped over. "I didn't think you liked it."

"It's very distracting." He moved closer to me. "And I've been wanting to do this all night."

"Frighten me in the kitchen?"

"Not that."

He came closer still, and put his hands on my hips, and my bones turned to water as he pushed me backward, gently, until I collided with the kitchen table. He lifted me up and sat me on the edge of it, not without an intake of breath that I realized later was down to his cracked rib. I slipped my arms around his neck as he stepped between my knees, closing the distance between us. My skirt slid up my thighs an extra inch or two. He said my name in a low voice, and then we were kissing and it made the room spin as if we were on a carousel. I couldn't think, couldn't speak, couldn't even worry that it was a bad idea. Dizzy, I put one hand on the solid wood of the table, bracing myself as he dropped kisses down my neck. He trailed his fingers along my spine and I felt it in the pit of my stomach. I gasped as he dipped under the edge of the dress, his fingertips skimming over my skin. He pulled the material off my right shoulder and leaned in to kiss my collarbone.

"You would not believe how much I missed you."

"Me too." I touched his face, trying to make myself believe that this was really happening, and failing. "Kiss me again."

I was watching his mouth and saw it curve into not quite a smile as he leaned in to me, and it made my heart flutter. This time he ran his hand up the length of my thigh and I shivered, holding onto him as if he was the only thing that mattered in the whole world.

We could have kissed all night, and I would have been absolutely fine with that, but it was too good to last. He stopped kissing me and I opened my eyes to see he was frowning.

"You took a long time to say goodnight to Ryan."

I blinked, changing gear. "I had a lot to say to him."

"Like what?"

"Like thank you for taking me to the party." I dropped my hands from Will's shoulders.

"Did he kiss you?"

"Will, it's not—"

"Did he?"

"No." I tilted my head and waited for him to kiss me again, but he didn't.

"Did you tell him to leave you alone?"

"Not in so many words, but—" I shook my head. "What is this? Are you jealous?"

"Why do you think I punched him in the mouth?"

Will was still standing between my knees but the distance between us seemed to stretch for miles. I pushed him back and slid off the edge of the table, pulling my dress back into place. "Well done. Mood officially ruined."

"Sorry. I don't like sharing."

"First, it's not up to you to 'share' me. It's up to me to decide who I kiss, and when. And second, I like Ryan. Not in that way, but I like him. He flirts with me. You're the one who's making it into a big deal."

Will's jaw was clenched. "Really, what do you expect?"

"Less drama," I snapped. "But I keep being disappointed. I thought you and Ryan weren't going to fight anymore."

"I don't remember saying that."

"There is no need for you to be jealous. I can handle Ryan."

"That's what I'm afraid of," he said softly. "How do you think it makes me feel to know you're here with him while I'm at school?"

"I don't know."

"Yes, you do." He folded his arms, his expression remote. "Now seems as good a time as any."

"For what?"

"My second question."

"Oh, that."

"Yeah, that."

I waited, feeling very much as if I'd just run out of road. Will looked at me and I could see the confusion in his eyes. All of a sudden I knew what the question was going to be.

"Did you mean what you said when you broke up with me?"

"Which bit?" I asked carefully.

"The bit about not caring about me. The bit where you told me it was just a holiday romance."

Great. That *bit.*

"Yes," I whispered.

"Don't lie."

"I'm not." I shook my hair back, my expression bland. *Make it believable.* "What do you want me to say?"

"Say it didn't mean anything."

"It didn't mean anything," I repeated. "I had fun. But that's it."

I thought he was going to argue with me, but he didn't. He nodded slowly. Then he leaned in to kiss me on the cheek.

"What was that?"

"That was me kissing you good-bye." He went to the door and I couldn't say anything to stop him, or bring him back. The door closed behind him and he was gone. I sat down at the table, and I cried as if my heart was breaking, because it was.

All over again.

12

The next morning I woke up early, with a hangover, which was more than unfair since I hadn't had anything to drink at all. I got out of bed and saw my reflection: pale as paper, lank hair, dark shadows under my eyes. The classic post-break-up look. It wasn't even as if Will and I had got back together again. All of the misery, none of the fun. It was the story of my life.

Someone had put a note under my door and I bent to pick it up, wincing as my head throbbed. It was from Ella: an apology that she had got back so late from the party. She was going to sleep in, unless I needed her, in which case I should wake her up. I checked the time: she'd had three and a half hours in bed. Not really enough to justify disturbing her. There was an arrow to the other side of the page and I turned it over.

I kissed H! H kissed me! OMG!

In spite of everything I laughed. I was glad someone's romantic life was working out, even if mine was a disaster.

I went and had a long, very hot shower, ignoring Tom knocking on the door halfway through and shouting abuse through the keyhole. It had been a revelation to me that in a big family you had to hold your ground. I refused to hurry, emerging feeling altogether more human. Makeup helped too—wide-awake eyes, courtesy of mascara, and a healthy glow thanks to some blusher. No one would have guessed that I'd cried myself to sleep, slept badly, and woken up on the verge of tears before I even remembered why. I opened the curtains on a beautiful day, bright blue sky and a veil of frost turning the garden silver-white. Stepping over the hateful black dress, which I'd abandoned on the floor of my room, I found my oldest, softest jeans—the ones that were nearly falling apart—and boots, and a jumper that came down to my thighs. It felt better to be in my own clothes, instead of playing dress-up.

Downstairs, nothing was stirring. It was my day for getting notes: Mum had left one telling me she was going out to take some pictures before work. Tilly taught an art class in a local community center on Tuesdays and had already left. Jack was gone too. Hugo was asleep. Ella was asleep. Petra had eaten, judging by the crumbs on the kitchen table that had her napkin ring in the middle of them, but she had disappeared. Tom was going out to play football and was never exactly sociable anyway. The house was too quiet, and too full of memories. The previous evening haunted me, particularly the last bit. I averted my eyes from the table, standing up by the sink as I ate some cereal without tasting it. I washed the bowl, trying not to think about Will rinsing his mug there two days ago. Everywhere I looked, I saw something that reminded me of him. There would be no peace for me at Sandhayes. I couldn't stay, but there was nowhere I needed to be. No one was waiting for me. All I wanted was something to take my mind off the hollow feeling in the pit of my stomach.

It was traditional to go to the seafront in Port Sentinel if you had nothing better to do. I went and got my parka, then walked into town. The weather was too still for the surfers and sailors to be happy, but there would be *something* to see. There weren't many people around yet, because it was still early. I cut down Fore Street, seeing a couple of girls from the year below me. I didn't know their names and there was nothing notable about them—except for their hair, which was a delicate shade of pink. I stopped and stared at them, amazed. It shouldn't have been a surprise. I'd been mocking Immy when I suggested she might start a trend, but of course there was nothing too stupid to become a craze in Port Sentinel if the popular girls did it. Weirdly, I felt much better about life all of a sudden. It had something to do with thinking the worst of people, and being right. It was also to do with the pink hair looking surprisingly good. I was almost tempted to give it a whirl myself.

The gallery wasn't open yet. I kept walking, all the way down to a tiny public park that the Victorians had put at the bottom of Fore Street, mainly so they could surround it with municipal buildings. The council offices were on one side, the police station on another, facing the library. The fourth side was the town hall. The council offices and the police station were in Victorian gothic red brick, but the town hall and library were painted white, with Doric columns. All four buildings were too small to be properly grand, but then Port Sentinel was a rural backwater and had never been anything else. I wandered into the park, dodging predatory seagulls which assumed I was there to feed them. The leaves were beautiful against the very blue sky, in searing yellows and burning reds. I hoped Mum was taking advantage of the weather to capture the iconic image of Port Sentinel in the autumn, so we could afford to eat.

I sat on a bench for a little while, watching my breath plume in the cold air. A girl walked through the park, head down, her hands buried in the pockets of her coat. I glanced at her, then looked again as she ran up the steps to the library and slipped through the door. Lily Mancini, unless I was very much mistaken, and in a hurry. Without really thinking about it, I got up and followed her. I was curious about Lily. I really wanted to know whether Seb Dawson had anything to do with her spilling Ella's drink and leaving work early, or if it was all a coincidence. There was no harm in asking.

The library was warm and smelled comfortingly of much-read books. Four rooms opened off the central space, where once there had been long tables and wooden chairs under a domed skylight. The skylight remained but the tables were gone, replaced by work stations for the public computers that sat there humming to themselves. I checked the other spaces: the children's library, the periodicals room where some ancient crones were reading knitting magazines, the area for fiction, complete with armchairs, and, finally, nonfiction. It wasn't a popular bit of the library, and it was where I usually ended up when I had homework to do. I saw the fur-trimmed hood of Lily's coat. She was leaning over a table right at the back, talking to someone I couldn't see. Helpfully, the bookshelves were set at an angle to the room, so I could slide in behind them and not be seen. I regretted not wearing trainers, but I tried not to make too much noise, drifting up to stare at a shelf of maps. East Anglia. The Western Isles. The Dordogne. Fascinating.

"But I don't understand what happened. I thought he was fine when you left him."

"He was." Lily, sounding upset.

"Shh. Someone will hear." A third voice.

"There's no one here. Anyway, it's not our fault. It can't be. Nothing happened to him when he was with us."

"He hit his head on the door frame." The first person was speaking again. "When we were getting him into the car."

"Not hard enough to fracture his skull," Lily snapped. "But they say it's pretty bad. And he's still unconscious."

Well, that settled who *he* was. I needed to know who Lily was talking to. I went on tiptoe to peer through the shelves. Lily was standing beside a table covered in books, where Amanda Secombe and Ruth Pritchard were sitting, side by side. Finding Amanda and Ruth in a library wasn't in the least remarkable; the two of them vied for top position in our class and spent every possible moment studying. It was strange that they were sitting together, though, because as far as I knew, they were sworn enemies.

Ruth looked as if she'd hardly slept since I saw her on the cliffs. Her face was bloodless but her expression was fierce. Amanda, in contrast, looked calm. She was large, pale, slow-moving, and a regular victim of Ruth's sarcasm. And it was a mystery to me what they had in common with Lily, with her piercings and hair dye, who had a constellation of stars tattooed on the inside of her wrist and the word *Serendipity* in script across the nape of her neck.

"This was all your idea," Lily said to Ruth, who looked pinched.

"You were the ones who saw him last. I wasn't there. I don't know what you did."

"Nothing. Absolutely nothing. I got the number. I dropped the phone and I left."

"What about the others?" Amanda asked.

"They had to go to the fireworks," Ruth said. "They couldn't have done anything."

"You don't know what they did after they left. I knew we couldn't trust them." Amanda sounded morose.

"You're just putting the blame on them because they're not here." Lily bit her lip, almost in tears. "I know what you'll do if anyone finds out. You'll blame me."

"You were the last one with him," Ruth said. "You've got more explaining to do than the rest of us."

The voice behind me was loud enough to make me jump out of my skin. "Look who I found. What are you doing back here, Jess?"

I turned to see Immy peering at me from under a black fedora that almost hid her hair and made her look absolutely adorable. Claudia came up behind her.

"Well, if it isn't the face that launched a thousand punches."

"Indoors voice, Claudia," I hissed. "This is a library." I didn't dare look through the shelves to see if the three girls had overheard, but I couldn't imagine how they'd have missed Immy and Claudia braying at me.

"Going somewhere?" Immy pulled a book off the shelf and handed it to me. "May I suggest this one?"

"*The Sights of London*. Nice of you, but I've already seen them."

Immy gave a tinkly laugh. "I'm just messing around."

Claudia tilted her head to one side, sweetness and light personified. "How are you, Jess? You didn't stay long at the party last night."

"It wasn't my sort of thing."

"It was an *awesome* fight." Immy leaned against the shelves. "Didn't it give you the tiniest thrill to know that they were fighting over you?"

"Not really."

"You are such a joy-killer." Immy looked at Claudia. "Who knew Will Henderson was so hot?"

"Jess did."

I felt my face flame.

"Apart from her."

Claudia shrugged. To me, she said, "So what's the deal with the two of you? Are you seeing him or Ryan?"

"Neither."

"How come?"

"I don't want to talk about it. I'm sorry."

"We're just being nosy." Claudia half smiled. "This is what it's like to be on the other end."

"Funny." I glanced through the gap in the shelves but I couldn't see Lily any more. I assumed they'd finished their conversation. I made the best of things. "Speaking of being nosy, I hear Guy and Seb had a fight the other night, just like Will and Ryan. How come you didn't mention it to me when I asked you about him in the café?"

"I only just found out about it," Immy said quickly. "Last night. Someone was talking about it. I didn't see it happen."

"Yeah," Claudia said. "It was between the two of them, from what I heard. Not a big thing like last night."

"Did you happen to hear why they were fighting?"

Immy looked at Claudia for guidance. "No. Not really. Just rumors."

"Saying what?"

"They've never got on. Seb did something to annoy Guy, deliberately, and Guy snapped."

"What did he do?"

"I don't want to say." Claudia was looking stubborn. Less horse today; more mule. "I don't think it's any of your business. Or ours."

"I heard he pulled someone Guy fancied," I ventured.

"Then you heard plenty." Claudia caught her lower lip between her teeth for a moment. "It's not fun gossip, Jess. It's just unpleasant."

That was all I was getting, I could tell. "And you can't say who it was."

"Sorry."

"Not one of you two, though."

"No way." Immy looked outraged at the very suggestion.

"How's the hair?" I asked.

She flipped her hat off to show me. "Still pink. I actually like it, I think."

"You and a few other people." I told her about the girls I'd seen and she laughed.

"Amazing. I'm going to have to go purple next. Change it up."

Claudia sniffed. "We should go, Immy. I need to find that book."

"Oh yeah." Immy looked around vacantly.

"Which book?" I asked.

"*A Passage to India*. It's by E. M. Forster." She said it as if she didn't expect me to have heard of it. "Is this the travel section?"

"You need fiction. This is nonfiction."

Claudia gave me a bright smile. "*So* confusing."

"I can imagine."

"Let's just see if there's a film of it. You can watch the DVD," Immy said, stifling a yawn.

I watched them walk off, waiting until they were out of sight before I spun round and looked through the shelves. Amanda sat on her own, hunched over a book that was propped up in front of her. She was reading intently, her mouth slightly open, her hands in fists on either side of her forehead. There was no sign of Ruth or Lily. I'd missed my chance.

I came out from behind the shelves since there was no point in hiding anymore. Amanda didn't acknowledge my presence in any way. So much for stealth: I could have been wearing a gorilla suit and jumping up and down for all the attention she paid me. I moved casually to a point where I could see the books on her desk. Medieval history. About which I knew nothing. Scrapping the idea of getting into a conversation about what she was reading, I sauntered past, close enough to knock a stack of books off the edge of her desk with a well-timed swipe.

"I'm so sorry." I knelt down and started to pile them up again. "That was so clumsy."

"Don't worry." No smile on Amanda's face, but her demeanor wasn't actually hostile. Just blank. And Amanda was a girl of few words normally, so I'd have been surprised if she'd been chatty.

"What are you reading?" I asked.

"*The Waning of the Middle Ages*. Huizinga." She showed me the cover of the book. "It's a classic."

"I'm sure it is." *Feeble . . . Think of something else to say.* I stood up. "Is it for school?"

"Not really. I'm just interested."

"Oh. That's . . . great." Inspiration came at the last possible moment. Amanda had already put the book back down and was leaning in to continue reading when I remembered something. "Have you ever been in St. Laurence's Church?"

"What?" She actually jumped. "What did you say?"

"You know, in St. Laurence Square. It's got this incredible iron door that dates from the Middle Ages, covered in animals and leaves. It's really beautiful." Tilly had taken me to see it during a brief but intense period of sightseeing, just after I came to Port Sentinel for the first time. Most of what I'd seen had blended into one hazy muddle—there were only so many rood screens and baptismal fonts and important architectural features I could remember. The door had stayed in my mind, though, probably because it featured two grinning Plantagenet lions that reminded me of the Sandhayes cats.

"I'd forgotten that. I have seen it, but I'll go and have another look some time."

"St. Laurence Square is so pretty too. I loved sitting there under the tree when the weather was warmer."

Amanda stared at me stolidly.

"Did you know that's where Seb Dawson ended up the other night? When he was injured, on Halloween?"

"I heard. Are you friends with him?" she asked abruptly.

"No. Not at all. I don't know him. Just to see."

She nodded. "I don't really know him either."

"Really? Have you ever spoken to him?"

"Probably, but I can't remember the circumstances." Her face was bright red now, her eyes fixed on mine as if she was trying to make herself look honest and direct. The effect was more alarming than reassuring. "I'm not friends with him or his friends. I don't know any of them."

"Even from school?"

"None of them would talk to me." There was the faintest touch of bitterness in her voice. "I wouldn't expect it. I don't think we'd have much in common."

"I doubt Seb knows much about the Middle Ages. You're too clever for the likes of him."

She raised her eyebrows. "That's not it and you know it. They don't talk to me because I'm a freak."

"No, that's not—"

"They call me A-*man*-da. Or Sea Cow. Seb came up with those names."

I sat down on Ruth's abandoned chair, pulling it in to get closer to her. "Look, from what I've heard they're horrible to everyone. If he said something like that to you, I'm really sorry. But you're not the only one."

"I know that. It doesn't actually help when someone says

something like that to you and you know it's true. And don't try to tell me I'm not odd-looking, because I am. I know I am."

I felt really, intensely awkward. No one was going to make nasty remarks to me about my appearance, and if they did I could ignore them. I couldn't begin to imagine what life was like for Amanda, who was tall and broad-shouldered, with a square jaw and big hands and bushy eyebrows that met over her nose.

"Seb asked if I'd ever done any shot-put competitions or weightlifting. He told me I looked like an East German athlete from the 1970s. A man, basically. The reason everyone laughed was because they thought so too." She was watching me intently, waiting to see if I laughed too. I'd never felt less like laughing but I didn't want to be patronizing either. She would know if I lied to make her feel better. So, the truth.

"If someone asked me to describe you, the first thing I'd tell them is how brainy you are, not what you look like. And you look fine, anyway. Only someone mean-spirited like Seb would make fun of you. He picks on everyone."

She sighed. "You're just being nice to me. Why are you being nice? What do you want?"

I want to know what you did to Seb. I want to find out who else was involved and why. "Do I have to want something?"

"Everybody wants something."

"Not me." I waited a second. "I'm guessing you haven't spent much time weeping over what happened to Seb, though."

"Not a lot."

"Do you know who did it?"

"No." We were back to the direct stare. I hadn't noticed

before but her eyes were lovely—pale blue with an indigo circle around the iris.

"Have you heard anything about it?"

"Just that he's in hospital."

"His little sister is really worried about him." It was worth a try.

Amanda's face remained impassive. "It must be very upsetting for her."

"She'd like to know what happened to him, and why."

"She's probably better off not knowing."

I pounced. "Why do you say that?"

"So she can think the best of him, instead of knowing the truth."

"Which is?"

"He had it coming."

I was about to answer her when I stopped. Someone else had said that to me, using that exact phrase. "Have you been talking to Claudia Carmichael?"

Amanda looked at me as if I was insane. "She's one of Seb's gang. Look, I have to read this. I'm sorry I can't help."

I stood up. "On the contrary. You've been a big help. Really."

I could see her running through the conversation in her head to try to work out what she'd given away without realizing it. I left her to think about it. The truth was that the more I found out, the less I understood.

The only thing I knew for sure was that something bad had happened on Saturday night, and no one wanted me to know what it was.

13

I came out of the library and wandered into the park, sitting down on the same bench as before. One thing was bothering me: Claudia's expression when she'd avoided telling me why Guy was angry with Seb. So few things counted as off limits for gossip that it had to be something truly awful. I wanted to know what it was, but I was almost reluctant to find out. If Beth hadn't been depending on me, I might have stopped asking questions there and then.

In fact, it didn't matter whether I wanted to investigate what had happened to Seb or not, because I'd hit a wall. I hadn't the faintest idea what to do next. I could try to speak to Ruth, but I shrank from it. Amanda had been hard enough. I couldn't imagine persuading Ruth to tell me all she knew.

Footsteps approaching with great speed made me turn my head and my heart sank all the way to the soles of my boots. A grim-faced Dan Henderson was striding toward me.

"Jess. I need to speak with you."

"Oh, really? Why?" I was trying to think what I could have done to upset him—apart from the usual—and coming up blank. I stood up, anxious to avoid a tête-à-tête on the bench.

He stopped a little bit too close to me. In the bright sunshine he looked tired, his face drawn. "Have you been asking questions about Seb Dawson?"

Oh, crap. "Just to see if anyone knows what happened."

"I thought you'd have learned your lesson. Leave the police stuff to me and my officers."

"OK." I was already in trouble, and Dan was never going to like me. Recklessly, I said, "But I didn't think you were investigating it at all."

"That's where you're wrong. I've got someone in custody."

"Seriously?" My voice came out as a squeak.

"I arrested him last night."

"Who? I mean, how? Who?"

"Someone who had a row with Seb. A lad called Guy Tindall."

"*Guy?*"

"You know him."

"Not well. But I know that's just impossible." I was shaking my head. "Completely wrong."

"He's got fight injuries. He told me he'd argued with Seb. He admitted losing his temper with him."

"So you're willing to accept Seb wasn't injured in a car accident."

Dan had the grace to look sheepish. "It was a preliminary assumption."

"It was wrong. And it's also wrong to think that Guy could

have injured him so badly. He's not like that." I was talking to Dan as if I wasn't scared of him. But I was.

"When people lose their tempers they're capable of doing terrible things. Things they would never do if they weren't angry. Guy doesn't have an alibi for Saturday night. He admits having had a fight with Seb. He won't tell us why, but there's obviously bad blood between the two of them." Dan shrugged. "I've got him now. I can take my time with interviewing him and other witnesses. I don't have to charge him yet, but I can, and I will."

"Are you looking for anyone else?"

"Why should I?"

"Because Seb had lots of enemies."

"I've got a credible suspect. I don't need to go looking for any more."

"What about Seb? Aren't you even a little bit curious about why he got a beating?"

"No."

I pounced. "Because you know already?"

"Stay out of it, Jess. I'm handling it. And his mother and father don't want anyone spreading rumors while Seb isn't able to defend himself."

"His mother? Is she here now?"

"I meant Stephanie Dawson, his stepmother. She's very concerned about his reputation being damaged."

"Why would anyone bother if he hadn't done anything wrong?"

"Because people are malicious."

"Or because he'd done something to deserve what happened to him."

"Blaming the victim?" Dan raised his eyebrows. "That's not very nice, Jess."

"Doesn't it make you a tiny bit suspicious that Mrs. Dawson doesn't want you poking around in Seb's private life?"

"A bit," he admitted. "But I can see why."

"Because Mr. Dawson would be heartbroken if he knew his son was a bully."

"That sort of thing."

"Who suggested it was a car accident? He'd have had to be blind and stupid to believe it. I know he didn't think it's true."

"That came from Stephanie." He sighed. "She just wants all this to go away. You know she doesn't get on with Seb. He's caused her a lot of trouble and grief. She's trying to protect her husband and keep her family out of the public eye. I have been investigating what happened, Jess, even if you don't believe I've done enough, but I've been doing it quietly, behind the scenes. And I really do think I've got the right person in custody. When Seb wakes up, he can confirm it."

"Is he still unconscious?"

"No change." Dan held onto the bridge of his nose for a second, frowning, as if he had a headache. "Where were you going when I interrupted you?"

"That way." I pointed toward town.

"Me too."

We started walking toward Fore Street, side by side. He looked exhausted. I had always been terrified of him and avoided talking to him if I could, but I'd learned something from dealing with Claudia and Immy. Sometimes being nice could work wonders. And I wanted a miracle. "Busy week?" I risked.

"You could say that. Vandalism and underage drinking and some public disorder to deal with. The usual, for half-term."

Not to mention your son getting into trouble. "Have you seen Will today?"

"Not yet." A quick glance. "He wasn't up when I left. Why?"

"No reason." At least Dan didn't yet know he'd been fighting. He'd see the bruises on Will's face, though, and I didn't think he'd be all that pleased, fake fight or not. I carried on. "At least you have him back. To help with his mother, I mean. That must take some of the pressure off you."

Instant suspicion. "Not really. He's been out a lot."

"Not with me."

"No?" Dan frowned down at me.

"I promise you, we haven't been together." Deep breath. "And we're not going to be."

"Is that right?"

"I wouldn't lie about it." I waited a moment. "So I was wondering if—"

"No."

"But you haven't even heard—"

"You're going to ask if Will can leave his boarding school and go back to Sentinel College, and the answer is no. It's a great opportunity for him academically, and socially. He's lucky to get to go to Stonehouse."

"I think he'd rather be here."

"I'm sure you're right."

"It just doesn't seem fair to send him away." My bottom lip was trembling. "His mother . . ." *Also known as your wife.* "She might not be around for much longer."

"I know. She's dying," Dan said coldly. "She's been dying

for a while now. She'll probably still be dying when he finishes his exams. And when he graduates. I'm not encouraging Will to hang around here just because of that."

"You sound as if you wish she'd get on with it."

He actually laughed. "Sometimes. The progress of her disease is so uncertain. It could be soon, or it could be years. I remember when she got the diagnosis. It took ages because there's no test for motor neurone disease. They have to rule out every other possible cause for the symptoms. We were hoping and praying it would be something else."

"Really?" I couldn't help sounding skeptical.

"Yes. I wouldn't wish it on anyone. Horrible disease." He tucked his chin down into his chest for a moment, then straightened up. "I don't want Will to put his life on hold while she takes her own sweet time about dying. He has a chance to do something with his brains, but in three or four years it will be too late for him."

Like it was for you. I thought it but I would never have dared to say it. The reason Dan hadn't achieved his dreams was because of Will and, at least in part, my mother.

As if he'd been following my train of thought, Dan said, "How *is* Molly? I haven't seen her for a while."

"She's fine. Working hard."

"Nick's keeping her busy."

"I suppose."

As if he couldn't stand not to, he asked, "Does she ever talk about me?"

Oh my God, no. "Um. Not to me, really."

"But to Tilly?"

"I have no idea." I stared up the street, desperate to find

something that I could use to change the subject. The answer to my prayers was right in front of me. It was also, potentially, a total disaster. "I don't believe it."

"What?" A couple of seconds too late, Dan looked where I was looking. "I don't see anything."

"Nothing to see." I picked up speed. "He's gone into the gallery now."

"Who?"

"My dad." I left Dan standing as I ran.

I don't know what I was expecting to find when I burst in through the door, but it wasn't the sight that greeted me. Mum was sitting on the edge of her desk with her arms folded while Dad leaned toward her with one hand on either side of her hips. She had a familiar, dazed, rabbit-in-headlights look on her face, and Dad was saying something in a soft voice. It could have been nice; it could have been vile. There was just no way to tell.

"What are you doing here?" I demanded, slightly out of breath from pelting up the street.

He turned round. "Jessica. I was just asking your mother where I could find you."

Mum glanced at him, surprised.

"Elementary mistake, Dad. If you're going to lie, don't involve Mum in it."

He held his arms out expectantly. I went over and submitted to a kiss on the cheek. I'd got my fair hair from him, but not his height. He was strikingly like my uncle Jack—the sisters had chosen men who were physically very similar—but he was better looking. To balance that, Jack was infinitely more pleasant than him.

"Why are you here?" I asked again.

"To see you."

I raised my eyebrows. "Really? Now?"

"Why not now?"

Because maybe you could have done the decent thing and visited when I almost died, *instead of sending me a get-well-soon card written by your girlfriend.*

Which reminded me. "How's Martine?"

He looked uncomfortable. "Gone back to Germany."

"Permanently?"

"As far as I know. We're not in touch."

I was sorry to hear it. Martine had been nice. She'd tried extremely hard to be my friend, and it wasn't her fault that Mum and Dad had split up. She was the girlfriend after the girlfriend after that.

"Is this relevant to why you decided to visit?" Mum sounded uncharacteristically tough.

"I had some time off. I wanted to use it wisely. See the people I love." He was looking at Mum as he said "love," watching for the blush that, inevitably, turned her cheeks pink.

The door opened behind me and Dad looked past me. His expression changed. "I wasn't expecting to see you, Dan."

"Really? This is where I live. And work."

Dan's eyes were always a muddier shade of gray than Will's, but at that moment they were the inky color of thunderclouds in a heat wave. *Storm a-coming*, I thought.

"Still a policeman?"

"Just an ordinary copper," Dan said, leaving out the fact that he was the local inspector and they didn't come more important than him for a good thirty miles. "Why are you here?"

"Are you asking in your official capacity?"

"I like to know what's going on in my town."

"*Your* town," Dad repeated. "Certainly something to be proud of."

"I think so." Dan was visibly bristling.

"You must really love it here. Since you never left."

Good old Dad, straight in with the killer line. I'd have enjoyed Dan getting to see what it was like on the receiving end of snide comments, but it made me uncomfortable to know why they hated each other. Mum and Dan had been madly in love until they broke up over a stupid argument. He took up with Karen, who then announced she was pregnant with Will, and Dan married her. Devastated, Mum had run away with my father, who was practically the first man she'd ever met who hadn't been brought up in Port Sentinel. No wonder it hadn't worked out.

Mum was so tense she was digging holes in the desk with her fingernails. I felt much the same way.

"I had reasons to stay."

"Yes, you did. How's the little boy?" Dad asked, in what might have been a non sequitur but wasn't.

"Taller than you."

Dad looked surprised for a moment, then glanced at me and obviously did some mental arithmetic. "Time goes by, doesn't it?"

"Yeah, but some things don't change." Dan's voice was heavy with meaning.

"No. They don't."

The two of them stared at each other and the air was so charged a spark would have been enough to send us all sky-high.

"What are you doing here?" Dan asked again.

"I had some news I wanted to share with Molly and Jessica."

Oh no. What now? From the look on Mum's face, she felt much the same.

Dad turned his back on Dan, the better to stand a bit too close to Mum. At least he'd given up on the creepy leaning. "I might as well tell you this now. They're winding up the firm. I'm getting a decent lump sum and I'm using it to set up on my own."

Dad was a financial adviser, which was exactly as interesting as it sounded. He loved money more than sunshine, even if it was someone else's money rather than his own. He'd always wanted to have his own company, with his own name on the door. Living the dream, Christopher Tennant–style.

Mum's face lit up. "I'm so glad. What a wonderful opportunity for you."

"It shouldn't affect my income if you're worried about me providing for Jessica. I've got several clients lined up already."

"I wasn't worried." Mum, as usual, had total faith in everyone but herself. "You'll do brilliantly."

"Thanks, Molly." He looked at her without saying anything more, until she ducked her head, embarrassed. It was as if that was what Dad had been waiting for. "Can I ask you a massive favor?"

"What is it?" I asked, on Mum's behalf, since she didn't seem capable of speech.

"Can I stay with you? Just for a couple of days?" Dad ran a hand through his hair, looking hassled. "I'm going to be busy with work for the foreseeable future. I won't be able to take a break and I'd like to have some time with you first."

"With Jess," Mum prompted, seeing my face.

"With you too. I missed you, Molly."

She looked stricken. "Christopher."

He reached out to touch her and Dan snapped.

"Get away from her."

"Are you still here?" Dad glared at him. "This is a private conversation."

"Yeah, whatever, but seriously, don't touch her," I said, moving forward to get between them. I hated being on Dan's side, but I couldn't stand to see Dad playing games with Mum. "You got divorced. You divorced her."

"Thank you, Jessica. I remember." He looked back to Mum. "Do you want me to leave?"

"No. I don't know." Mum was huddled on the edge of the desk, miserable. "Of course I don't want you to go. You should spend time with Jess."

"Don't stay on my account," I said. I was trying to work out what game Dad was playing, because there was definitely a game, even if he wasn't prepared to tell us the rules.

"That's nice." He nodded, his eyes cold. "I'll remember that."

"I don't want to be your excuse." *Because I know it's a lie.*

He must have seen what I meant from the look on my face, because he backed off straight away. "It's not just you. Of course not. I want to see the whole family."

"*My* family," Mum checked. "Tilly and Jack and everyone."

He shrugged. "Why not?"

Because they hate you? No one said it. Everyone thought it.

"Doesn't seem to me as if they want you to stay." Dan was thoroughly enjoying the moment, awkward as it was.

"I haven't had an answer yet." Dad turned back to Mum and his voice softened. "Molly? Are you really going to turn me away?"

He so knew what he was doing. Put on the spot, she gave in immediately. "N-no. I mean, I'll have to check with Tilly. But how long were you planning to stay?"

"Just a couple of days."

"So you're leaving on Thursday," I said. "To be specific."

"Probably."

"Why don't you just leave now?" Dan asked.

"Why don't you just back off?" Dad snapped.

"I'm saying what Molly won't. You need to hit the road." Dan folded his arms, looking both muscular and murderous. "There's nothing for you here."

"I wouldn't say that." Dad was looking at Mum as he said it, but then he turned back to Dan and his expression hardened. "Anyway, I'll go when I'm ready. You can't make me leave."

"Watch me."

"I'm not breaking any laws." Dad took a step toward Dan, who moved forward too. They reminded me of old lions, all roar and no bite.

"That's not why you have to leave."

"What the hell's going on?" Nick had arrived in the front gallery and sounded more annoyed than either of the other two. "Who are you?"

"I'm Christopher Tennant."

"My dad," I said, for the second time that day, and with even less enthusiasm.

Nick swung round to Mum. "Your husband?"

"My ex-husband."

"And why is he in my gallery? Why is Dan here?"

"He and Dan—" Mum broke off and held up her hands, giving up the attempt to explain the situation.

"They have a lot in common," I said. "So obviously that means they hate each other."

I saw Nick work out what I meant, looking from Dad to Mum to Dan. He frowned, his expression forbidding. "Molly, do you mind if I ask your ex-husband and Dan to leave?"

"Be my guest."

"Nick, come on," Dan said. "You don't mean me."

"Yes, I do. This is my gallery, not somewhere for you to air your grievances."

"But—" Dan began, and Nick held up a hand to cut him off.

"I'm not interested."

"And I'm not impressed." Mum's expression was stern. "It's time for you to go."

"Go where? I need to know if I can stay at Sandhayes." Dad was looking at her with puppy-dog eyes.

"I have to speak to the others. Go and find somewhere to wait until I can call you."

"Any suggestions for where I could go in the meantime?"

"Don't tempt me," Dan said under his breath.

"Mario's is nice," Mum said. "Down by the beach."

"Don't go there," I said quickly. "Lots of people I know go there."

I got my very own glare from Dad for that. Dan grinned at me appreciatively, which was almost more unsettling.

"Time to leave." Nick held the door open. Dad paused for a moment to kiss Mum on the cheek, then walked out, head up, as if he owned the place.

Dan blew out a lungful of air. "He hasn't changed."

"I meant what I said, Dan. You have to leave too." Nick's face was stern.

"Yes, please go," Mum said, her voice wavering a little.

Dan moved over to stand beside her and said, in a low voice, "Can I come and see you, Molly? Later?"

I looked from Dan to Mum with a thud of dismay. *Is meeting up a regular thing?*

"I'm busy," Mum said.

"Tomorrow."

"Busy. I'll let you know."

Nonplussed, Dan gathered himself together and walked out, heading in the opposite direction to Dad.

Nick shut the door and stood with his back to us for a moment, as if he had to gather his strength. I'd been hoping he might see the funny side, but when he turned he looked grim. "Molly, I can't pretend to be pleased about that."

"I didn't know Christopher was coming. I certainly didn't expect him and Dan to be here together, at the same time."

"This is where you work, not a place for you to deal with your family dramas. You should have told them to go."

"It's not that easy," I said, nettled. "They don't listen to her."

"That's not true. I could have made them leave. I can stand up for myself," Mum said, and there was a little silence as Nick and I thought the exact opposite.

When Nick spoke again, he was more gentle. "I'm not blaming you, Molly, but I am tired of your private life taking over what should be a calm, peaceful, professional environment." He rubbed his eyes. "I think you should just go."

Mum stood up. "Am I fired?"

"Take some time off. Get things sorted. Come back when you're ready to work." He strode off toward his office. The door closed behind him.

Mum looked at me. Before I could say anything at all, she burst into tears.

14

I headed back to Sandhayes to see if Ella had surfaced yet. She was still out cold, snoring lightly. I loitered in the doorway of her room, hoping she would hear me and wake up, but there was no chance. Downstairs, Hugo was locked in the bathroom. He liked to read while he was in the bath, adding hot water every so often, and it was utterly impossible to get him out once he was installed. I carried on down to the kitchen, where Tilly was doing laundry in a towering rage.

"You've heard the news. Your father is in town."

"I saw him. And the fight."

"What fight?" Tilly stopped halfway through folding a fitted sheet. "With your mum?"

"With Dan." I told her what had happened and her anger turned to amusement, which was far more like her.

"Your poor mother. She does attract drama. And bastards." She clapped a hand over her mouth. "I shouldn't have said that."

"I couldn't agree more," I said. "They were squabbling like kids with a toy. No one even asked Mum what *she* wanted."

"They think they know best." Tilly went on folding. "This is the problem. Molly attracts men who want to look after her. They think she's helpless. She'd be one of the most capable people I've ever met, if she'd only believe in herself."

"Did she come back here?"

"I haven't seen her." Tilly sighed. "I haven't seen Christopher, either. But he's coming over later. He's having dinner here."

"Oh, great."

"Don't sound too enthusiastic."

"It's just that—well, you know him." I could see trouble brewing. "Is he staying here?"

"On the sofa bed in the study. There's nowhere else to put him. Also, it's tremendously uncomfortable." Tilly smiled at me sweetly. The oven timer beeped and she jumped, then clutched her head. "Oh no. I'd forgotten about that."

"What is it? Can I help?"

"I made something for the Hendersons. Macaroni and cheese." Tilly was lifting it out of the oven, so she didn't see my face. "Can you take it round? Do you mind?"

"Um . . ."

"You just have to leave it in the kitchen. I've got a key so you don't even have to ring the bell. Just let yourself in. Dan will be at work anyway. I haven't seen Will today."

"Me neither." *And I don't want to start now.* "What about Will's mum?"

"Karen? She'll be upstairs. She lives up there now." Tilly checked the time. "Will or Dan will be in by one o'clock to help her with lunch, so if you take this over now she can have some."

"Oh. Right. But I don't have to see her."

Tilly stared at me. "Why would you not— Oh. Are you worried about what she'd say to you?"

I wriggled. "No. I mean, I haven't done anything to her. It's just that I haven't met her." *And her husband is still in love with my mother, which she probably knows. So.*

"You won't see her," Tilly said confidently. "Or Dan. If you see Will, tell him he's welcome to come over for dinner, Christopher or no Christopher."

"I'm not sure that's a good idea." I was desperately trying to think of a reason why Will wouldn't want to come to Sandhayes without having to explain our painful little scene the previous night.

"Your dad will be perfectly nice. And Karen will be just as nice to you if you do meet her. We are all grown-ups, and we can all behave ourselves," Tilly said firmly. Then, "Well, you're not a grown-up. But you know what I mean."

While we'd been talking, she had been wrapping up the dish of macaroni. She lowered it carefully into a cardboard box. "You should be able to carry that. Don't go over the wall, will you? I don't think you could manage it with this."

"I wasn't going to try." I took the box, and the key she handed me. I couldn't think of a single thing I could do to get out of going to Will's house, and every step I took felt like one closer to the scaffold. "So I just leave it in the kitchen and go."

"That's it. Thank you, Jess." Tilly winked at me. "It'll be all right, you know."

"If you say so."

It took five minutes to walk round to Will's house by road, but I spun it out to nearer ten. I could feel my heart thumping as I got closer, my palms damp against the cardboard of the box.

Will's house was much smaller than Sandhayes, a white cottage with a big overgrown garden and ramshackle outbuildings covered in peeling paint. It looked unloved, neglected, and I shivered as I walked up the path. The houses on either side had been knocked down and rebuilt in the best Port Sentinel tradition, and the Hendersons' house looked even smaller and dirtier in comparison.

I didn't want to let myself in without giving them any warning. I knocked on the front door with my knuckles, a compromise that I hoped wouldn't be loud enough to wake Karen if she was sleeping. There was no answer. I knocked again, then turned the key in the lock. I still felt tense but this was overlaid with curiosity, and as I walked in I had a good look around. I'd been in the house before, but in Dan's company, and only once. It wasn't the most exciting hallway in the world, with old-fashioned wallpaper and a bottle-green carpet that I would have hauled out and burned. Of most interest to me was the row of hooks, where I saw Will's coat. But it was a nice day, bright and clear, warmer now that it was midday. He might have gone out without it. *Clutching at straws . . .* I carried the box through to the kitchen and set it down on the table. The view from the window held my attention for a moment—the top floor of Sandhayes, including my bedroom, in plain view above the treetops. Maybe Will thought about me every time he looked out.

Or maybe he didn't. I wasn't going to waste any more time on snooping around; the thought of getting caught was too appalling. I tiptoed back to the hall, closing the kitchen door very quietly behind me.

But not, as it turned out, quietly enough.

"Will? Is that you?"

The voice was distant and not terribly strong. I went to the bottom of the stairs.

"It's not Will, Mrs. Henderson. It's Jess Tennant. My aunt made some food for you and she asked me to come round with it."

Silence. I waited, chewing my lip, not knowing if I should go or if I should wait. Then:

"Come up."

It was just not my day. I started up the stairs, full of foreboding.

"It's the second door on the left."

I walked along the landing to the second door and pushed it open to find a large, light-filled room overlooking the garden. I stopped just inside the door, looking around. Looking everywhere except at the bed, where Will's mum lay. There was a chest of drawers in an alcove by a small fireplace, and the top of it was covered in framed photographs. I glanced at them, then looked more closely, seeing an adorable baby with round cheeks, sweeping eyelashes, and a pout. He became a sturdy, muddy toddler, then a boy with knobbly knees, a gap-toothed grin and a deep fringe, and then, incredibly, he turned into Will—a younger, thinner version of him, but recognizable all the same. I couldn't stop staring at the photographs, trying to recognize his features in the baby pictures. It was painful to see the wariness develop in his eyes over time. My heart ached again, but this time on his behalf rather than my own.

"Come over here." Reluctantly, I did as I was told, keeping my eyes trained on the floor. Karen was propped up against lots of pillows. There was a wheelchair by the window and the bedside tables were loaded with books, a jug of water, medicine bottles—all the paraphernalia of the chronically unwell. I'd never seen Will's mother—not even a picture of her—and he was so like his father in appearance that I had no idea what to expect. When I couldn't avoid it any more, I looked at her.

Karen was thin and pale, but she didn't look as if she was at death's door. She had dark hair and a narrow face with a pointed chin and finely arched brows. I couldn't help comparing her to Mum, who was the same age. Karen looked much older than her, which had to do with the set of her mouth and the lines around her eyes. Her skin was very fine, almost translucent, and time had creased it like tissue paper. Her long, narrow hands lay on top of the sheet, folded over one another, and they reminded me of Will's. She would have been attractive if she had been more animated, but currently she had all the vitality of a marble statue.

If I'd been staring at Karen, she'd been doing exactly the same to me. "I was expecting you to look different."

"Different?"

"More like *her*."

Instantly, I was on my guard. There was something in her tone that was deeply unsettling. "Do you mean my mother?"

Karen nodded slowly. "But you must be more like your father."

That was so not the way to make me like her. I grimaced, taking refuge in the fact that adults never really expect teenagers to be able to speak English or interact in a socially adequate way. "I look a lot like Freya, so there's a bit from Mum's side of the family."

"Yes. So you do." She lost interest in the subject. "And why are you here?"

"Because Tilly sent me."

"Not because you wanted to come."

"I didn't not want to come. I mean, I didn't mind." My face burned.

"Will's not here."

I didn't know what to say. *Good* sounded rude, even if it was what I was thinking. "I didn't come to see him. I was just delivering the food."

"Tilly always cooks for us when she's feeling guilty about something." Karen stretched out her hands and stared at them, then laid them back down on the coverlet. "I wonder what that could be."

"She likes looking after people. She likes to help."

"She disapproves of the way my husband and your mother have been carrying on. This is her way of making it up to me. It's pretty inadequate. She knows that, and yet she keeps cooking."

I went hot, then cold. "What do you mean? Mum would *never*—"

She interrupted. "Molly is weak. She always was. She would always do whatever Dan said."

"Not if it meant cheating."

"You are so young." *And stupid* was the subtext.

"I know my mother. And I know that she would never do anything with a married man. Dad cheated on her and it almost killed her."

Her eyebrows went up an inch. For the first time, she looked happy. "Did it hurt her feelings because he preferred someone else? How perfect. I could have told her what that was like."

I held onto my temper with great difficulty. "It's not the same and she doesn't deserve that remark. She didn't do anything wrong. You married Dan even though he was in love with her—which you knew—and she left town so she wasn't in your way. How is your situation her fault? Blame Dan by all means, but leave Mum out of it."

"Of course Molly always knew how to make it look as if she'd done the right thing." Karen's hands clenched on the coverlet for a moment, then relaxed. "There's nothing I can say that will convince you you're wrong, but just open your eyes. Look at what's in front of you. I'm stuck in here and even I know they've been sneaking around."

"You're wrong."

"You should think it's romantic. Star-crossed lovers. Love will find a way, no matter what." Her voice was bitter. "Which leads us back to you."

"What about me?"

"You hanging around Will. I don't want you to have anything more to do with my son."

"You as well? Everyone is so concerned about this and there's really no need to be. We're not together. We're not going to be together." If I kept saying it, I might even learn not to mind.

"Dan told you to leave him alone but you kept sniffing around, didn't you? You don't like being told what to do."

"It wasn't an act of rebellion. We just spent some time together. Being friends." All right, a bit more than friends, but I wasn't prepared to go into it with her. As it happened, I didn't need to.

"Don't pretend it was all innocent. I saw you together, in the garden." She looked over at the window. "That view is all I have to look at. I spend a lot of time watching the birds. And anything else that moves. I saw Will climbing over the wall to be with you. I saw you and him in our garden. You were all over him."

"We didn't do anything wrong. We kissed a few times. That was it."

"You thought you could hide what you were doing, but I knew all along that you were lying," Karen spat.

"What I've just said is the truth."

"I don't believe you. Lying is in your blood. Sneaking around comes naturally to you. And you snared Will, didn't you? It was the first thing you did when you got here. You made him fall for you, the same way your mother got her hooks into Dan."

I ignored the bit about Mum. "I didn't make him do anything. I liked him and he liked me. But it's over now."

"Over?" She gave a brittle laugh. "I don't think so. I saw your face when you were looking at the photographs."

"It's not about how I feel. I'm pretty sure he doesn't have feelings for me anymore. I've done my best to make sure he doesn't." I shook my head. "You're making assumptions about me that aren't fair. I was the one who broke up with him. I wanted him to be able to stay here, so he could be with you." *Because you're dying.* At that thought, my temper began to fade. Why shouldn't she be bitter, with her ill health, horrible sham of a marriage, her vindictive, uncaring husband, and her beloved son far away most of the time? What had I expected? Kittens and roses? I took a moment, then said, "I was just trying to do the right thing. I know you must hate me because Will's not here, but it's really not my fault that Dan sent him away."

"Dan didn't send him away. I did."

"What?" I stared at her. "But Will thinks—"

"I know. He assumed it was Dan and I let him think it. Dan can take it." She glared at me. "Don't even think about telling him. He'd never forgive you for telling him the truth."

"And you're lecturing me about lying?" I shook my head. "How can you?"

"I want what's best for him. And I want him to stay away from you."

"So you broke his heart by making him leave Port Sentinel, and you. Do you know how much he worries about you?"

"He would never have left of his own volition, no matter how good the opportunity was. I made it easy for him. I made the sacrifice on his behalf." She looked proud.

"You should tell him."

"Absolutely not. You mustn't either. It would only confuse him."

"Confuse him? Yeah, that's one way to put it. What you've done is evil."

"He's a good boy. Too good for you." She tried to sit up, leaning forward. "I would rather die without him than see him with you."

"Listen to yourself," I said, appalled. "How can you be so cruel? I'm not my mother, and Will isn't Dan. You're not fighting the same fight all over again. You don't win anything if you keep us apart. You're hurting Will and you're depriving yourself of his company, for no reason."

"I think I'm doing the right thing." She looked stubborn. "You have your own agenda. I have mine."

One last try. "Look, if this is really about me, you're not doing the right thing because there's no reason to send him away. Will and I are never getting back together. Please, for his sake, just let him come home."

She stared at me for a long moment. "How can I be sure you're not lying again?"

"Because I'm not," I said lamely. "I don't know. I really care about Will. As much as you do, even. I want him to be happy."

"He's not coming back." Her voice was flat.

I was furious. "All right. Then there's no reason for us to be apart, is there? I can see him in the holidays, when he's at home, and we can do the long-distance thing the rest of the time. Thanks, Karen. You've made it really easy for us."

"It won't work."

"Why not?"

"Because he'll resent you. When I die, whether he's here or not, he'll regret that he chose you and not me. He'll blame you for being sent away. He'll hate you. Is that what you want?"

"No. Of course not. But—"

"I've waited for years for Dan to forget about your mother, and he never has. Now it's your turn to wait." She turned away from me to look out of the window. "You can have him when I'm dead. Not before."

I could think of a lot of things to say in response. With great difficulty I managed to stay silent. I walked out of the room and down the stairs. The bitterness I'd seen in Karen's eyes burned me. All I wanted was to get out into the fresh air and shake off the horrors.

I had my hand on the latch when I heard the tap running in the kitchen. I turned and saw that the door, which I had closed, was wide open. I hesitated, then decided to go. Whether it was Dan or Will, neither of them would be pleased to see me.

And then Will walked over to the sink, silent in his trainers, and I froze.

Too late.

I must have made some noise because he looked round, startled.

"What are you doing here?"

"I brought the food." I walked as far as the kitchen door. "Macaroni and cheese. Tilly made it."

I didn't have to be Miss Marple to deduce he'd been out for a run. He was wearing shorts and a T-shirt that was limp with sweat. His breathing was still a little fast, as if he'd only just come in. Maybe he had. I hadn't been listening to anything except Karen's poison.

"And you delivered the food because . . ."

"Tilly was busy. She couldn't spare the time." I remembered another bit of our conversation. "She said you should come for dinner tonight. If you want to."

"How do you feel about that?" He leaned back against the sink and folded his arms.

"I don't mind."

"I see."

"It's up to you."

"Great."

"Do you think you'll come?"

"I'll have to see." With his back to the window he had the

light behind him, but I could still see the bruise on his cheek. It looked painful.

"How's your face today?"

"Sore." He put a hand up and touched his cheek gently.

"And your rib? I'm surprised you were able to go running."

"It was fine. I needed to get out." He hesitated for a second. "Did you hear about Guy?"

"Being arrested?"

His eyebrows shot up. "I didn't think it was common knowledge."

"Your dad told me."

"Why was that?"

"Because I was having a go at him about not investigating the attack properly."

"Not because you told him about Guy and Seb."

"I didn't. Absolutely not."

"Oh, so it's just a coincidence."

"Yes, it is." I glowered. "I wouldn't do that. And I'm surprised at you for thinking I would."

He was still staring me down. "I'm just worried about Guy."

"They'll question him and let him go."

"Not if he confesses to something he didn't do." Will ran his hands through his hair, standing it on end. "He'd throw his life away to be a hero."

"A hero to whom?"

"Whoever injured Seb. Guy's going to take the blame and they're going to get away with it. What were you doing upstairs?"

I blinked at the change of subject. "Your mum asked me to come up. She wanted to meet me."

"Why?"

"You'll have to ask her. I don't know. Maybe she was curious. She knew Mum, back in the day."

"All too well."

"Don't start," I snapped. "Mum doesn't deserve that and you know it."

He held the hard stare for a moment, then dropped his eyes to the floor. "If you say so."

I shouldn't have said anything else, but I couldn't help it. "Do you know . . . Your dad and my mum . . ."

"What about them?"

"Do they meet? Secretly, I mean? Have you heard anything about that?"

"Oh, Jess." He sounded very tired all of a sudden, and sorry, and there was still that edge of anger. "Don't ask me that. Ask her."

"What do you know? Why didn't you tell me?"

His mouth twisted. "Because I didn't want you to get hurt."

Suddenly I couldn't stand to be there any more. Operating on auto-pilot, I headed for the door. Will was right behind me. He got his hand to the door before I could and held it shut.

"I want to go."

"Wait. Jess . . ."

I turned to look at him and I had the feeling he was going to say something but changed his mind halfway through.

"Did you tell Mum about us?" he asked.

"Firstly, there is no us. Secondly, she knew anyway."

I saw it hit him; he actually stepped backward. "Was she upset?"

"I don't know." Bitter, yes. Upset? Maybe.

"You shouldn't have come here. You shouldn't have spoken to her." Anxiety about his mother made him angry with me, as Karen had predicted. In the old days they'd have burned her as a witch.

Which made me think the old days weren't all that bad.

"It wasn't my idea to be here," I said. "Or to speak to your mother."

"No. Nothing is ever your fault. I forgot." He reached past me again, but this time it was to open the door for me. "I don't think you should come back."

"You and me both."

I stalked down the path, dry-eyed for once, and headed for home. I got there in one piece, but afterward, when I thought about the walk back, I couldn't remember a single step.

15

Dinner at Sandhayes was usually a fairly rowdy affair, just because of the number of conversations that went on at the same time. That night, with two extra people at the table, the only sound was cutlery clinking on plates. Jack hated conflict and had already left, with a pat on the arm from Tilly to show that she understood. We would all have left if we could. Ella had moved to sit beside Hugo so all she could do was look at me meaningfully, but she did that a lot. The problem, not unexpectedly, was sitting opposite me. Since he'd arrived at Sandhayes an hour earlier, Dad had managed to offend everyone, separately and together. I couldn't decide if the worst moment had been when he laughed at one of Tilly's paintings, or if it was when he asked Jack what he earned these days, or when he told Hugo to get a haircut.

I looked up and caught Dad's eye. He was chewing. "Did you make this, Tilly?"

She put down her knife and fork, ready for battle. "Yes, Christopher, I did. Why?"

"Just asking. It's very interesting."

"It's chilli."

Dad drank an entire glass of water in one swallow, then held it out for a refill. "Your own recipe, I suppose. It has that . . . inventive quality."

Tilly looked down at her plate, then checked everyone else's. No one had eaten much of it. The tension was getting to all of us.

"Usually everyone likes it," she said in a very small voice.

Instantly, there was a babble around the table as we all rushed to tell her how good it was and how much we were enjoying it.

"Really, Mrs. Leonard," Ella said earnestly. "I'm not all that into mince but this is awesome."

"Why don't you like mince?" Hugo asked, for a new entry in his comprehensive Ella encyclopedia.

She pulled a face. "It could be anything, couldn't it? Eyeballs and—and bits."

Tom looked panicked. "Mum, I'm not eating it."

"Don't be silly." Tilly tried to smile at Ella. "This isn't that sort of mince. I got this from the butcher's this morning."

Dad snorted. "Of course you did. You'd never go anywhere as banal as a supermarket. I bet you know the butcher by name. I bet he keeps the best cuts of meat for you, because you're such a loyal customer."

"Why is that a bad thing?" Tilly's face was flushed. She took a gulp from her glass of wine, as if she needed it. "Why do you have to make fun of everything? It's not a bad thing to support small businesses, Christopher. Just because you don't have the same values as my family, why are we in the wrong? Why can't you be wrong?"

Dad shrugged. He was smirking as he put his knife and fork together in the middle of the plate, having made a little well in the food. I looked at Mum, who was completely silent, her eyes cast down, as if she was pretending she wasn't even there. I usually avoided confrontations with Dad but I couldn't stand to see him walk all over the Leonards unchallenged.

"Mum, aren't you going to say something?"

She looked up, dazed. "What?"

"Let's see. Something about how Dad is a guest in this house and should be more grateful would work."

"He doesn't listen to me," she said simply.

"That's not true, Molly. Of course I do." His voice was soft. It raised the hair on the back of my neck. *Don't fall for it, Mum.*

I wanted his attention anywhere but on Mum. "Seriously, Dad. You can't be so horrible. You invited yourself to stay here and you're acting as if everyone should be grateful."

"Tilly and I understand one another. She's never been keen on me. She tried to tell your mother to dump me. And if she'd done that, you wouldn't even exist. So whose side do you want to be on?"

"Sorry, you're not going to win an argument with the whole 'I gave you life' angle. Your contribution was pretty minimal."

"But important," Dad said, his eyes bright with pleasure. What could be better than a jolly old argument? He loved the drama.

I turned to Tilly. "I forgive you for not wanting me to be born, Tilly."

"It wasn't like that," she said, distressed.

"I know." To Dad, I said, "I don't even have to think about which side to pick. You're on your own. Which, if I remember correctly, is what you wanted when you walked out on us—to be on your own again, without any boring responsibilities. I've never been sure how the hundreds of much younger girlfriends fitted into that scenario. Feel free to explain."

"*Pas devant les enfants*," Dad said, looking down the table to where Tom and Petra sat, saucer-eyed. "You'll understand when you're older."

"I understand now, and I think it's disgusting."

"You can't possibly." He leaned back and folded his arms. "Molly and I loved one another but our relationship was complicated. We needed some time apart."

"*You* did, you mean."

"I needed some time to work out how I felt about things."

"And now you have, is that it? Is that why you're here?" I was actually shaking I was so angry.

Dad was about to answer me when he looked up. "Who's this? Another of your brood, Tilly?"

Will was closing the back door quietly. He glanced at Dad. "I'm just a neighbor."

Tilly stood up, looking relieved to have something to do. "Come and sit down. I laid you a place."

She had; his usual place, which Ella had taken. Will had already started toward it when he noticed. He grinned at her. "Cuckoo."

"I can move," she offered.

"No need."

Ella's abandoned chair was beside me. "You can sit here," I said.

"Thanks." He didn't even look at me. This meal was getting better and better. He sat down, his shoulder brushing mine. I sat very still, wanting to move closer to him, while at the same time wanting to run away. Tilly put a loaded plate in front of him.

"I hope it's all right."

"Bound to be." He ate as if he'd last seen food months ago. It took him a minute to realize everyone was watching him. "This is lovely, Tilly. Hope you made enough for seconds."

Tilly beamed at him. "Of course I did."

"As long as there's some left for us." Hugo picked up Ella's plate and his own and headed to the cooker, whistling thinly. Neither of them had come near to finishing their food, but I got it. There was a principle at stake.

Dad was watching Will with a curious expression on his face. "What did you say your name was?"

"Will."

"No surname? Just Will?"

"It'll do," Will said, having swallowed his mouthful of food. "And I didn't catch yours."

"Christopher Tennant. I'm Jessica's father."

"Sperm donor," I said under my breath. The corner of Will's mouth lifted, so I knew he'd heard, but he didn't miss a beat.

"Pleased to meet you, Christopher. What brings you to Port Sentinel?"

"Visiting old friends." Dad was staring and I thought he'd worked out who Will was. But he said, "What happened to you? You look as if you've been in the wars."

Tilly leaned out to look at Will's face and exclaimed in horror.

"It's nothing. It looks worse than it is." Will stood up. "Did you leave any food, Hugo?"

"A bit."

"I should never get here late." Will shook his head sadly as he went to get seconds.

"There's apple pie for afterward," Tilly said. With a look at Dad, she added, "I picked the fruit from our apple trees."

"Brilliant." Tom hopped up and down on his chair. "Can I have some now?"

"Wait until everyone else is finished," Petra said, disapproving of her little brother as usual. For a moment it felt like an ordinary Sandhayes dinner, but of course that couldn't last, because it didn't take Dad long to find a new target.

"You're very quiet, Molly."

"Just tired."

"Why are you tired? You don't do anything all day."

"I work," she said, stung.

"In the gallery?" He laughed. "I've never seen such a collection of dross in my life. I can't imagine your pretty-boy boss ever sells anything. Why he needs you to assist him, I can't imagine. Well, I can, but . . ."

"What are you implying?" Mum looked furious. "Say it."

"You're just part of the décor. Something nice to look at while people are browsing. That's not a real job."

"Mum's job is so much more than that," I said. "And Nick gives Mum time off to take pictures. He sells them in the gallery."

"Like I said, dross. He obviously has no taste."

"Molly's a great photographer." Will had finished the second plateful in record time. He looked down the table at Mum and gave her a smile that you would have wanted to keep, somehow, so you could take it out and look at it again when you needed to. "I've got one of her pictures in my locker at school."

Mum took a deep breath, then smiled. "Thank you, Will. But Christopher is never going to admit that I have any talent. He never encouraged me when we were together. It was all about him and his career, not mine."

Dad laughed. "You don't have a career. You just point your camera at something and click. Call it art if you want, but you and I know it's amateurish rubbish."

"You haven't even seen Mum's portfolio," I said. "You don't know what you're talking about."

"Anyway," Tilly said, "what makes you the person who decides what's good art and what isn't? Money is all you care about."

"That's my job!" Dad snapped. "I've got other interests. I'm going to have more time for them now. Everything is going to change. There are going to be a lot of changes, one way or another."

"I'll believe it when I see it," Tilly said flatly. She handed Petra and Tom bowls of apple pie and ice cream. "Take them away. Go on. You can watch television."

They ran, balancing the bowls carefully. Hugo looked at Ella. "I don't want any apple pie."

"Me neither."

"Can we leave the table?" Hugo asked his mother.

"Absolutely."

The two of them were gone before Tilly had finished the

word, and I saw Hugo catch hold of Ella's hand as the kitchen door closed behind them.

"I'd like some, please, Tilly." Will sounded completely unperturbed. He was probably used to searing tension.

She handed him a bowl. "Don't feel you have to stay at the table."

"This will do fine."

Dad looked at Will with dislike. "Don't you have somewhere better to be?"

"Nope." Will carried on eating. He was completely serene. It surprised me how glad I was that he was staying beside me, a solid and somehow reassuring presence, even though he hadn't said a word to me.

"What are you doing here, Christopher?" Mum sounded tired, but also defiant. "What do you want?"

"I'm not going to talk to you about it here. Not now." He looked around. "Somewhere a bit more private would be better."

"I just want to know. And whatever it is, Jess and Tilly will hear about it anyway. So you might as well say it now."

Dad pushed his plate away so he could lean his arms on the table. "It's very simple. I came here because I want you and Jessica to come back. I want you to be my administrator. Help me build my new business into a success."

Mum shook her head, looking dazed. "After everything . . . now you want me to come back."

"I miss you."

"You miss me."

"That's what I said." There was an edge of irritation in his voice.

"So this isn't about you getting an employee who you don't have to pay properly?" I asked.

"Of course not."

"What would you pay her? Would you pay what Nick's giving her for working in the gallery?"

"It's none of your business, Jessica."

"It is, actually. Because you're trying to take her independence away again. You liked it when she depended on you and looked after the two of us and didn't have time to do any of the things that mattered to her, like taking pictures. You want things to go back to how they were."

Mum gave me a faint smile. "You said it better than I could, Jess."

"Complete rubbish," Dad snapped. "Can't you see I'm trying to help you? Both of you. Molly, you're living in a dream world. You're wasting your time in a joke of a job. You think taking pictures is going to make your name, but what makes you better than anyone else? Why should anyone buy your photographs? You don't have training. You don't have a reputation. The people around you won't tell you the truth in case it hurts your feelings. I'm not going to play that game. It isn't fair to you to let you fool yourself."

"Outrageous," Tilly said, bristling. "Ignore him, Molly."

I looked down the table at Mum, and saw that she had gone very still. She was staring into space. Dad had always known how to play on her fears. Everything he'd said was what she thought about herself and her work, and he knew it. During their marriage, she'd barely touched a camera. It would happen again, I knew, if she went back. She would give up hope.

Sensing his advantage, Dad carried on. "You know, I didn't

say anything when you told me you were coming here on holiday. I thought it was fair enough. Jessica needed to get to know your side of the family. But if I'd known you were planning to stay, I'd have made sure she didn't go. I rescued you from this pathetic backwater. I can't believe you'd drag Jessica back here without even thinking about her prospects. Her education too."

"My new school is so much better than the one in London." I was really angry now. "Moving here was the best thing that could have happened to me."

"Jessica, you can't hope to achieve anything if you stay down here. You'll never get into a decent university. Look at what happened to your mother and aunt. They haven't a qualification between them."

"I'd be completely happy if I turned out like either of them," I said defiantly.

"You're too clever for that. Being pretty will only take you so far, as I think they have conclusively proved."

"How I look has nothing to do with anything." *You sexist idiot.* "What I do depends on me. If I want to go to a good university, I will. If I want to stay here and paint pictures, I'll do that." Leaving aside the fact that I couldn't begin to draw a straight line. The arty side of things had missed me out completely. I knew it would annoy him, though, to suggest it. "Being in London won't make any difference to me. Except that I'll miss being here."

"Don't you miss it at all? Our old life?" Dad's eyes were fixed on mine. "Doesn't it mean anything to you?"

"It used to."

"Until I ruined it?"

"You said it."

"What if I want to fix it?"

"You can't just fix things because you want to. Sometimes things are broken and it's better they stay that way." As I said it I realized how it would sound to Will. He had been tapping his foot under the table, but now it was still.

"Your mother has you where she wants you, doesn't she?" Dad sounded bitter. "I can understand her wanting to stay down here. She wants to be with her old boyfriend. The policeman." He sneered the word and I felt Will react, but he didn't interrupt. "It's what she's always wanted."

"That's not true," Mum said faintly.

"She's not thinking about you, Jessica. She hasn't got your best interests at heart."

"That's not true, either," I said. "And there's nothing going on between them."

"You saw him today. He went for me. Why would he do that unless he still has feelings for her?"

Will looked at me. "My dad hit your dad?"

"Unfortunately not," I said. "They just did a lot of shouting."

"OK." Will nodded. "Just wanted to be clear."

"That's why you look familiar." Dad was catching on at last. "You're his boy."

"Undeniably, more's the pity." Will stretched. "You know, there's one possibility you haven't considered. Maybe he had a go at you because you're a pain in the—"

"Will!" Tilly said, just in time. "No!"

"You were all thinking it. I don't mind saying it."

"He's not," I said. "You don't know him."

Dad smiled at me triumphantly. "Good girl, Jessica."

"He's much worse," I said. "He's a bully. A selfish bully. He manipulates everyone around him and he never apologizes for anything."

Will grinned at Dad, whose face had darkened. Mum had one hand to her mouth. She looked distraught.

"Mum, don't even think about going back to him." I turned to Dad. "Don't expect me to come back, either, because it's not going to happen. We have a new life now and it makes us both happy."

"Really? Because you don't look happy, Jessica."

"I'm fine."

"I doubt that. All you've done since you got here is get into trouble and run around with boys." Dad's eyes went to Will, then back to me. "You're more like your mother than I thought. And frankly, I find that disappointing."

"You just can't stand losing," I said. *Disappointing.* No matter how much I told myself not to mind, the word stung.

"I can't stand to see you throw your future away."

"You don't care about me. You've never put me first. You just want your own way and you'll do anything to get it. You're using me to hurt Mum and you don't care if you hurt my feelings too."

"You'll look back on this, and you'll regret it, Jessica."

"The way you regret leaving us so you could have your midlife crisis?" I stood up, aware all of a sudden that my knees were shaking. "I would have done anything to bring you back. I begged you to come home. You never listened. You broke Mum's heart and now you want to do it again."

"You're wrong, Jessica," Dad said, and his eyes were suddenly sad. "Her heart was never mine to break."

At that, Mum got up and ran out of the room. I followed, only pausing to glare at Dad. She was quicker than me, though. By the time I got to her bedroom door, she had locked it, and nothing I could say got a response from her. I leaned against the wall for a bit, then slid down to the floor. There was no reason for me to be there but I couldn't move, somehow. I was shivering as if I had a fever.

Someone was running up the stairs. They stopped at the landing, then came toward me. I didn't look up. I knew who it was.

Will sat down beside me. "Are you all right?" he asked, very quietly, so Mum wouldn't be able to hear.

I nodded.

"That was pretty fierce."

I nodded again.

"Is your mum all right?"

"Probably not."

Will looked up at the locked door. "Has this happened before?"

"She doesn't like to cry in front of me." I locked my arms around my knees. "Dad used to make her cry a lot."

"So that's a yes."

"I suppose. It was worse when I was younger. Then it just got to be normal."

"Normal," Will repeated. "I see."

"Normal is whatever you're used to and I didn't know any different. As far as I was concerned, we were just a normal family. Just like yours."

He gave me a look. "It's not quite the same."

"Not quite. But similar."

"Why didn't you tell me? You know all about my family. Why didn't you talk to me about yours?"

"Because I like to pretend it doesn't bother me," I said.

"Whereas actually . . ."

"I'm fine."

Will nodded. "They did a good job of messing things up, didn't they?"

"Except us. We're all right."

"Better than all right."

"Pretty amazing."

"Go us." Will took a second, then said, very carefully, "I understand why you're so protective of your mother. And I understand why you don't think she would do anything to break up my parents' marriage."

"Do you think I'm right?" I couldn't look at him.

"I don't know. She has scruples but my father doesn't. It depends on whether she can stand up to him."

The two of us sat in silence for a moment, considering it. I sighed. "Based on this evening's showing, the answer is no."

"You never know," Will said.

"I kind of do know. But I wish I didn't." I put my head down on my knees. "I'm sorry."

"It's not your fault. You don't have to apologize."

"Not for that," I said, and then wished I hadn't said anything. I could sense Will looking at me, deciding whether to pursue it or not. And then, for whatever reason, he didn't.

In fact, he didn't do anything. We just sat there, not talking, not touching, for a long time.

I could have stayed like that forever.

16

One of the best things about living by the sea is that you have a perfect place to go when you want to be moody and think dark thoughts. The next day I sat on a bench, alone, looking out across Port Sentinel's deserted beach to the gray waves rolling in to the shore, feeling dismal. It was Bonfire Night. *Remember, remember, the fifth of November*, but all I wanted to do was forget about my worries. I'd left a grim house, where Mum was still hiding in her room and Dad was lurking, trying to corner one or both of us so he could continue his lecture. In sympathy, Ella had brought me breakfast in bed and stayed in my room for a while, listening to music and talking about anything except family issues. The closest she got to controversy was when she asked, all innocence, if Will had stayed for long the previous evening.

Not long enough was the answer I didn't give her. He'd left after some friendly *I-hope-everything-works-out* remarks, without trying to talk about our relationship or our breakup or anything else. Maybe he thought I had enough to deal with as it was. I would almost have been glad of some distraction from the gnawing worry in the pit of my stomach that Mum was about to make some very bad decisions indeed. I was desperate to talk to her but she wouldn't talk to me. There was nothing I could do except wait to see what happened.

It was quite nice to be on my own with my thoughts. Ella was with Hugo, who had been impatience personified while we were shut away. Eventually, he'd stormed up the stairs and demanded that I let her go.

"She is my friend. She came to see me," I pointed out, standing in the doorway of my room while Ella giggled behind me.

"And then she met me. The end."

"She didn't get much of a chance to meet anyone else."

"So it was first time lucky. So what?" Hugo bobbed and ducked, trying to see round me to where Ella was sitting. "Come on, Ella. The day is wasting."

"In a while."

She sounded amused, and embarrassed, and I took pity on both of them, shooing her out to join him. I loved seeing them so happy together. It was all so cute and straightforward that I felt envious. None of that for me. Nothing as easy as liking someone and being liked in return. I couldn't help wondering what would have happened if I'd met Ryan first, when I arrived in Port Sentinel. If I had fallen for him instead of Will, I could have saved myself maybe half the trouble I'd got into so far.

"Jess!"

I looked round to see Beth rushing toward me along the promenade, her face pink, one hand in the pocket of her coat.

"What's up?"

"I've been looking for you." She sat down close beside me and leaned in, her Harriet-the-Spy glasses sliding down her nose. "I've got Seb's phone."

"What took you so long?" I patted her head. "Good work, sidekick."

"I thought it would be somewhere obvious, like Seb's room, but it wasn't there. I had to go to Mum's ultra-secret hiding place to find it."

"Where's that?"

"On top of her wardrobe." Beth rolled her eyes. "She couldn't actually be any more obvious about it. She might as well have a sign pointing at it, saying *Interesting Things Here*."

"What sort of things?"

"Diet pills, mainly. Money. Letters from her old boyfriends." Beth shrugged. "I've been through it a zillion times. She's never noticed."

"What if she notices the phone is gone? Won't she go mental?"

"She'd put it right at the back. I don't think she was planning to go looking for it for a while. Anyway, she's distracted. Séverine is here."

"Seb's mum?"

"The one and only. Mum's really tense about her and Dad spending so much time together. She thinks Seb's mum is trying to flirt with Dad."

"Is Seb's mum very glamorous?"

"Think Angelina Jolie. Older than her, obviously, but like that. All hair and drapy clothes and big lips. She's really up herself."

"Is she upset about Seb?"

"I suppose so." Beth sounded dubious. "Anyway, Mum is so busy trying to be superwife she's not really that interested in what I do. Mum can't stand Séverine. And it's totally mutual."

"I suppose it must be hard for her to see your dad with a new wife."

"Especially since she was the one who broke them up," Beth said calmly. "No, I don't blame either of them for being a bit twitchy. But it's very useful if you want to nick something."

I regarded her with awe. "You look so innocent."

"Appearances can be deceptive." She grinned at me. "People always underestimate me because I look young."

"I won't," I promised. "And I'm really grateful. This is exactly what I needed." In more ways than one. I was feeling far more cheerful already. Emotions were messy. Facts I could deal with. This mystery had a beautiful simplicity compared with everything else in my life.

"It's freezing here. Why are you sitting on the promenade?" She looked up and down the seafront, at the dog walkers and joggers who were the only people mad enough to be out. "No one else is sitting."

"I like to be different. Anyway, I like the cold."

"We were supposed to be going to St. Lucia." Beth sounded doleful. "I bet we won't be able to, if Seb is still ill."

Or the unthinkable alternative; if he was dead. "Probably not."

"It's so unfair." She gave a weighty sigh. She was shrewd and startlingly mature, but when all was said and done Beth was thirteen, I reminded myself. And Seb had not been the most pleasant older brother so far. I couldn't blame her for being disappointed.

"Beth. The phone?"

"Oh yeah." She took it out and handed it to me furtively. "I don't want anyone to know I took it."

"Your secret is safe with me." *Seb's secrets, on the other hand . . .* I looked at Beth sternly. "Have you switched it on?"

"Yes. But just to check it was working. I wasn't sure. I mean, look at the state of it."

The phone was incredibly dirty, the casing gritty and smudged from being in the drain. "Are you sure the police don't want it?"

"Positive. Dad asked. Dan told him to keep it for when Seb wakes up."

It sounded as if Dan didn't want to know what was on the phone. Hear no evil, see no evil.

"Aren't you going to switch it on?" Beth asked.

I weighed it in my hand. "I'll do it in a second." This bit was awkward. "But, Beth, I'm not sure if you want to see what's on here."

"Why?" Her face paled.

"I've found out a couple of things about Seb. Things he did to people. I'm absolutely not saying he deserved what happened to him, but I'm not having any difficulty finding enemies who might have wanted to hurt him."

"I knew it." Her shoulders slumped. "Dad is going to be so upset if it turns out he was to blame for all of this."

"Look . . ." I hated to say it, but I had to. I was starting to see this from Dan's point of view. Investigating crimes wasn't a harmless little hobby. Seb was a real person with people who loved him, who wanted to think the best of him. It wasn't up to me to shatter their illusions. On the other hand, Guy was in custody, potentially in a world of trouble.

I had to ask.

"Do you want me to stop asking questions? Just leave it? If it's going to do more harm than good to know, maybe it would be better to quit now."

Beth was made of sterner stuff than I'd thought. "No way. Whatever he did, he chose to do. That's his responsibility. You're not making any of this up, are you?"

I shook my head.

"Well, then. He thought he was untouchable." She sniffed, and I couldn't tell if it was the cold that was making her nose pink, or if she was trying to hold back tears. "He was wrong."

"OK. If you're sure."

"I'm sure." She stood up. "But I don't want to see it. You're right. You can tell me about it if you like, but seeing it is different." All of a sudden she looked very young.

"Good idea."

"Do you remember the PIN?"

"Six nine six nine." I grinned. "Hard to forget."

"That was his idea." She huddled into her coat. "Thanks, Jess. Don't get too cold."

"I won't," I promised. I watched her walk away, her legs spindly and too long for her body, like a wading bird. She'd grow into them, and her looks, even if she never became as spectacular as Seb. As he had been, I reminded myself, thinking of the battered face I'd seen in the hospital. It was anyone's guess how he would look when he recovered. *If* he recovered.

I switched on the phone, still amazed that it worked. It took a few seconds to warm up, then demanded the PIN. I put it in, sure that Beth would have got it wrong. It would be too easy if it just worked at the first time of asking.

Except that it did. I stared at it for a second, then tried to work out what to look at first. The phone beeped as hundreds of missed calls and unread text messages and e-mails downloaded off the server. Then it beeped again, more urgently, and a big "low battery" warning flashed up on the screen.

I made up my mind to start with texts. I scrolled past all of the *Get-well-soon* ones, and the *OMG-I-just-heard* ones from the previous Sunday, until I got to the ones Seb had read and answered. Guy Tindall's name jumped out at me and I clicked to see the conversation, scrolling down past a couple of messages confirming the arrangements for Saturday night's pre-disco party to one that made me stop.

You are dead.

My heart rate shot up and then slowed as I read Seb's response. It was a grinning smiley-face, so maybe I was overreacting since I knew what had actually happened. So what had provoked Guy's message? There was nothing in the messages before that. It had to have been an e-mail, or a phone conversation, or something relating to the pictures he'd sent. Which might, it occurred to me, be on the phone. I zoomed through some more texts, seeing names I knew and nothing much that was interesting. There were some flirty ones from Immy where she went as far as suggesting that he take her to the fireworks. Judging by his side of the conversation, I didn't think Seb had been all that keen, but she got her way in the end, promising that she would make it worth his while.

"Oh, Immy," I said out loud, "he can't be that amazing." Seb Dawson was toxic, it seemed to me. She should have been running away from him, not trying to get him interested in her again. Some people never learned.

The phone displayed the first line of the last text in each conversation, which was quite useful for quick scanning, and that was all I could really do. The battery indicator was a thin red line, almost invisible. I'd get a few minutes more out of it, and then I'd have to find someone who had a phone like this who could lend me a charger since mine wouldn't fit. That was a problem I would have to deal with, but for now I scrolled up and down, trying to guess from the names and the messages whether it was worth my while to click. One of them caught my attention because it was just a number, with no contact information. The last text began: *Good choice, mate.* Which wasn't the sort of thing you texted to a random number, I thought. It was the sort of thing you said to someone you knew. I opened the message to read the whole conversation, and was immediately disappointed. There were only two messages. The first read: *You win. Cash?*

And then Seb had replied, *Good choice, mate. Cash is fine.* So what had Seb won? And what was the choice the other person had to make?

I put the questions on hold, and the texts, as the phone flashed up another warning. I had only two percent of battery remaining, apparently. Not nearly enough. Hurrying, as if that would make a difference, I opened the photographs and found two folders. I ran through the first folder of images in thumbnail form, squinting to try to make sense of the pictures. Parties, random girls, approximately one million selfies. Nothing surprising there. The second folder only had seventy images in it and was called *Fun and Games*. I started to scroll but stopped almost immediately, my attention caught. I sacrificed some battery life to open a picture that turned out to be Seb kissing Amanda—*Amanda!*—on a sofa. The body language was weird. She had her hands in her lap and was turned away from him, as if he had grabbed her head and pulled it round to kiss her. Her eyes were half closed and it was hard to tell if she was enjoying it or not. Two of Seb's friends, Phil and Raj, were standing behind the sofa. Raj was cheering and Phil was sticking his fingers down his throat.

Oh, Amanda. And oh, Seb, too, because if he needed to be able to boast he could pull anyone, any time, he was more insecure than he looked.

I went back to the thumbnails, looking for the banner. I found it almost immediately and opened the image to see Seb all over Julie Drake. Julie, who walked with crutches because she had lost a leg in a car accident when she was twelve. Julie, who was stunningly pretty and used crutches instead of a prosthetic limb because the amputation had been so high up her thigh. She said she didn't mind. She could move faster on crutches. In the picture a couple of boys I didn't know were crouching down, pointing at the gap where her leg should have been, laughing. She obviously had no idea.

I went back to the thumbnails, dreading what I would find next. It was Claudia in a field, at night, with Seb. Her eyes were closed, so she couldn't see the bale of hay Raj and Phil were placing behind her. But she'd have opened them sometime, and she was too clever not to know that the hay was fodder, for her. I felt sorry I'd ever told her to trot back to her stable, once upon a time.

Immy was in a few pictures, generally as the victim of a practical joke. Ruth was there too, blushing in a sadly unbecoming way as Seb stroked her face and murmured something into her ear. Phil and Raj were back, along with a guy called Eddie Gray, and all of them were standing behind Ruth, laughing hysterically. There were more jokes, more victims: not just girls, either. Where one of his friends had passed out drunk, there Seb would be, armed with a roll of cling film to wrap around them or a permanent marker to scribble on them. Humiliation was the aim.

I was really pushing my luck with the battery. I paused on a series of ten or twelve pictures that were too hard to make out in thumbnails: they were very dark and indistinct. Knowing it was my last chance, I opened one, just to see what was going on.

"Seb, you are a turd." I really meant it. The lighting in the picture was terrible but I could see a girl lying on her back on a rumpled bed, one arm over her face. She was topless. I was also fairly sure she was unconscious. And I knew exactly who she was, because of the stars tattooed on the inside of her wrist: Lily.

I scanned through two more of the collection before I stopped. I couldn't go on. The images were a grotesque invasion of privacy. She had been wearing knickers but nothing else apart from her jewelry, and she seemed totally out of it. He hadn't shown her face in any of the images I saw, but I had recognized her straight away; anyone who knew her would. Her tattoos were so distinctive.

The last three pictures were different, but I could see they were of someone lying on white sheets, in daylight. The person looked very naked in the thumbnail image and I hesitated to open them, but curiosity won out.

"Good grief."

I'd been right about the person being naked. I hadn't even come close to imagining who it would be. This time there were no tricks: she knew the pictures were being taken and she was posing for them. There was no mistaking her, or Seb, in the picture he'd taken of the two of them kissing. And he was pretty obviously naked too, so it didn't take a genius to work out what was going on.

I still couldn't believe it.

Stephanie Dawson.

Seb's stepmother.

Suddenly her reluctance to let Dan investigate Seb's private life made perfect sense. Of course she wanted everyone to think it had been a car accident. Of course she was determined to get hold of Seb's phone, if she knew it had incriminating evidence of what she'd done. Betrayals didn't get much bigger than cheating on your husband with his son, even if you'd only met the son when he was sixteen and a massive flirt.

Two things occurred to me, more or less simultaneously.

One: Beth must never find out what her mother and her brother had done.

Two: Stephanie Dawson had the perfect motive to harm her stepson. Maybe the fact that she'd slept with Seb wasn't all she was covering up.

In which case the Dawson family's problems were about to get a whole lot more complicated.

The phone's screen kept going dark. I thought fast about what I needed before it died. There was no point in trying to forward anything to my own phone; that would kill it straight away. I shrank from copying any of the pictures. I didn't want them on my phone, especially the ones of Lily.

I didn't want them to exist in the first place. I also didn't want a souvenir of the Mrs. Dawson pictures. I was pretty sure they were burned on my brain for all time anyway. In the end I settled for going back to get the number for the mysterious text message without a contact. I could call it, I thought. If nothing else, I might recognize the voice of whoever answered it.

The phone whirred and died more or less as soon as I got back to the right screen, and I had only had time to glance at the number. The prefix was the same as my own, which was useful. I thought I'd got the rest, but I needed to write it down or I'd forget it.

". . . seven, four . . ." I was scrabbling in my pocket for my own phone, but found a pencil first. "Double-three, five, one."

I pulled a handful of receipts and rubbish out of the other pocket and stared at it for a second, wondering where I'd got it. The doorway of Fine Feathers, when I was there with Ella. I didn't know whether to be glad I hadn't thrown them away or disgusted. *Get on with it, Jess.*

"Double-three, five . . ."

I separated out a sheet of thin, almost translucent paper. It was blank on one side, but there was something written on the other. Automatically I turned it over to check what it was before I wrote on it, in case it was something important.

"Seven . . . four . . ."

I stopped. I stopped everything. I might even have stopped breathing. I definitely stopped repeating the number, because I didn't have to any more.

Someone had already written it down on the sheet of paper I held in my hand.

17

On such a cold day, Mario's was doing a brisk trade. The warm, steamy air made my face tingle as I came through the door. I had to wait for a table, and while I stood in the queue I watched Lily writing down an order. She had her back to me, her head bent over her notepad as she scrawled, and even from the door I could make out the word that scrolled across her neck. There was just no doubt that she was the person in the pictures. And there was no doubt that I had come to the right place.

The turnover in tables was high and it didn't take long before I had my own, a booth near the back of the café that suited me perfectly. I sat facing the back of the room, keeping a low profile. I really didn't want to see anyone I knew. Except one person.

"Can I get you anything?"

Lily was standing beside the table with her pen poised to

take my order, her expression as blankly pleasant as if we'd never met. I knew she recognized me.

"I'd just like a word with you, if you have a second."

"I'm working."

"I know. I won't take long."

She frowned. "What do you want?"

"I think you know."

"Sorry. Drawing a blank."

"I've got Seb Dawson's phone," I said quietly, and watched her expression change to the guarded, guilty look that told me I was right.

"What's it got to do with me?"

"Pictures."

Her response came immediately. "I'm not going to talk to you about it. Why should I?"

"Because of Guy." I saw it hit home. "He's in a lot of trouble for something he didn't do."

"I know."

"And you know why he's not saying anything to the police, don't you? He's trying to protect you."

She looked stubborn. "I can't help."

"Look, I don't think you did hurt Seb—at least, not enough to put him in hospital. But I know you did something last Saturday night and you're scared of being found out. I heard you talking to Ruth and Amanda in the library yesterday."

"Then you know everything and you don't need my help."

"I got interrupted," I admitted. "I didn't hear your whole conversation. Enough to know you did something to Seb. Enough to make a connection between the pictures on this phone and you wanting to get revenge on him."

"Revenge is a hard word. We wanted—I mean, *I* wanted him to admit he'd been wrong."

"And it didn't work out the way you'd expected?"

"You could say that."

I dropped my voice even further. "You know, if Seb dies and Inspector Henderson actually bothers to investigate it, he'll start with Seb's enemies. There are a lot of you. Getting your story in first seems like a good idea." I saw her wavering. "I know you said you couldn't help, but Guy doesn't deserve to take the fall for what happened. He'd do anything for you. Can't you tell the truth for him?"

"He doesn't want me to."

"Oh, OK, then," I said, irritated. "Let him rot."

She bit her lip, then looked round at the counter, where the manager was talking to another waitress. "I'll have to ask Mum."

"I'll wait," I said.

"She'll get cross if you don't order something."

"All right. Black coffee."

Lily nodded and headed for the coffee machine. Her mother came and stood beside her, cleaning the counter. Lily spoke to her, leaning in so she could murmur in her ear. Her mother listened, then looked over at me. Lily was still talking. I tried to look pleasant and unthreatening and it must have worked because in the end she nodded.

Lily came back with my coffee and dumped it on the table, sliding into the seat opposite me. She looked sulky, and on edge.

"What did you tell her?" I asked.

"Homework."

"How long have we got?"

"For homework, you've got as long as you like. Try to look

as if we're talking about maths, or something." She put a hand up to her hair, then toyed with one of her many earrings. She was looking everywhere except at me.

"So you said you had Seb's phone."

"That's right."

"You said you saw the pictures."

"Just a couple of them. I take it they're the ones Seb sent to Guy."

She looked surprised. "How did you know about that?"

"I heard about it. I didn't know it was you in the pictures until I saw them, but I knew Guy had a crush on a girl and Seb persuaded her to go out with him, deliberately, to annoy him."

"I didn't go out with him. It wasn't even a date."

"But you ended up in bed with him."

"I made a mistake. And *he* made me into a joke. Do you know what he said to Guy? He said he didn't know what his problem was. He said he hadn't had any problems getting me to go out with him. He said I was easy."

"Not very nice."

"No, it wasn't. And it wasn't true, either. At least Guy knows that." She corrected herself. "I think Guy knows that."

"The pictures . . ." I almost didn't want to bring them up. "You can't see your face in the ones I saw. Your arm is over your face. It looks as if you're asleep, actually. Or passed out." Her face twisted as she struggled not to cry. "Was that what happened?"

A nod. She put her hand over her eyes. "I can't cry here. Is Mum looking?"

"She's in the kitchen," I said quickly. "Don't worry."

"OK. OK." She wiped her cheeks. "Do you really need me to give you the details?"

"Not many." I felt like the worst person in the world. "But I'd like to know how he got away with it."

"Oh . . ." She swallowed. "That was my fault. I was so stupid." She closed her eyes for a second, gathering her strength. "It was about six weeks ago. Just after the start of term. I bumped into Seb in school. I mean, literally—I went round a corner and he was there. He made a big deal out of how I'd knocked into him. Then he said he'd accept my apology if I'd go to a party with him."

"And you said yes."

"No. I said no. I didn't like him. Never have. But then he went to work on me. He kept leaving notes in my locker, and staring at me in class, and texting me. He walked me home or to work a few times, even though I told him not to. There wasn't much I could do about him walking beside me. I wasn't keen, at all, but he didn't really listen."

"I know the thing," I said dryly. "Go on."

"He said I'd misjudged him and I wasn't being fair. He asked me to give him a chance. I said his sort of parties weren't my kind of thing and he said they weren't his kind of thing, either, and me being there would make it bearable." She looked up at the ceiling, trying to stop the tears that filled her eyes from falling. "I told him it was too awkward because of Guy."

"Because Guy wanted to go out with you?"

She nodded. "I'd turned him down. A lot."

"He seems like a really sweet person." I said it diffidently, though. On paper, Ryan was perfect too. But to me, he was about as exciting as paper. I wasn't going to judge Lily just because she didn't want to go out with Guy.

"Our backgrounds are too different. We don't like any of the same things." She listed the issues dully, as if she'd thought about them too many times. "His mother would freak if I turned up and said I was his girlfriend."

And I knew what that was like too. Oh, the irony. Unaware of all we had in common, she went on, "I'm a working-class girl with a nose stud and three tattoos. Guy is like my polar opposite."

"Didn't your mother go mad when you got your nose pierced? Not to mention the tattoos?" I was curious. Mrs. Mancini looked like the type to disapprove just as much as Guy's mother might.

"It was worth it," she said dismissively. "I really thought about it before I had any of them done and I paid for them with my own money. Anyway, she didn't know until afterward so there wasn't a lot she could do."

"I thought you had to be over eighteen."

"Well, technically." Lily looked amused. "I have fake ID. And money can buy you anything in this town. Haven't you learned that yet?"

Anything except happiness. "Go on. You kept turning Seb down, because of Guy."

"And because I didn't like him. He's always been smug. Just because he's good-looking he thinks the world owes him whatever he likes." Lily shook her head. "I should never have said yes."

"Why did you?"

"I told you. Stupid. He bought tickets to a gig I really wanted to go to in Plymouth. He said Guy wouldn't find out because he was back at school, and anyway Guy didn't really have a claim on me when I'd turned him down too. I said I'd go as long as he was clear it wasn't a date."

"It seems fair enough so far," I said. "Not stupid at all."

Lily sighed. "Well, stupidly or not, I went to the gig with Seb. I didn't think it would do any harm. And then I went to a house party in Plymouth after the gig because Seb was driving us back and he wanted to go, so I really didn't have much of a choice. It was a good party. At first."

"What happened?"

"I'm not totally sure. I think he spiked my drink. I don't usually have very much and I only remember having a few sips of beer that night. I passed out. I woke up there the next morning, with him." She was shivering. "We were in bed. I was wearing my pants and a T-shirt that didn't belong to me. Nothing else. I asked him what had happened and he said I'd been sick on my outfit so someone had lent me the clothes. The people who had the party let us stay over and Seb had stayed in the room with me in case I became ill, he said. I was mortified." She put a hand over her eyes.

"It happens all the time," I said.

"Not to me. I couldn't believe I'd got into that sort of state. And I wasn't thinking straight—I was really worried about my parents and what they would say about me staying out all night. I had about twenty messages on my phone from them. I just found my jeans and coat and asked him to drive me home. I never even thought to look for the rest of my stuff to see if he'd been telling the truth about me being sick. I didn't make a note of the address—I've no idea where it was, even. I didn't see anyone else that morning, or speak to anyone else who'd been at the party who could tell me what happened. They weren't people I knew. They were friends of Seb's. I don't think they'd have been very helpful anyway."

"But you were upset."

"I kept asking him what happened and he kept saying, *Nothing, nothing*, but he was smirking all the time, and sending messages on his phone. Now I know he was sending pictures of me to all his friends. No wonder he was laughing."

"Do you think . . . Do you know . . ." I couldn't think how to ask, but she knew what I was implying.

"Did he do anything else apart from take pictures? No. I don't think so. But I don't know." Her eyes welled up again. "I asked him, when I found out what he'd done. He just laughed at me."

"How did you find out?"

"Guy told me." She saw the look of shock on my face. "Not to upset me. He thought I should know what had happened, since everyone else did. He couldn't stand that people were talking about it behind my back."

On the surface, Guy was all rich-boy charm, but dig down deep enough and you found a moral center that was as hard as rock.

"I'd already noticed there was something going on. People were laughing at me. Making comments about posing for pictures and getting drunk at parties, and even the color of my underwear, which was pale green." She looked exasperated. "That was the stupidest thing. Asking me if I liked mint ice cream, or if I'd ever been to Greenland, and then sniggering."

"What did you do when you found out? Did you talk to Seb?"

"Tried to. All he would say was that nothing had happened and he didn't know what I was talking about. He said the pictures that were doing the rounds hadn't come from him and it must have been someone else, another time." She laughed bitterly. "Because I'm the kind of girl who goes out and gets drunk and strips off in front of near-strangers every Friday night."

"Obviously not."

"That's what people think of me."

I felt terrible for her. "Did you go to the police?"

"After a couple of weeks. I shouldn't have bothered."

"Who did you speak to?" I knew the answer before she said it.

"Inspector Henderson. I went right to the top."

"I bet he wasn't interested."

"He took a statement. Then he told me I had to take responsibility for my own behavior. He said I'd put myself at risk by going to a party with people I didn't know. He said I should have looked after my drink to make sure it wasn't spiked, if that was really what had happened. I said Seb wasn't a stranger. Inspector Henderson said I'd chosen to be there with him. I'd agreed to go out with him, and to go to the party. He basically called me a liar. He said I'd got drunk and done things I regretted, and now I was looking for someone else to blame so I didn't get in trouble." She sounded bitter, unsurprisingly. "He told me no jury would ever take me seriously, especially when I don't know where it happened or even what happened. The pictures on their own aren't proof of anything because I might have agreed to pose for them."

"But you wouldn't have."

"I know. He didn't believe me. He said no one else would believe me." She sniffed, holding back tears again. "It was so humiliating. He said he'd talk to Seb and scare him a bit so he stopped circulating the images. He said he'd have a word with Seb's parents too, just to encourage them to keep a closer eye on him. He told me to tell him or a teacher if I was being bullied about it. You could see him trying to work out whether he'd get the blame if I tried to kill myself. All he was interested in was covering it up and covering his ass."

"Dan doesn't do blame," I said, thinking about what Beth had told me. "Did you ring Seb's mobile? About a month ago?"

She nodded.

"Did you say you'd never forgive him for what he'd done?"

"Something like that. Why?"

"It was his sister who answered. That's why I started trying to find out what happened to him and why. She needs to know what he did."

"She doesn't need to know about me." Lily's eyes were lifeless, as if telling the story had killed her spirit all over again.

"Maybe. Maybe not." I fiddled with the phone, turning it end over end. "Lily, what did you do to Seb?"

"What do you mean?"

"You're the person who's suffered most from Seb's behavior. And you were in the library yesterday, talking to Amanda and Ruth. You said Seb was fine when you left him. What did you do?"

"Just talked to him."

"I don't believe you. When I saw him he was almost naked, and he'd been tied up, and beaten up, and he had a fractured skull. Guy beat him up."

"Not that badly."

"And you did what, Lily? Stripped him? Tied him up? Did you take pictures of him?"

Her face was red. "We just wanted to show him what it was like."

"We?"

"Me and Amanda and Ruth. It was Ruth's idea. I persuaded him to meet me. Ruth had pepper spray—you know, for muggers. She sprayed him in the face and he was too busy screaming about his eyes to care that we were getting him into a car and driving him to Ruth's house and taking off his clothes and tying him up."

"But he wouldn't mind being photographed naked."

"He did when he had to hold a sign saying what he'd done to us. He was pretty angry." She rubbed at a scuffmark on the table, avoiding my eyes. "We wanted him to apologize to us, and he did, eventually. But it took a while."

"What were you going to do with the pictures you took?"

"Keep them. Use them if he told the police what we'd done. If you put stuff like that on the Internet it lives forever. He'd never get rid of all of it. So it was our insurance policy."

"What did you do with him afterward?"

"I let him go. He walked away. I didn't see him again."

I shook my head. "No. Sorry. That's not what happened."

"What do you mean?"

I took the paper out of my pocket and flattened it out on

the table. "I found this on Fore Street on Monday, in the door-way of Fine Feathers. It's a page from your order pad. Look." The Mario's logo at the top was unmistakable.

"You don't know it's mine."

"I can compare it to this." I held up the docket she'd given me for my coffee. "That's your writing. The sevens are really distinctive. I don't know anyone else who does them like that."

Her face was flushed again. "OK. So what?"

"So that number is on Seb's phone. No contact details. I rang it just now and it's out of service. Who does it belong to?"

"I don't know."

"Come off it."

"I don't!"

"Then why did you write it down?"

She crumpled. "I called it. From the phone box near Fine Feathers. I must have dropped the piece of paper afterward." She bit her lip. "Basically, we dumped Seb in St. Laurence Square. I took his phone and told him he had to pick one per-son who would come and get him—if he could think of one person who genuinely cared about him. He gave me that num-ber. I dropped his phone in a drain, out of reach. I said I'd call the number but if they didn't come, he'd have to stay there un-til someone found him. I wanted to show him that he'd hurt too many people to have any real friends he could count on."

"What happened when you rang the number?"

"A guy answered. He didn't say much. There was music in the background, really loud. I just said where Seb was and that he needed help and I hung up."

"Did you recognize the voice?"

Lily shook her head.

"Can you tell me anything about him?"

"He sounded really irritated when he answered, which seemed weird to me. I was ringing from a phone booth so he didn't know who it was. If you didn't want to answer your phone, wouldn't you just let it ring?"

"Absolutely. Let it go to voicemail."

"That's what I was thinking."

"You say you didn't recognize him, but did it remind you of anyone?"

"Oh. No. I mean, it just sounded like a rich boy to me. One of Seb's friends." She gave me a one-shouldered shrug. "Maybe I just thought that because I was expecting it to be one of them. It could have been Eddie Gray or Harry Knowles. It could have been any of them."

I knew what she meant. There was a generic quality to the way they spoke. The cadences were all the same, and the vowel sounds.

"After you called him, what happened?"

"I went home."

"How was Seb when you left him? What sort of injuries did he have?"

"His eyes were really inflamed. His face was bruised where Guy had hit him." She thought for a second. "The rope had rubbed his wrists, and he'd bruised himself trying to get free. And he wasn't wearing many clothes. But he was conscious and talking."

"He could have died of hypothermia," I pointed out. "You were taking a big risk, leaving him there."

"Not really. We picked a public place, even if it's not busy. And the cops patrol a lot on Halloween. We actually took a big risk putting him somewhere so obvious." She looked up. "Oh no."

I twisted round in my seat to see Claudia and Immy striding toward us. "What's wrong?"

"Nothing," Lily said. She jumped up. "I should get back to work."

"What are you doing?" Claudia had reached our table. She put out a hand, shoving Lily back so she overbalanced and sat down again. Claudia sat beside her, and Immy slid into the booth beside me. Cozy, except that it wasn't. Both the new arrivals looked furious.

"What's up?" I asked.

Claudia ignored me. She got very close to Lily and repeated, "What are you doing?"

"Nothing."

"We talked about this. You don't tell anyone anything about the other night."

"Look, shut up," Lily said. "I haven't done anything wrong. It was just because of Guy. He—"

"Why am I not surprised? Boys before friends. This always happens," Immy said.

"You'd know. You've always put boys first." Lily glared at her.

"And since when were you two friends with Lily?" I asked.

"What do you know about anything? You've only been in Port Sentinel for about two minutes," Immy sneered.

"I've literally never seen you speak to Lily." I looked across the table. "Am I wrong?"

Lily shook her head. "Look, just forget about it. You too, Claudia."

"I want to know what you've told her, Lily."

"She hasn't told me half as much as you just did," I said, and watched Claudia get the picture, pixel by pixel. Download speed: slow.

"You didn't know."

"Not until you charged in here shouting at Lily. All I knew was that Amanda and Ruth and Lily had a crisis meeting in the library about Seb. And then you turned up and stopped me from hearing what it was about. I was a bit surprised to see you in a library. I really should have guessed you were involved."

Immy gave me a level-five hate-stare. "You still don't know anything about what we did."

"I can guess," I said slowly. "There are messages from you on Seb's phone. You persuaded him to go with you to the fireworks. You were the bait, weren't you?"

"You've got his phone." Immy looked across the table at Claudia. "You read the messages."

"I thought they were needy and desperate, but now I get it. You had to make sure he met you so the others could trap him."

"Me wanting to go out with him isn't proof of anything."

"No, but you and Claudia hanging around in a dark alley two minutes from where Seb was dumped looks a bit suspicious from where I'm sitting."

"You two went to the fireworks," Lily said, surprised. "What alley?"

"After I saw Seb being scraped up and taken away, I bumped into this pair playing Halloween pranks." I frowned. "You weren't supposed to double back, were you? No one thought you'd be there when Seb was dumped, but you knew the plan and you knew the timings and you made sure you were nearby.

What did you want to do? Get an apology from him? Make fun of him once he'd been humiliated?"

"Did you hurt him? Afterward?" Lily looked from Claudia to Immy, her eyes wide. "Did you think I'd be blamed, or Ruth, or Amanda? Or poor Guy?"

"We didn't do anything," Claudia snapped. "We'd made ourselves obvious at the disco. We sneaked off while everyone was watching the fireworks and went to see him. We were too late. The cops were already there."

"You said you didn't go back. I *asked* you." Lily still looked outraged.

"We didn't go back properly. Like she said, we didn't speak to him." Immy looked sulky. "Anyway, we weren't the only ones."

"What do you mean?" Lily and I asked in unison.

"We saw Ruth when we left the fireworks," Claudia explained. "She was running up the street, away from St. Laurence Square. She didn't speak to us. She didn't even really look at us."

"In shock," Immy said. "She'd probably just whacked him on the head. She probably thought she'd killed him."

"Ruth is five foot nothing. How would she hit him hard enough to fracture his skull?" I demanded.

"You'll have to ask her." Claudia looked at Lily, who was staring at the table, her forehead furrowed. "Didn't she say anything about being there? Or about us?"

"No."

Claudia shook her head sadly. "Who can you trust these days?"

"Not either of you two," I said tartly. "Why didn't you say anything about it before?"

"None of our business." Claudia sniffed. "You could take a lesson from us, Jess. We know when to keep our noses out of trouble."

"I don't think I'm the one in trouble here."

Claudia smiled, and not pleasantly. "Then you need to think again, because *we* didn't try to kill Seb but someone did, and they're not going to be pleased to have Jess Tennant, Super Sleuth, on the case. They're going to be angry as hell when they find out you're asking questions—if they don't know already."

"I'll take my chances."

"Brave. But they're prepared to let Guy go to prison instead of owning up. They were prepared to hit Seb hard enough to fracture his skull. I don't think they're going to be too impressed if you run across them."

"Are you threatening me?"

"Warning you. I told you, I don't know who did it." Her voice was colorless. I couldn't tell if she was lying or just really hung over.

"Thanks for the tip."

"Any time."

"Speaking of tips, I'd better get back to work." Lily stood up again, and this time Claudia let her out of the booth.

The two other girls sat there for a moment. Then Claudia sighed. "I never thought I'd say this, but I like you. I don't want you to come to harm."

"I thought being friendly with me was all an act."

"What can I say? You've grown on me."

"Like a fungus," Immy said. She seemed unmoved by my potential plight.

"Thanks, Claudia. I appreciate it." I meant it too. "I just want to clear Guy's name and find out what really happened."

"Just don't get us in trouble. I'll deny everything," Immy said.

"Me too," Claudia said quickly. "It's one thing saying it here. I'm not going to admit anything to the police."

"I didn't say you had to. All I'm doing is following the trail back to the person who is actually responsible. That's the only one I'm interested in."

They stood up, preparing to leave. Before that blissful event happened, though, Claudia looked down at me.

"Really, Jess, be careful. I think whoever did this is prepared to do whatever it takes to get away with it. You don't know who you're looking for, but they probably know all about you."

"There's nothing I can do about that."

Claudia nodded. "Just keep your wits about you. And don't walk into any traps."

My heart was racing. I didn't want to be scared, but I couldn't deny that Claudia had a point. I watched her walk out with Immy. I looked around at the people sitting at the other tables, trying to see if anyone was watching me. Paranoia kicked in and I felt as if everyone was. The café didn't feel like a safe place any more.

Actually, nowhere did.

And the only thing I could do was try and find Seb's attacker before they found me.

18

Life being what it is, I walked out of the café and straight into the path of the other person I really didn't want to see.

"Jessica!" Dad sounded pleased. I couldn't manage the same. "Hi, Dad."

"Is this the place your mother was talking about?" He looked up at the Mario's sign. "God, it's like time travel. Please tell me there's a Starbuck's somewhere in this hole in the ground."

"The locals voted against it. They don't want chain coffee shops. They felt that would ruin Port Sentinel's unique identity."

"Oh, please."

"The coffee in Mario's is good. But I've just had some," I added quickly.

"I can manage without it." Dad put his arm around my shoulder. "Where are you off to?"

"Just wandering about."

"That's a good use of your time."

"I'm on holiday," I protested.

"You should make the most of having your freedom. Do something exciting." Dad shook his head. "You've got no drive. No get-up-and-go."

"Thanks very much." I felt defensive immediately, and hurt. Top parenting. "Was there something you wanted, Dad?"

"I wanted to talk to you." He steered me toward the seafront. "Come for a walk."

"Do I have any choice about this?"

"None."

"I don't want to talk about you and Mum," I said. "It's none of my business."

"It is, because you're part of the family."

"We're not really a family any more, Dad. We're an ex-family. A broken home."

"That's not true."

"It is. There's me and Mum, and you and me, but me, you and Mum aren't a group now. And we never will be again."

"Don't be so sure about that." He sounded incredibly pleased with himself.

I stopped walking. "What have you done?"

"Nothing. Absolutely nothing."

"Have you spoken to Mum this morning?"

"No. I promise. She's still locked away, considering her options."

"You are not one of them. It would be a disaster. For both of you."

"So wise and yet so young." Dad patted my head. Being patronized had never sat well with me.

"You are toxic, Dad. You should have *Warning: Harmful to*

Health written on your forehead. Mum suffered the whole time you were married and then you threw her away. Now you're trying to get her back because you've decided she'd be useful. It makes me sick." I ducked out from under his arm. "And I told you, I don't want to talk to you about her."

"And *I* told *you* I didn't want to talk to you about her." He was holding onto his temper with some difficulty, I thought. "That's not what this conversation was supposed to be about."

"OK." *Give him a chance*. "What did you want to say?"

"The Henderson boy."

My stomach flipped as if I'd just walked over the edge of a giant pit and hadn't hit the bottom yet. "I don't want to talk about him."

"Too bad. I do. I want you to stay away from him."

"You too? That makes everyone, I think."

"What do you mean?"

"Will's parents aren't keen on me, either."

"Idiots," Dad said crisply. "They should be glad you've shown an interest in their son. You're far too good for him."

"Dad, you don't know him."

"I know enough, and I'm telling you it's a bad idea for the two of you to be together."

"I don't have to explain myself to you, but we're not together. We had a bit of a thing in the summer and it ended."

"I saw the way he was looking at you last night."

"He wasn't."

"Exactly." Dad looked smug. "I know the signs."

"Well, you've had plenty of girlfriends, I suppose. You would be an expert."

"Ouch."

"Why is everyone so worried about whether the two of us are together or not?" I felt like crying. "Not that it even matters when we aren't. But I don't get it."

"Jessica, you're too involved to be able to see what we can see."

"Which is?"

"It would be a disaster. It would be history repeating itself."

"Not necessarily."

"I can see the appeal. It's romantic to think of giving the Romeo and Juliet story a happy ending. You're Molly, and Will is Dan, and you're playing the same parts in the same old film. But your mother's feelings for Dan blighted our marriage."

"You did that all by yourself."

"No. I didn't. I meant what I said last night. Your mother was never in love with me. She was in love with Dan. And the sad thing is that it wasn't really him she loved—it was her idea of him. You've met him. You know what he's like. She thought he was perfect and she hated me for not being as good as him." He sounded sad. "I couldn't live up to the idea she had of him."

"She's never said anything like that to me."

"She's in denial. But she has never been happy since she left Port Sentinel. She never allowed herself to be happy with me. She drove me away."

I stared. "You're seriously saying it was her fault you cheated on her."

"I have to take some responsibility."

"Given that it was you who decided to sleep with other women."

"That kind of thing, yes." He looked sideways at me. "I

know. I made a mess of it. I did things I shouldn't have done, but I was frustrated."

"What do you want, Dad?"

"I want to stop you from making Molly's mistakes out of some misplaced romantic idea."

"I know. You said. I want to know what you want with Mum."

He stopped walking. "I want her back."

"You are out of your mind."

"I have never stopped loving her. Ever. I hated myself for doing everything I did."

"Not as much as I hated you, I bet."

"I was desperate to get her to notice me. Just for once. Just to realize that I wasn't a second-best loser." He shook his head. "I got it all wrong with her. Now I want to put it right."

"Why now?"

"Midlife crisis, probably. I need a new start. New business. New life. I wasn't happy. I want to be happy."

"So find someone who makes you happy. Leave Mum alone."

"She's the one, Jessica. She's always been the one. I can't stand the thought of her being back with Dan."

"She isn't," I said sharply. "Dan's married."

"That won't stop them. When I heard she was staying down here, I knew."

"I don't think she would do that." I was feeling faint.

"I don't think she could stop herself. But he'll crush her if he gets his hands on her. You thought I was a bad husband—you were right. But I can change. A lot of the things I do and say are to get her to notice me. If I thought I had persuaded her to care for me, I would be a different person."

"Is that what you think?"

"You should be on my side, Jessica. Dan's rotten to the core. The best thing I ever did was take her away from him. You've got to help me to stop her from falling for his lies again."

"I don't want her and Dan to be together either, but it's not up to you to decide what she does. Or me. She needs to make her own decisions."

Dad raised one eyebrow. "That's a recipe for disaster."

"Stop putting her down. And stop trying to interfere in my life."

"I just don't want you to do what Molly did. I don't want you to miss out on what's right in front of you because you want something—or someone—you can't have."

"I won't." I thought of Ryan, though, and felt unbearably confused. Dad was right. I hadn't even given him a chance. And he was far nicer than Dad had ever been. I pulled myself together. "OK, I've listened to you and I have three things to say. One: Will and I are not together, so that part of the lecture is pretty unnecessary. But I note your concern. Two: you and Mum were terrible together and I'm not going to help you get her back. I don't want her to get involved with Dan, but you are not the safe option. Just back off. And three: this has been an excellent father–daughter chat but let's not do it again."

"Jessica, you do not speak to me that way." Dad's jaw was clenched. "I have your best interests at heart."

"So you say." I looked past him. "Dad, I'm not being rude, but I've got to go."

"Why? Where?"

"There's someone over there I need to talk to." I ran before he could say anything else. I didn't have time for him to say a long good-bye when Ruth was scurrying along the seafront, moving fast in the opposite direction. And I didn't have time to think about whether it was a good idea for me to talk to her. Historically, I had difficulties with looking before I leaped, but it had worked out fine before.

Sort of.

Even though I was running and she was walking, she moved fast and it took me a surprisingly long time to overhaul her. When I got close enough, I called out, "Hey. Wait."

She swung round. "What do you want?"

I was panting. I leaned forward, hands on my knees. "I have got to get fitter."

"Join a gym." She turned and walked away, her curls bouncing.

"Wait, please."

She didn't stop. I jogged after her. "It's about Seb."

The brakes went on. Her expression was just as hostile, but she was listening. "What about him?"

"I spoke to Lily, and Claudia, and Immy, and Amanda. I know everything that happened. More or less," I added, thinking about it. "I know it was your idea."

"Did they say that? They're making this *my* fault?" She actually bared her teeth, looking as friendly and approachable as a feral weasel. "I don't think so."

"Look, the one thing I do know is that Guy isn't to blame. He shouldn't be in custody. He hasn't done anything wrong."

"He won't be charged. There's no evidence."

"You don't know that. You don't know they won't make something up. Ruth, you have to come clean."

"Sorry. Not sorry."

"Ruth!"

"It's his problem."

"You've set him up."

"Not deliberately. If the police are too thick to look beyond the obvious, I can't help that."

"Yes, you can."

"Well, I don't want to. I'm not all that worried about Seb—or Guy, for that matter. He's never been nice to me. He's never even spoken to me."

"So he deserves to have his life ruined? For something you did?"

"I didn't do anything. I played a joke on Seb, along with a few other people. We didn't hurt him."

"Much."

"We bent him a little." A tiny smile curved the corners of her mouth. "He cried."

"Lovely."

"He deserved it. You don't know."

"I do. I spoke to the others, and I saw his phone. No one is saying he's a nice person, but he's in a coma."

"Which isn't anything to do with me. That was someone else."

There was something about the way she said it. "You know who, don't you?"

"What?" She looked unsettled for a moment. "No."

"Claudia and Immy saw you walking away from St. Laurence Square. What were you doing there?"

"Just checking the plan was all working."

"You were supposed to be at home. That was your alibi."

"I wanted to be sure everything was as I'd planned. I'm a

control freak. I don't like leaving things to other people. They get it wrong."

"So why did you let them do it on their own?"

"I can't drive. And I wasn't strong enough to lift him. I was supposed to pretend Amanda and Lily were at my house, to be their alibi."

"What about Claudia and Immy?"

"They did the first part. Trapping him. Then they handed him over to us so they could go back and be noticed at the disco. We thought the police would be looking for one person, not a group."

"Especially not the five of you, who have nothing in common except that Seb Dawson was unpleasant to you."

"Which you could say about most people he knew."

"What did you see, Ruth? What made you so upset? I saw you on the cliffs the next day and you were in a state."

She looked down so I couldn't see her eyes. "Nothing."

"Someone you knew?"

"No."

"Then what?"

She gave a tiny sigh, as if the air was being squeezed out of her. "I went to see if he was still there about an hour after Lily and Amanda dumped him, and he wasn't. There was no sign of him. I was sorry he'd been rescued. Then I heard a car. I ran and hid in the doorway of the church."

"Whose car?"

"I don't know."

"What make?"

"It was an Audi. Silver."

That narrowed it down for me, especially in a place like Port

Sentinel, where silver Audis were as common as street lamps. "OK. Then what?"

"Someone got out. They dragged Seb out of the back seat and put him on the ground, where we'd left him. Then they got back in the car and drove off."

"One person."

"As far as I could tell. I only heard one door open and close."

"Male or female?"

"I don't know. I was hiding. I could only see the front of the car and the headlights were shining in my eyes. I could barely see the logo."

"Did you get the license plate?"

"No."

"Was it a sports car? A saloon? A hatchback? Four-wheel drive?"

"I didn't see."

"Ruth!"

"Sorry. I was hiding, remember. I could only peek out. And when it moved away I was mainly looking at Seb." She looked utterly sick at the memory. "He was destroyed. It wasn't how he'd been when we were with him. I knew he was in serious trouble."

"What did you do?"

"Once I was sure they'd gone, I checked that Seb was still alive. He had a pulse, just. It took me ages to find it and I got blood on me." She rubbed her hands on her jacket, remembering. "I ran away. I stopped at the nearest phone box to call 999 and then I ran. That must have been when Claudia and Immy saw me."

"It was nice of you to call an ambulance."

260

"I didn't want him to die."

"He didn't deserve that."

"No, *I* didn't deserve the stress of a murder investigation. They never let them drop. I'd never be able to relax. Always looking over my shoulder." She shivered.

"OK. Well, you did the right thing for the wrong reasons. We'll give you half-marks."

"Oh, shut up. You'd have done the same."

"I'd probably have called from my mobile so I could stay with him and do first aid."

"Then the police would have known you were there."

I shook my head, irritated. "You were more worried about saving your skin than saving Seb's life."

"I put myself first. It's human nature."

Without expecting much, I asked, "Did you see anything else that might be useful?"

"No. But I heard the car scrape a wall as it drove off."

And I could think of two silver Audis owned by people who knew Seb that had recent, serious damage to their bodywork. "At last, a useful detail. You're a great plotter but you're a terrible witness."

"There's no need to be rude." Her face was flaming.

"Sorry," I said. "Not sorry. As you might say yourself."

I wasn't massively surprised when she walked off. I didn't mind all that much. You could have enough of Ruth's company. I found the one-minute mark was usually when that feeling kicked in.

I started jogging up toward the center of town. I still had more questions than answers, but the questions weren't *who* so much, more *why*. Though the more I found out about Seb, the more I thought *Why not?* I could find a motive for Mrs. Dawson without having to work too hard. I shrank from confronting her, though. Better to rule out the second of my two suspects and then hand the whole thing over to Dan, who would surely do his job this time, when the case was all but solved already.

I was absolutely in my own world, hurrying up Fore Street, when someone shouted my name. I turned to see Nick standing in the doorway of the gallery.

"Where are you off to?"

"I need to see someone."

"Urgently?"

"Fairly." I walked back toward him, though. "What's up?"

"Where's your mother? She's supposed to be here."

"Honestly? Hiding."

Nick frowned. "From whom?"

"Life, generally. It's what she does when everything gets too much for her."

"Everything being her ex-husband and her—" He broke off.

"Her nothing. She has nothing to do with Dan. Absolutely nothing."

"All right. I get the picture." Nick grinned at me. "You don't like Dan a lot, do you?"

I remembered that it was through Dan that Mum had got the job at the gallery, so he and Nick were probably besties. It would be seriously undiplomatic for me to say what I really thought. On the other hand, I wasn't in the mood to lie. "Nope. Can't stand him."

Nick nodded. "How does your mum feel about him?"

"I haven't asked her lately," I said truthfully.

"I see."

I thought he probably did; he was clever enough. "So should I tell Mum it's safe for her to come back to work?"

"Of course. Why wouldn't it be?"

"Because you told her not to."

Nick looked surprised. "She didn't take that seriously, did she?"

"She takes everything to do with the gallery seriously. She really loves working for you."

His face softened. "She's good to have around."

"Even if she doesn't sell much," I said, wary of mentioning it but wanting to know what he would say.

Nick laughed. "You might not know this but the gallery is my pet project. It's not how I make my money."

"How do you do that?"

"I started up a software company when I was twenty. I was bought out a few years ago and I used the money to start up another one. Then that company was taken over and I got a pretty sweet deal."

"So you're rich."

"I do all right."

"And the gallery?"

"A hobby. Losing money on it makes my accountants happy."

"So you actually don't care about selling things."

"I like my artists to feel they're doing well. I like seeing people fall in love with art that I like. Otherwise, not bothered."

"I should tell Mum. She's in a constant state of fear that she's going to get the sack."

"Is she that scared of me?"

"Scared of messing up." I hesitated, not sure if I was saying more than Mum would have wanted. "This job is the best thing that's ever happened to her. She loves it and it means she has time to take pictures and I can see her getting more confident every day. Or she was, until Dad turned up."

"I don't know your father, Jess, but I have to say, he makes a pretty terrible first impression."

"It's all downhill from there, believe me."

"Well, you can tell your mother that her job is safe. And if she needs more time to take pictures, she can have it. She's exceptionally talented."

Pride made me glow. "I'll tell her. It might even get her to leave her room."

He said good-bye and went back into the gallery, and I headed up the street again. A couple of minutes later a low, sleek sports car rumbled past me and pulled in to the curb. The top was down and Nick was driving.

"Jess, get in. I'll give you a lift. Make up for holding you up."

"Oh, that's OK."

"Get in," he insisted. "It's no trouble. I have somewhere to be. I can drop you on the way."

I did as I was told. "Where have you been hiding this?"

He laughed. "I never drive it. Parking is a nightmare around here. I save it for weekends and trips."

"It's beautiful." It was navy blue. Even sitting at the curb with the engine idling, it looked as fast as a bullet.

"It's a Lamborghini. My one indulgence."

"But you save it for weekends."

"Everything in moderation."

He moved off and I leaned back against the seat.

"Like it?"

"It's like they strapped the most comfortable armchair in the world to a jet engine." I had to shout over the noise the car made, and the wind was whipping my hair around my face.

"So where am I taking you?"

I told him where I wanted to go and he nodded. I wondered if he would ask why but his attention wasn't on me. "This room where your mother is hiding—is it at Sandhayes?"

"Yeah."

"I thought I might have a word with her myself. See if I can get her to come out."

I looked sideways at him, a thought forming very unexpectedly in my mind.

"What?"

"Nothing," I said quickly. "Nothing at all."

"Until she comes back, I have to open my own post. Which is clearly unacceptable."

"Clearly."

"No point in getting you to pass on my messages when I can do it myself."

I nodded. "I'd probably get it wrong."

"No, you wouldn't. But hopefully I'll get it right." The car coasted to a stop. "Is this where you need to be?"

"Perfect." I jumped out. "Thank you."

"Likewise." He waved and drove off, the rumble of the engine hanging in the air for what seemed like ages. The sun had come out and the birds were singing. A light wind scattered the fallen leaves and sent them dancing down the road. I let myself enjoy it, just for a moment. Then I took a deep breath and rang the bell by the high wooden gate.

19

I was all set to introduce myself but I got buzzed through the gate as soon as I said my name. A woman holding a duster opened the front door.

"Yes?"

"I came to see Harry. Is he here?"

She nodded and stood back to let me pass. The door at the end of the hall was open, and as I went toward it Harry appeared.

"Jess Tennant. What a surprise." He looked tired, his hair flat on one side as if he'd just woken up. He was in shorts and a T-shirt, despite the chill in the air, and his feet were bare. "Consolata, you can go."

"Sorry?"

"You. Can. Go." To me, he said, "She barely speaks English. They never do."

"I not finish yet." She was clutching her duster to her chest, looking nervous.

"It's fine. I forgive you. Go on. Go home. Have a day off for once."

She hurried past him, her head down.

"I won't stay for long," I said to Harry.

"It's a good excuse to get rid of her. I am not able to cope with the sound of the vacuum cleaner this morning."

"Technically, I think it's the afternoon. It's just after twelve."

"You could be right." He yawned. "My morning, though."

"Big night last night?"

"And every night." He ran his hands through his hair, standing it on end. "I'm just tired."

"Not hungover."

"I don't drink."

"Really?" I followed him through the massive living room, stopping to look at the view in daytime. I could see the entire sweep of the bay, dotted with little white sails. I side-stepped one of the big sofas to get closer to it. "This is incredible."

"I never really notice it."

"How is that possible?"

He yawned. "You can get used to anything."

I stared out at the horizon, imagining the scene later, when the sun had set and the torches were all burning. This would be the best viewpoint in Port Sentinel. I thought about asking Harry if I could come back here to see it, but decided against it, at least until I'd asked him about his Saturday night.

"Drink?"

"I'm OK."

"Have some orange juice. Consolata squeezes it every morning and I never drink all of it."

"Thanks."

He went down the hallway to the kitchen. The house was so quiet I could hear the sound his bare feet made on the marble floor as he walked. I went back to looking out. The garden was not all that big compared to the size of the house, but that was typical of Port Sentinel. Land was too expensive to waste on trees and shrubs. It was immaculately landscaped, though, with a terrace that led down to a pocket-size swimming pool that was currently covered over. To one side there was a long, low building that looked like a pool house.

The main feature, however, was a temporary one. At the end of the garden, with plenty of space around it, there was a huge pile of wood, at least five meters high and the same across.

"Admiring my bonfire?" Harry had come back without me noticing. "Tonight's the night."

"It's going to be a huge fire."

"It's going to be epic," he said happily, handing me a glass. He clinked it with his own. "We always have a bonfire for Bonfire Night but we've never had one as big."

"Are you allowed to have a massive fire in your back garden?"

"If no one calls the cops." He laughed. "Don't worry. I got some guys to set it up. They know about that kind of thing. It's properly stacked and it's away from any buildings and it'll all be fine."

"Sorry. Was I sounding too sensible?"

"A bit." He laughed again. "But that's possibly a good thing, given that I am literally playing with fire."

"I don't know how your parents can leave you alone in charge of the house."

"They're used to it." He knocked back his juice in one go. "Now, what can I do for you?"

I rubbed condensation off my glass. "It's a bit awkward."

"Sounds interesting." He sat down on one of the sofas, his arms stretched along the back, one foot propped on the opposite knee.

I sat down on the other sofa and sipped my juice, wondering how to start. "You and Seb are friends."

"Absolutely. He's my boy."

"Is this your telephone number?" I handed him the sheet of paper I'd found and he glanced at it.

"Why do you ask?"

"On Saturday night, Seb called that number asking for help. Someone came and got him. Later, he was dumped back in the square with serious head injuries. I think it was you who picked him up and took him to his house, but I can't prove it." I waited a second. "The police could prove it, though. Easily."

"How did you know it was me?" A muscle was flickering in his arm.

"You took your car to the fireworks. I saw it by the gate to the recreation ground. There was no reason for you to drive. You'd been at Guy's house, then at the recreation ground, and neither of them is far enough from this place for you to need your car." I drank some more juice, letting Harry think about the consequences of admitting I was right. "Look, I know who did it. I know what happened. I just need you to tell me where you took him."

"I took him home." He said it quietly, as if it was no big deal, but it was another little bit of proof for me that my theory was right.

"Did you see anyone there?"

"At his place? No."

"Any cars outside?"

"I don't remember. I just dropped him at the front door. Why?"

"I think it was Mrs. Dawson who hurt him and dumped him back in the square."

"Why would she do that?"

"Personal reasons." I wasn't inclined to encourage Harry to ask any questions about it.

"They must be pretty important reasons."

"They are to her."

"She nearly killed him, though." Harry shook his head, stunned. "A real wicked stepmother. How did you find out?"

"Talked to people. I got Seb's phone. I noticed a few things that night. I don't know. It all fits together." I leaned forward and put my half-empty glass down on the table. The sofa was soft and deep, and it was a big stretch to get to the table. "I have to tell the police, Harry. She has to be brought to justice. Will you tell Dan Henderson about your bit? To help Guy?"

"He'll ask me why I didn't own up before."

"It's a fair question."

"I know. I feel bad about it. I just didn't want to get involved. I didn't know Guy was going to get himself arrested. That's crazy. I've been waiting for the cops to admit he didn't do it. I mean, there's no way he's getting convicted when he had nothing to do with it."

"You'd hope not, but you really have to come clean now. You can't let Mrs. Dawson get away with it."

"No. You're right. I see that now."

I picked up my glass again. It felt like a huge effort to lift it and sip from it. Now that I'd said my piece, I was utterly exhausted. This was not the most relaxing conversation I'd ever had. I didn't know Harry at all, and it wasn't as if we could go from *Your friend's stepmother almost killed him* to *What sort of music do you like?*

"I should probably go."

"You really haven't explained how you worked out it was Mrs. Dawson. Take me through it from the start," Harry said. He was watching me with that close attention I'd noticed before. Total focus. It made me edgy.

"Another time." I drained the last of the orange juice and leaned forward again to put my glass back down. I stopped mid-stretch. "What's that?"

"What?"

"On the rug. By your feet." The sofa had moved back a little when Harry sat on it, so I could see a brownish-red stain matting the pale gray rug.

"Oh, someone spilled a drink last night. Terrible. I'm going to be losing all my pocket money so my parents can get it cleaned professionally."

"What were they drinking? Tomato juice?"

"Looks like it." His knee was jumping. "I've made up my mind, Jess. I'll go to the police. Come clean, as you said. It's only fair."

I ignored him. I was looking up at the walkway over our heads. Then I stood up. My head felt light, my feet impossibly heavy. I went to the end of the sofa and looked at the constellation of little brownish-red spots on the side of it. And the other sofa, the one Harry was sitting on—it was in the wrong place.

I had had to go round it to see the view. Logic told me it had been moved to cover the carpet.

"What are you doing?" Harry sounded intrigued.

"Working out how Seb got injured." My voice sounded very small, as if I was a long way away from myself. I dragged my arm up to point at the walkway. "He fell off it, didn't he? And landed here. And smashed his head on the ground."

"No. He didn't."

"That's blood on the rug, and the sofa. You haven't been able to get it off so you've tried to cover it up. You like betting, don't you, Harry? What odds will you give me that it's Seb's blood?"

"Have another drink."

"I'm OK." I wasn't. I felt sick. I sat down on the arm of the sofa to disguise the fact that my legs were shaking. "What happened?"

"It *is* blood, but it's from a fight."

"You stop the fights as soon as there's blood. That's your rule."

"When two guys are beating the tar out of each other, they don't always stop because I say so."

"The police will test it. They'll be able to match it to Seb. Why did you hurt him? You two are friends. What happened?"

I could see his mind working as he came up with a different story. "It was an accident."

"Then why didn't you call an ambulance? Why did you try to cover it up?"

"I panicked. I had half an hour before people started arriving here for a huge party and I had Seb half dead on the floor. I just wanted him gone."

"You shouldn't have moved him. You could have killed him."

"So what's worse? Being dead or being a vegetable for the rest of his miserable life? He's screwed. He's not getting back to normal from that." Harry's voice had risen. "They should have let him die."

"It's not up to you to decide that kind of thing." I blinked, trying to clear my head. "You put him back where you found him and drove up to the fireworks display. You made a big deal out of being there, so everyone would remember and give you an alibi, but you only turned up at the end."

"People believe what you tell them. I told them I'd been there all evening and everyone remembered me being there all evening. Easy."

My voice sounded as if it was coming from far away. "What did he do to you?"

Harry wavered, then broke. "He was blackmailing me, OK? This poor victim who you're so worried about was a blackmailer. He found out something about me and he threatened to tell everyone. My parents. My friends. He wanted to destroy me. Or have me pay for everything he wanted for the rest of his life. He made me get that phone so he could always get in touch with me. The Harry Hotline, he called it. Very funny." Harry thumped his fist on the back of the sofa. "It was never going to stop. I couldn't say no to him, ever, no matter what he asked, and he was never going to stop."

"What were you trying to hide? What did he find out that was so terrible?"

"I slept with a girl and I shouldn't have."

"That sort of thing happens all the time, though." I shook my head, bewildered. "Why keep it a secret?"

"She wasn't aware I'd done it." He looked up at me, gauging my reaction. "She was pretty out of it at the time."

"You raped her," I whispered.

"That's a very technical term for what we're talking about. There were no consequences for her. She didn't even know it had happened, and neither did anyone else. I wore a condom. I was respectful. I didn't take pictures or video. I didn't make fun of them."

"Them? There was more than one?"

"Slip of the tongue." Then he grinned at me, a naughty little boy caught in the act. "All right. More than one. But it's harmless fun."

"It's rape," I insisted. "If they couldn't consent, you don't know that they would have consented."

"How could they say no to me?" He really meant it.

"Did you drug them?"

He held up his thumb and forefinger a few millimeters apart. "Little bit."

"If they wouldn't have said no, why did they need to be drugged?"

"I can't be bothered with girlfriends. This is less hassle."

I was thinking back to the party—to Lucy Blair with her head lolling as the bouncer carried her up the stairs, at Harry's request. In front of everyone. I felt sick.

"How did Seb know what you'd done?"

"He hid in my room. He wanted to play a trick on me." Harry folded his arms. "Got more than he bargained for."

"Did he try to stop you?"

"No."

"Did you know he was watching?"

"No. Of course not."

"Did he record what you were doing?"

"On his phone." Harry's jaw tightened. "I couldn't get him to delete it. He said it was proof."

"And he blackmailed you."

"Yes. For months."

"But you kept doing it."

"I like it," he said softly. "Anyway, Seb didn't care. He just wanted money and attention and power."

"And access to your drugs. He used them on Lily."

"He needed them. He couldn't stand losing a challenge. He liked to brag that he could pull anyone he liked, and it was a good game to come up with the worst girls imaginable. Once you'd said it, he had to do it. He kissed a few shockers, let me tell you. Lily was different. She was a tough one. She didn't want anything to do with him." Harry shook his head. "I didn't know he was going to take pictures. Amateur hour. My rule is that I never leave any evidence that could be used against me."

"Very sensible. Seb is bad. You're worse." I was struggling to think in a straight line. My thoughts were weaving in and out of one another like drunken Morris dancers. "You tried to kill him."

"We had an argument about how indiscreet he was being. He was showing off too much. He behaved as if he could get away with anything. He'd learned nothing from what happened to him on Saturday night. He was just obsessed with getting revenge on everyone who'd wronged him. He wanted me to make it happen and we argued."

"How did he fall?"

"He was following me to my bedroom. Shouting at me. I

couldn't deal with it and I just turned round and pushed him to make him stop. He fell back against the rail of the walkway. Then he was gone. Over the edge."

"So it was an accident."

"Of course." But he wouldn't look at me.

"Then you can say that to the police. You don't have to say why it happened. But the least you can do is get Guy off the hook." I put one hand to my head. "Oh."

"Are you all right?"

"I feel a bit strange."

"I'm not surprised." He stood up and walked toward me. "All this talk of me drugging girls and you're sitting here as if you're not in danger. What do you think was in the orange juice? Apart from Consolata's perspiration, of course."

"Did you spike my drink?"

"You tell me."

"Stay away from me," I managed to say.

"The hardest bit was keeping you interested while I waited for it to kick in." He looked thoughtful. "It felt good to tell the truth. Like counseling. I should have tried that."

I tried to stand up and he caught me as I fell forward.

"Don't do that. You'll hurt yourself." He pushed me back onto the sofa. It felt like much too much trouble to try to stand up again. I blinked at him a few times, feeling my eyelids getting heavier and heavier. He nodded.

"Just let go."

I didn't want to.

I didn't have any choice.

The room went dark around me, and I was gone.

20

I woke up without the least idea where I was. The sun was slanting in through the window, bathing the room in red light. Sunset. How long had I been asleep?

And why was I on the floor?

I sat up, and wished I hadn't. My head was thumping and I was struggling to focus. I shut my eyes, then regretted it as I felt the room spin around me. Eyes open. Better, but not much.

I looked around, wondering where I was. It was a small room. Wood-paneled walls. A big window. A wooden bench. A rectangular box with a metal tray in the top. A wood-paneled door. A bucket with a ladle in it.

"A sauna. I'm in a sauna." I almost laughed. What a ridiculous place to sleep. I got to my hands and knees and crawled over to the door. I reached up and tried the handle.

Locked.

A fact that was surprising enough to get through the fog that was filling my mind. It made me wonder if I had chosen to sleep in the sauna, or if I had been put there. I jammed the heels of my hands into my eye sockets and sat still for a moment, trying to remember. I had been at Mario's. I had talked to Lily. I had talked to Claudia and Immy. I had talked to Nick. Nick had driven me to—

I sat up. I couldn't remember everything that had happened after I arrived at Harry Knowles's house, but I remembered him watching me as he sat, apparently relaxed, on his big sofa. And that had been around midday. It was the last memory I could be sure of. Everything else was in bits.

But what I could remember made my blood run cold. I ran my hands over my clothes, checking that everything was where it should be. I didn't think I'd been undressed and dressed again. I didn't feel any different.

I couldn't be sure.

Feeling sick, I checked my watch: just after nine. So it was possible, if not likely, that I'd been unconscious for nine hours straight. My mouth was dry, my throat raw, and I looked around for water while I checked my pockets. No water. No phone. No key to the sauna door, magically. Nothing useful.

Nothing that could get me out.

I rubbed my eyes, then squinted at the room. It wasn't me. The sunset was *flickering*. And it was too late for sunset anyway, if my watch was right. I held onto the window ledge and pulled myself up so I could see out.

"Oh. My. God."

It was dark out, the sky as black as tar. The sunset was nothing of the sort. It was the bonfire.

And it was burning out of control.

Even as I watched, the wind pulled a sheet of flames sideways, catching the top branches of a nearby tree. Sparks danced around it, and tiny chips of blazing wood dotted the grass, as if the stars had fallen out of the sky.

The sauna, it occurred to me, was mainly wood too. And it was far too close to the fire for me to feel happy about being locked inside it. I made myself stand unsupported, peering out with my hands cupped around my eyes so I could see if there was anyone in the garden. A friendly fireman, preferably. Someone who could get me out.

The only living thing in the garden was the fire.

And I recalled, with a sick feeling, that Bonfire Night was the one night of the year when a giant blaze at one of Port Sentinel's most exclusive addresses would attract no attention whatsoever. I could see a tiny bit of the bay between two shrubs. The black water made an ideal background for the blazing torches that drifted around the sea like fireflies. Anyone who wasn't looking at the boats would simply assume that Harry's bonfire was like everything else he did: big, dramatic, and over the top.

I needed a plan. Two plans, actually. Plan A was get rescued, which was not going to happen. Plan B was pretty simple. Get out.

I stood up, ignoring the spinning sensation in my head and the fact that my muscles seemed to have been replaced with cotton wool. Now was not the time to faint. Waiting patiently to be saved was just not an option. I was going to save myself.

After two circuits of the sauna looking for anything that might help me do that, I'd found nothing except the stupid ladle. It wasn't heavy enough to break the window, which seemed to be made of toughened glass. I could throw lumps of charcoal at it if I wanted. I could arrange them in a circle around myself and wait to burn.

Not appealing.

Which left the door, and me.

I stood and looked at it. The lock seemed pretty solid. So did the door. On the other hand, I was what you might call highly motivated, and I was wearing boots with heavy soles. I chose a spot just below the lock. The trick was to imagine I was kicking someone standing on the other side. The person who had dumped me in the sauna and left me to burn, ideally. I stood side on to the door, my right leg braced, and kicked the door as hard as I could, landing my heel right on the spot I'd intended to hit.

Thud.

Deep breath. *Thud.*

Deep breath. *Thud.*

The door didn't budge. A rattle on the roof made me stop and look up, which was stupid, because I couldn't see what it was, but I knew. The fire finding something new to burn.

Thud. Thud. Thud.

And the wood started to give. I kicked harder, sobbing under my breath. The frame splintered. The lock loosened. Another kick, and I was getting tired. I wasn't strong enough to do this.

I *had* to.

I took a second, choosing the exact spot where I was going to land the next kick to cause maximum damage. I was getting out.

I kicked, and the door burst open. I must have stared at it for two whole seconds before I went through it, I was so surprised. Surprised and wary, because instead of leading to the outside world, the door opened into a dark, windowless room, and only the light from the fire behind me showed that it was the changing room of the pool house. I half expected to be grabbed as I stepped into the darkness of my own shadow, but the room was empty, and quiet, and the next door I came to was unlocked. It took me a moment to realize that my luck, such as it was, had run out.

The last room in the pool house was fitted out as a gym. Three of the walls were mirrored, and I almost gave myself a heart attack as I saw a movement in the darkness, before I knew it to be my own reflection. There was a running machine, and an elliptical trainer, and an exercise ball and some yoga mats. No free weights. Nothing heavy that I could use to break the sliding glass doors that constituted the fourth wall of the room. The ones that were locked. The ones that showed me the heart-stopping view of the garden, and the house. I'd been wondering why Harry's uptight neighbors hadn't reported the fire, but they probably had. The trouble was, the house was burning too. All that sharply angled, silvered cedar was blazing merrily, as a couple of million pounds of real estate went up in smoke. No one, but no one, was going to be worried about a bonfire and a pool house with all that to look at. That was assuming the firemen even made it to the back garden through the house. I knocked on the glass with my knuckles, hearing the dull sound of reinforced glass. There was no point in kicking that.

I went back through the gym to the changing room and tore through it, looking for something heavy that I could lift and throw. I found towels and laundry baskets and toiletries in quantity, but nothing useful. The air was getting hard to breathe as I got nearer the sauna, and I peered in to see that the roof was starting to go, glowing red, throwing off thick black coils of smoke that made me cough.

Back to the changing room to discover that the water was switched off, so I couldn't even soak a towel and use it to protect myself from the flames.

Back to the gym. Back to the view of hell. I hammered on the glass and called for help, and I might as well not have bothered, except that I couldn't just give up. Giving up was the end, and I wasn't ready for the end yet.

A shadow moved in the dark garden. It flitted in front of the flames so I could see a brief silhouette, and disappeared against the darkness. A man, running. A few endless seconds passed before I saw him again, nearer the fire. I hit the glass again with the flat of my hands, shouting, and either the movement or the sound made him twist round to look at the pool house, then at me. Right at me. He saw me. He ran toward the door and I realized it was Dan Henderson, his face blackened by smoke.

"Jess! Are you all right?"

He was my last hope of survival, but it was still a stupid question. "Not as such."

"I mean, are you injured?" He was pulling at the door.

"No. It's locked," I said, pointing at the handle. I wasn't even sure he could hear me, but he seemed to get the idea.

"Stand back." He pulled a short black stick out of his pocket and shook it, and it turned out to be the police-issue extendable baton.

"Now that would have been useful earlier. I need to get me one of those," I said to myself, moving smartly to the back wall of the gym. I was lightheaded from the aftereffects of the drugs, and the smoke, and the relief of being rescued.

All of which would have been fine if I had actually been rescued. Dan hit the door five or six times, then stood back, shaking his head.

"Oh, you are kidding. Hit it harder!" I yelled, coming over to push on the glass—as if that would make any difference.

He dropped the baton on the ground and held up one finger, then turned and sprinted away. I watched him go. One minute, he'd said. Sixty seconds. I wasn't sure I had that much time left. I was coughing almost constantly.

He was back within the minute, as he'd promised, dragging a wrought-iron patio chair with him. He pointed to me, then to the back of the gym. I went. It was really hard to breathe now.

Dan picked up the chair, hefted it, and threw it as hard as he could at the glass. It smashed through, quite low down, and the whole wall turned to frost. He bent to yell through the hole. "Get over here, Jess. Right now."

I went, crouching, and allowed myself to be dragged through the gap in the glass. Mum's leather jacket bore the brunt of the edges, which was one reason to be glad I couldn't wear my coat. It would have been in ribbons.

"Thanks," I wheezed, collapsing against Dan's chest in a most embarrassing way. "That was not fun."

"Can you walk?"

"I learned ages ago." Still lightheaded. Still coughing too. "I can probably do it. This foot, then that foot—am I right?"

For a second I thought he was going to laugh, but he shook me instead. "Come on, Jess. Sober up. We've got to go."

"OK. I'm fine. Let's go." I almost fell over. "Oops."

"Do I have to carry you?"

"No," I squeaked. "Definitely not."

He put his face close to mine. "Then walk."

I did as I was told. He wrapped an arm around my shoulders, holding me close to him as he did his best to shield me from the fire.

The way out lay through a tiny dark alley that ran along the side of the house. The house was in danger of collapsing, I found out later—which was why the firemen hadn't made it to the back garden. We shouldn't have been anywhere near it, but it was the only way out.

Dan put his mouth to my ear. "Put your head down and run. Don't stop. Don't look back. Don't wait for me if I get held up."

I nodded and did as I was told, for once, with the last of my energy. I came out in front of the house, on a path that ran between tall stands of bamboo. After a few steps it seemed like too much effort to go all the way along it. I sank down to my knees, waiting for Dan. It felt as if I was standing in a furnace, inhaling super-hot air, but I was far enough from the fire to know that the problem wasn't with the air I was breathing, but with me. I tilted my head back and struggled to breathe.

"Bit of help over here!" Dan yelled it over my head. I was glad he'd made it out too. I tried to say as much, but I couldn't think how. Suddenly we were surrounded by people lifting me up, half carrying me to an ambulance beside the gate, where there was oxygen, and a blanket I didn't really need, and paramedics who seemed to know what they were doing and how I was feeling. Dan stood just outside the door, breathing hard, waving away offers of medical assistance every time a paramedic came near him. Every fire engine between Port Sentinel and London seemed to have turned out for the show, and the view I had from my seat in the ambulance was of a sea of big men in high-visibility jackets and helmets unrolling hoses and shouting a lot. It was like watching a film. It was nothing to with me, or what had almost happened to me.

Trudy, the paramedic who was looking after me, was a nice, motherly lady wearing purple mascara. I really wanted to ask her about it but I was too fuzzy-headed.

She fiddled with my oxygen mask. "You're going to be just fine."

I just nodded at her, as if to say, *I know, thanks, lucky old me*, and she seemed to get the idea. She smiled, then leaned out to talk to her crewmate.

"This one is doing well—we can transfer her to hospital when you're ready."

"Good. At least we got one of them."

I struggled up onto my elbows, pulling my oxygen mask away. "Who else?" My voice sounded ridiculously weedy and I coughed, then tried again. "Excuse me, who else were you talking about?"

Dan heard and came to stand in the doorway of the ambulance, glowering. "Never you mind. Concentrate on getting better."

"Tell me." I could feel my heart starting to race.

"The fire crews have found one casualty so far."

"Who?"

"We don't have an official ID at the moment."

"What does that mean? Do you actually not know or are you just being official about it?"

Dan pointed at me, back to being stern. "This doesn't go any further."

"Who am I going to tell? I'm stuck in this ambulance."

"It looks as if it's one of the residents at this address. Harry Knowles."

"And he's dead."

"I'm afraid so."

"Are you sure?"

Dan grimaced. "Am I sure he's dead or am I sure he's Harry Knowles?"

"Both."

"I am very sure he's dead. I am fairly sure he is who I said he is."

"Was he . . . was he burned?" I was shaking.

Dan stared at me, and his expression slowly changed from the usual hostility to something approaching sympathy. "They think he was overcome by the smoke. He was beside the front door."

"He almost made it." I sank back against the pillow Trudy had tucked behind me. "Did he leave any clues? Anything that might say why he started the fire?"

"He started it? Deliberately?"

"Excuse me, can you leave my patient alone?" Trudy clambered back into the ambulance past Dan, her expression stern. "She's not able to talk. She's supposed to be resting."

"I asked him," I said. "I wanted to know."

"With all due respect, young lady, you don't know what's

good for you. Now just be quiet and calm and take nice deep breaths for me."

"I'll be asking you about what happened, Jess. When you're well enough." Dan, marking my card. He wanted to know what I knew. He probably wanted to know all of it. I sat silently, letting Trudy fuss over me, thinking about all the people who had brought me to Harry's door, and how I couldn't possibly tell Dan what I knew about them, and the part they had played in Seb's downfall.

The next minute, all that flew out of my mind as Mum came running toward the ambulance. "Jess? Are you all right?"

I nodded, smiling at her to prove it. She whirled round and hugged Dan, which instantly made me feel worse. "Thank you for saving her."

"Anytime."

"Hopefully not." Mum turned back to me. Dan still had a hand on her back, as if he'd forgotten to take it away. "What were you doing in there?"

"Coughing a lot." I put a hand up to my head, not having to pretend it was throbbing. "Sorry, Mum."

"You can come with us in the ambulance," Trudy said. She looked past Mum. "Not you, though."

Dan nodded. "I thought as much. I'll see you at the hospital, Molly."

"OK."

"I won't be long."

Mum nodded, trying to smile. Dan pulled her into his arms and held her for a moment, the doors of the ambulance hiding the two of them from everyone but me and Trudy. Trudy, who didn't know or care that he shouldn't have been touching her. I glared, outraged, and was ignored. When he let her go, she climbed up the steps and sat on the seat Trudy indicated. She concentrated on putting on her seat belt for so long that my raised eyebrows started to ache.

"What was that?"

"What?" All innocence.

"That. You and Dan."

"Don't start." It was not like Mum to snap. "You don't know what today has been like for everyone else, Jess, because of you. Dan got me through it, and he saved your life. So don't even think about having a go at me. If you're able to talk, you'd better tell me what you were doing here in the first place."

I backed off, all the way. "Sorry, Mum. I'm just really tired."

"Let her rest for now." Trudy, an angel in a green boiler suit. Her crewmate flipped up the steps and she helped him to close the door. "Plenty of time to talk when you're feeling better, Jess."

I nodded. Mum gave me the look—the *I-know-I-let-you-get-away-with-a-lot-but-I*-am-*your-mother* look. Then she reached over to hold my hand, and I knew I wasn't in too much trouble, really. I closed my eyes and gave myself up to the simple enjoyment of being scorched but alive as the ambulance took the road out of Port Sentinel.

21

They kept me in overnight for observation, which is what they do when they can't really find all that much wrong with you but they don't think you should go home yet, just in case. I yearned for my own bed, my own room, my own things, but I couldn't really complain about the narrow, hard hospital bed, or the fact that the room was sweltering, when I was the one who had got myself into hospital in the first place. Mum slept in the chair by my bed, curled up in a ball, and we both woke up every time a nurse came to check on me. Breakfast arrived at six, and even though it was still dark outside, and long before I would usually choose to wake up, I was almost glad it was the end of the night so I could give up on the pretense of getting some rest. From that point on, everyone who came to check on me got the same answer: I was feeling fine. All better. I actually felt like someone had had a barbecue in my throat but it wasn't bad enough to make me want to stay in hospital. I had to wait to be discharged, though, and no one seemed to be in any hurry about that except me.

I wanted out. I wasn't ill and I didn't feel like lying in bed being wan. Lying in bed meant time to think, and I didn't want to think about what had almost happened to me. Every time I closed my eyes I was back in the pool house with no way out, trapped.

When Tilly arrived with Ella and Petra midmorning, I was immensely relieved to see familiar faces, but I was almost more pleased to see they'd brought me some clothes.

"Thank you, thank you, thank you," I said in my new husky voice. I grabbed the bag and disappeared into the bathroom to change out of my horrible hospital gown.

"Feeling better?" Ella asked from outside the door.

"Completely." Then I ruined it by coughing, but shouting wasn't the ideal way to test my voice. I was pale and tired but in clothes I didn't look *ill*.

I came out of the bathroom. "Ta-dah. Oh."

The "oh" was because Dan had arrived while I was in the bathroom. He was leaning against the windowsill, arms crossed, grinning at something Tilly had said. He reminded me very much of his son, and I blinked, making myself focus on the differences between them.

"You do look more like yourself," Mum said. She was holding a cup of coffee tenderly, her hands wrapped around it as if she was actually in love with it. We'd both had a tough night; I wasn't surprised she was feeling emotional about a caffeinated beverage. "Does this mean you're ready to start answering some questions, young lady?"

I sat on the edge of the bed, Ella beside me with her arm around me, Petra on the other side holding my hand.

"Don't be mean, Mrs. Tennant. She's still recovering," Ella said.

"You can't have it both ways," Tilly said. "Either you're better and you're in trouble, or you're ill and you have to stay in hospital. Which is it?"

"Trouble," I said dolefully. "Get it over with."

"What happened?" Mum said.

"I'm not totally sure." I had to be careful, knowing that Dan was listening. I felt fine, but I wasn't as alert as I might have been, and I didn't want to give anything away that I shouldn't about Lily and the others. There was no sense in getting them into trouble. "I went to see Harry because I'd heard he might know something about what happened to Seb Dawson, and I wanted to ask him about it."

"What did he say?"

"That it was an accident." That was one of the things he'd said, anyway.

"Are you sure about that?" Dan asked.

"I'm not sure he was telling the truth, but I remember him saying it." I shook my head. "I can't believe he's dead."

"He tried to kill you," Mum said.

"I think he just wanted me out of the way. He couldn't have known the fire would take hold as it did."

"Except that it seems pretty clear he used an accelerant to spread the flames from the bonfire to the pool house," Dan said.

I considered that and felt sick. Petra squeezed my hand, her face pale.

Dan went on, "The fire investigator is absolutely certain the fire in the house was deliberate. The house was fitted with a sprinkler system and fire alarms that should have triggered an automatic call-out of the local fire station, but the sensors were all switched off. The house is a shell. Everything in it was completely destroyed. Everything burned. The investigator is working on the assumption that whoever set the fire used petrol to get it started, probably in the living room."

Harry had decided to destroy the evidence that he'd injured Seb. He'd decided to kill me so I couldn't share his secret. "The fire . . . was he trying to kill himself?"

"We think it was an accident. We found the remains of a suitcase in the hall, near his body. It looks as if he was leaving but was overcome by the smoke before he could get out."

Which was better than burning to death, I thought. "I wonder where he was going to go. He hated flying."

"I wonder why he felt he had to go." Dan's eyes were on me.

"Guilt, maybe, about Seb."

"Oh, that's the good news." Ella squeezed my arm. "We heard yesterday morning. Seb's awake."

"Awake is one thing. How is he?"

"He's doing well," Dan said. "The doctors say he's likely to make a good recovery. It's too soon to tell how he might be affected in the long term but he seems to be lucid. I'll be having a word with him later."

"Did Harry know he was awake?"

"Would that matter?"

"It would if he thought Seb was going to tell everyone Harry had injured him. Assuming Seb remembers why it happened."

"And why was that?" Dan asked.

"Harry had been drugging girls at his parties for—for fun."

"Fun?" Dan repeated.

"Fun," I said, and glanced at Petra, very briefly.

He got the hint. "I'll have to talk to you about that again."

"I don't know any details, like who, or when. I don't think the victims would know it had happened. He was pretty clever."

Mum and Tilly were both frowning. I reckoned I was about ten seconds from someone working out that he'd drugged me too, and asking the kind of questions I specifically wanted to avoid asking myself.

"What are you going to tell Harry's parents?" I asked Dan. "They'll be devastated."

"I don't want to say anything until I have some evidence of what he did."

"It was his secret," I said. "Maybe it should die with him."

His eyebrows went up. "I didn't think you were a fan of hiding the truth, Jess."

I took the hit. I deserved it. "What good would it do if people knew what he'd done? Or suspected it? They'd have to live with the possibility he'd done something to them. Better not to even know anything like that happened. He's been punished, after all."

I saw Dan work it out and I held his gaze, warning him not to say anything in front of Mum and the others. You can say a lot with a look, when you have to.

"What's the last thing you remember?" Dan asked.

"Sitting on the sofa drinking orange juice."

"What time?"

"Just after twelve."

"And when did you wake up?"

"Around nine."

"In the pool house."

"Locked in the sauna," I said.

"Properly locked in."

"Yes. No key."

"Did you try the door?"

"A couple of times." *Believe it or not.*

"How did you get out?"

"I kicked the door until it broke."

Mum made some exclamation and I turned to check she was all right. Tilly was kneeling beside her chair, her head leaning against Mum's shoulder.

"It was fine, Mum. I just aimed for the wood near the lock. That's where it's most likely to give, because the lock is stronger than the wood so when you kick it the wood gives way. The doorframe goes or the door does. Either way, you get out."

"I don't want to know where you learned that," Dan said. "Or why."

"We did self defense in school in London. The teacher was pretty amazing. He was ex-SAS. He showed us all sorts of things about how to escape if you were kidnapped."

"I'd have tried to pick the lock," Ella said.

"I was all out of hairpins. Besides, I'd still be there, probably. Much easier to boot it open."

"If I'd known you had SAS training I'd have been a lot less worried," Dan said.

"I still couldn't have got out of the pool house without your help."

Mum gave a little sigh, as if she was on the verge of tears but holding them back.

"We had a bad time of it yesterday, Jess," Tilly said. "No one knew where you were."

"I'm sorry."

"It was just like when Freya went missing. Except with a happier ending."

Mum reached out and held onto her twin, the two of them looking more alike than ever. Both looked strained, with shadows under their eyes. I felt guilty, and ashamed of myself for having taken the risk of confronting Harry without even thinking I might have been putting myself in danger.

"You need to be more careful," Dan said. "You should have spoken to me."

"You had Guy in custody and you didn't want to hear about anything else," I pointed out. His face flushed with anger but I wouldn't back down. I didn't have to feel bad about that. He hadn't given me the least encouragement to come and talk to him about what I'd found out, probably because he was so keen to hush up Seb's less-than-perfect past.

Still, I did owe him one. "Thank you for rescuing me. How did you know where to find me?"

"Luck," Dan said.

"We were looking for you from early afternoon," Ella said. "You didn't show up for lunch and your phone was off and it just wasn't like you. Hugo called Will to see if you were with him and he said he hadn't seen you since the night before. He was crazy worried about you."

"Everyone was concerned." Dan's voice was heavy with disapproval.

"We went all over town trying to find you," Ella said. "No one had seen you since yesterday morning. Those two girls from the party—Claudia and Immy—they helped. So did Ryan. And loads of people from your school."

"Did they?" Weirdly, I felt like crying.

"We knocked on a lot of doors."

"I had my men out looking for you too," Dan said. "It wasn't just the Famous Five and friends."

"You didn't find her, though." Ella blinked at him, all innocence. "We did. Or rather, Will did."

Dan rubbed his chin and said nothing. Mentally, I awarded Ella all the points from that encounter.

"How did Will know where to find me?"

"He bumped into Nick," Mum said. "Yesterday evening. Quite late. Nick said he'd dropped you at Harry's house."

Ella took over. "Will just ran as soon as he heard where you were. Hugo and I went back for the car and followed him. By the time we got there we could smell smoke in the air, and Will had gone over the gate. He opened it up for us. The house was already on fire but he couldn't get inside—"

"Which was fortunate," his father interjected dryly.

"—so we called the police and fire station. They were there incredibly quickly."

"And that was when I turned up," Dan said. "I was not so keen on Will proving he could be a hero."

"You were quite scary." Ella was watching Dan as warily as if he was a fully grown lion. She was right. He might look tame but he could turn at any minute.

"When I have to be scary, I can be scary."

Or when you feel like it, I added silently.

"Well, you didn't give Will much of a chance to argue," Ella said.

"I didn't see you and Hugo at the house. Or Will," I said. It had been bothering me, a bit. Not that I had expected him to be the one who rescued me, but if he'd been there it was hard to know he hadn't even tried to come and see me.

"We were behind the cordon. And Will was . . ." She trailed off, looking from me to Dan.

"He was in the back of the patrol car," Dan said. "I locked him in there."

"Like a prisoner?"

"He wouldn't do what he was told. He tried to go round the back of the house, down that little alley. It wasn't safe. The wall was going to go at any minute."

"That was the way you went," I said. "Twice. That was how we got out of the garden, wasn't it?"

"That was different. We didn't have any choice."

"You had a choice when you went down there. You didn't have to go into the garden to check if I was there."

"On the contrary, I wouldn't have been doing my job if I hadn't." Dan smiled at me and I felt the warmth of his charm, briefly. "I don't think any of us could have forgiven ourselves if we'd missed the chance to save you."

"Well, you didn't miss it. And here I am."

"Yes, you are." Dan got off the windowsill. "I'm not finished with you, Jess. I want to talk to you about Harry again later. See if you can remember anything at all that might be useful."

"I will." I watched him walk toward the door and felt uneasy. "Are you going to talk to Seb?"

"Yeah. Later on. His doctor told me to give him as much

time as I could to recover. I can't really tell him it's urgent given that the main suspect is dead."

I refrained from pointing out that Dan had never really acted as if it was all that urgent to find out what had happened to Seb. Then again, his mind had been on other things.

As if he'd heard what I was thinking, Dan stopped at the door and looked at Mum. "Has your ex-husband been in yet? I thought I'd find him here."

"He's coming in later." She didn't look as if the idea made her particularly happy.

"What day is it?" I asked, suddenly suspicious. "Thursday? Isn't he supposed to be going back to London?"

Tilly sniffed. "No one's told you."

"Told me what?"

"Told her what?" Dan demanded from his position by the door.

"He's staying in Port Sentinel. He's going to start up his business here. He says there are great opportunities here for him— people who can afford to pay for his advice." Mum looked at me and shrugged. "We made living here look like too much fun, I suppose."

"I don't believe it," I said softly. "Why would he do that?"

"Because he wants to. Because he can," Tilly said. The only person who looked even less enthusiastic than her was Dan.

"This town has enough problems without adding Christopher Tennant to the list."

"I couldn't agree more," I said, and again had the unsettling experience of getting a proper smile from Dan Henderson and, stranger still, liking it.

22

Inevitably, Dad turned up at the hospital at completely the wrong moment. His instinct for being where he wasn't wanted amounted to a gift. I had been packing my things, hoping to encourage the doctors to get a move on with giving me permission to go, when there was a knock at the door.

"Come in."

Ryan leaned round it. "Are you sure? It's me."

"Especially if it's you. I thought it was going to be an annoying nurse."

He came all the way in, looking tall and stunningly handsome in a blue polo shirt that brought out the color of his eyes. "I thought you'd be in bed."

I grinned. "So you dashed here as quickly as you could."

"Any excuse." He stayed on the other side of the room and shoved his hands in his pockets, as if he was making doubly sure he wasn't tempted to try to touch me. "Seriously, shouldn't you be sitting down or something?"

"I feel fine." I paused to cough theatrically. When I could speak I said, "I just do that every so often. No big deal."

"You nearly died but it's no big deal."

"*Nearly* is the important part." I concentrated on folding a top Ella had brought in for me. "Thanks for trying to find me. I hear you were part of the search party."

"I'd never have forgiven myself if anything had happened to you."

"I don't know why." I was irritated in spite of myself. "It wasn't your responsibility to keep me safe."

"You didn't really give me a chance to try."

"I didn't know I was going to need rescuing. If I'd been calling for help, you'd have been on the list."

"That's something, I suppose." There was a bitter edge to his voice.

"I'm sorry," I said softly. "I'm just not that person."

"Which person?"

"The girl who needs looking after. You want someone who'll depend on you, who'll need you, and that's not me."

"You're wrong. I like that you're independent."

"It drives you mad."

"You do drive me mad. Completely." His voice was matter-of-fact, but the way he was looking at me . . . I felt a tiny shiver race over my skin. My brain was telling me to make a joke, to put him off, to change the subject and the mood, but my body was all about Ryan and whether I could get him to come a little closer.

Which was confusing. Because, after all, there was Will.

What I was thinking must have shown on my face, because he moved toward me. "Jess—"

"Jessica?" Dad breezed in without knocking. Seeing Ryan, he stopped. "Oh. Am I interrupting?"

"Dad, this is Ryan. Ryan, my dad."

Ryan shook hands with him. "Pleased to meet you, sir."

Sir. I could see from the look on Dad's face that he loved it. Was it possible for Ryan to be any more perfect?

"I just wanted to see if Jess was OK. I'll go," Ryan said, heading for the door.

"I don't want to get in the way." Dad was smirking. "I'm sure Jessica would much rather talk to you any day."

"I'd rather talk to anyone, actually. Up to and including any serial killers or dictators you can think of."

"Childish of you." Dad's face had gone tight with anger but he managed to smile. "Jessica and I have a relationship based on banter. You mustn't take her seriously."

Ryan looked at me, trying to work out what was going on.

"Banter? That's one word for it." I zipped my bag closed and dumped it on the floor. "Thanks for coming, Ryan."

"Give me a call."

"I will," I promised. I would too, even if it was just to explain why I was so hostile to my dad. It would be better to keep Ryan at the other end of a phone call, I thought. Face-to-face contact with him was getting to be distinctly risky. The more I saw of him, the more I liked him. I'd have wanted to see a lot more of him if I hadn't been worried about leading him on. I'd come perilously close to that already.

Ryan nodded to me, said good-bye to Dad and left.

Dad turned to me with a wide grin. "He seems like a nice boy."

"He's OK."

"Why don't you go out with him?"

"Why don't you stay out of it?" I took a moment to breathe. "Mum said you're staying in Port Sentinel."

"That's right."

"You hate it here."

"It's full of potential clients."

"And Mum's here."

"And Molly is here."

I was so angry, I felt as if I was choking. I managed to keep my voice level. "Do you know what I don't get? What makes you think she would be interested in picking up where you left off?"

"I won her once. I took her away from here, even though she was in love with Dan Henderson." Dad shrugged. "I think I can do it again."

"But why?"

"Because I love her. And I don't like losing."

I discounted the first sentence, but the second part had the ring of truth to it. "This isn't a game. She's not your prize."

"She's my wife."

"She was. You got divorced." I shook my head. "I don't know why you don't get this."

"Where is she, anyway?" Dad looked around as if she might have been hiding behind the door or in a cupboard all along.

"She's not here. And you've done your loving-father bit. I'm alive. You've seen me to check I'm all right. You've ticked that box. You can go."

"What about telling you off and warning you not to do it again?"

"I'll take it as read."

Instead of leaving, he sat down in the armchair by the bed. "I think I'll wait here for your mother."

"In that case, I'll go." I walked out, leaving him and all my things behind, and bumped straight into Dan Henderson just outside the door.

"What do you want?" I snarled.

Dan looked surprised, but then his face settled back into his usual expression: cold disapproval. "I wanted to talk to you in private, without an audience of family and friends."

"About what?" I was standing with my back to the door and he leaned round me to turn the handle. "Don't go in there," I warned.

"Why not?"

"Dad's in there."

Dan's expression darkened. "So he's turned up at last, has he?"

"And I wish he hadn't bothered." I looked down the hall. "Isn't there an empty waiting room somewhere we could borrow?"

"Yeah. This way."

I think Dan was surprised I was willing to talk to him, but I had questions of my own for him.

He didn't waste any time once he'd shut the door to the small, airless room he'd found. He stayed standing but I curled up on a chair. I wasn't feeling all that great, truth be told.

"Did something happen to you yesterday, Jess?"

"You mean apart from being drugged and smoke-damaged? I don't think so."

"But you don't know."

"I don't know."

Dan swore under his breath. He took a turn around the room, pacing like a big cat in a cage. "Can I take the clothes you were wearing for forensic analysis?"

"Why? What good would it do?"

"It could prove what happened, either way."

"I'd rather not know," I said, and meant it.

"I'm sorry."

"Why are you sorry? It's not your fault. Anyway, I'm almost sure he didn't do anything. He had all that fire-setting and packing to get on with."

"I didn't handle this case very well," Dan said. I stared up at him, surprised into silence. The next thing he said was much more in character. "But you should have stayed out of it."

"Harry would have got away with it," I pointed out. "He'd be choosing his next victim. And Guy would be looking at prison."

"He'd have got a slap on the wrist. He'd have pleaded guilty to assault for the fight, and everything else would have been brushed under the carpet."

"Why? Why would you want to hang everything on Guy? What did he do to you?"

"Nothing." Dan sat down. "I wanted to protect Lily Mancini. You know she came to see me to make a complaint against Seb Dawson. I told her to forget about it."

"Why didn't you just investigate what she told you?"

"There was no evidence. She'd have been destroyed in a trial. It would have done more harm than good."

"So you thought she'd taken matters into her own hands."

"I assumed that, yes." He leaned forward, elbows on his knees. "Look, Jess, I don't expect you to understand but I don't like seeing young girls like you and Lily get hurt. I wanted to help her. I want to help you."

"You were afraid you'd get in trouble for not taking Lily seriously when she made the original complaint. And then Mrs. Dawson discouraged you from investigating what really happened, which suited you fine."

"She wanted to protect her husband from finding out what Seb is really like."

"That's truer than you know."

Dan tilted his head to one side. "What does that mean?"

"Forget it."

"Still keeping secrets."

"This one isn't mine to share." I stood up. "Is that everything?"

"Pretty much."

"Can I go?"

"Be my guest."

I hesitated. "Mr. Henderson . . . please don't tell anyone about Harry and what he might have done."

"I won't."

"Anyone. Especially not Mum."

"I promise."

"Or Will."

He looked at me for what seemed like a long time before he nodded. I was expecting another lecture on keeping away from Will, but he didn't say anything. Maybe he felt he'd made his feelings clear already. Or maybe he'd realized there was no point in trying to tell me what to do.

I left him there and risked going back to my room, where I found Dad had got bored and gone home, as I had expected.

I decided not to tell Mum he'd been there. *Dad who?* was what I was going for from now on. It came to something when I would willingly have a tête-à-tête with Dan instead of spending time with my own father. Irritating though he was, I'd still choose Dan, every time.

I just hoped Mum didn't have to make that choice any time soon.

Later that day, I padded along the corridor in search of room 322. It was the private room where Seb Dawson was recuperating now that he was well enough to leave intensive care. I was packed and ready to go but I'd told Mum I had one last thing to do before we left the hospital.

"What sort of one last thing?" She pushed her hair back off her forehead. "Be specific."

"Don't you trust me?"

"Frankly, no." It was weird. One minute we were having our usual sort of conversation, bickering a little but generally cheerful. The next, Mum's face was streaked with tears. "I worry about you, Jess. You think you know what you're doing. You think you don't need any help from anyone. Sometimes it's a sign of strength to admit you need a hand."

"I know that."

"And I know you think I'm hopeless, but I might actually be able to help now and then."

"Not with this," I said and patted her knee. "But with other things, definitely."

"It breaks my heart that you think you have to look after me. That's not how it's supposed to be."

"I don't mind."

"I do."

"Look, Mum, I just want to go and see Seb, to wish him all the best with his recovery."

"I didn't even know you were friends with him. I am so out of touch with your life. I'm such a bad mother."

"Not really." Now I felt bad. "I only know him from school. But since we're in the same building and he's awake, I thought I might as well go and see him. You know how boring hospital is."

Mum nodded. "Off you go. I'll see you downstairs in reception. Don't be long."

I was doing fine until I bumped into Seb's dad coming out of his room. He looked so much more cheerful than the last time I'd seen him that I almost didn't recognize him, but he spotted me.

"Jess! I'm so glad you're here."

"Is he awake?" *Has he said anything about not having a girlfriend?*

"He's sitting up." Seb's dad rubbed his chin. "You know, he's probably still a bit confused. The reason we haven't been in touch to get you to come and see him is because he hasn't asked for you, I'm afraid. We should have reminded him, but—"

"Oh, don't worry." Weak with relief, I added, "You know what Seb's like. Always keeps his private life to himself."

"Yes, he does." Mr. Dawson beamed down at me. "Do you want to go in and see him?"

"Just for a minute . . ." I hesitated. "Is he on his own?"

"Stephanie is in there. Send her out, though. Don't take no for an answer."

Awkward . . .

Seb's dad was carrying on, blithely unaware of what I was thinking. "I'll make sure you get some time together. I'll keep guard on the door so no one interrupts you."

"Oh." I'd gone red. "There's no need. I mean, I just wanted a word with him in private."

"Of course. But you don't need any interruptions." I could tell he didn't believe we were just going to talk. He actually winked. "Don't tire him out."

I shot into Seb's room and shut the door. Even if I'd been nervous about talking to him, prolonging the conversation with his dad was unthinkable.

If I'd been worried about interrupting a tender scene, I needn't have bothered. Mrs. Dawson was sitting in a chair a long way from the bed, the ever-present magazine open on her lap. Seb was leaning against a stack of pillows. His face had healed a lot since I'd seen him on Monday but it was still pretty dramatically swollen and covered in stitches. It was hard to read his expression but I thought he looked surprised. "Hello."

"Hi." I walked over to the foot of the bed. "How are you feeling?"

"Like crap. Jess, isn't it?"

"That's right."

"I thought you two were going out," Mrs. Dawson said, suddenly suspicious.

"And I thought you two weren't having an affair," I said. "But then I saw Seb's phone."

Mrs. Dawson put her hand to her mouth. Seb sat up. "What do you want?"

"Straight to the point. I like it." I sat down on the edge of the bed. "Not to blackmail you, if that's what's worrying you. But for the record, I think what you did was disgusting and you should both be ashamed of yourselves. Especially you, Mrs. Dawson."

"Don't tell anyone," she said. "Please."

"I don't want Beth to know about it so I won't. But I think it was completely grim."

"It was a one-time thing. Bad judgment. It'll never happen again."

"Damn right it won't," Seb said, glowering at his stepmother. So the hostility wasn't faked, after all. At least Mrs. Dawson had been honest about that.

"I saw your husband outside," I said to her. "I think he's waiting for you."

She jumped up and hurried to the door. She didn't look at me or Seb as she left the room, but I saw her rearranging her face into a brittle smile for Mr. Dawson's benefit. I wasn't sure if I felt more sorry for him or for her.

"What do you want?" Seb asked again.

"Your little sister asked me to find out why all this happened to you."

"Did she?" He looked wary. "Did you?"

"I've been talking to lots of people about you this week. People you upset. People you hurt. People who had every reason to want to get back at you for the things you did to them. You ended up in here because of the way you behaved, and it's time for that to change."

"Is this going to be a lecture? Should I take notes?"

"Whatever helps you to remember it." I folded my arms. "I came to one conclusion, Seb. You are a really unpleasant person. You take advantage of people for your own fun. You started all this. If you hadn't been blackmailing Harry Knowles instead of reporting him to the cops, he wouldn't have tried to kill you. And me, for that matter."

"They told me he's dead."

"That's on your conscience too. I'd think twice about talking to the police about why he attacked you. You don't come out of it well."

Seb shook his head, but he wasn't looking me in the eye any more.

"Do you know what most people said to me? They said you had it coming. How does that make you feel?"

"I don't care."

"If I was in hospital, in intensive care, I'd like to think someone would worry about me." I looked around. "No *Get Well Soon* cards, Seb. You've been here for almost a week."

"Have you just come here to make me feel worse about myself? Seriously?"

"Pretty much. The things you've done are unforgivable."

"So?"

"So now would be the perfect time for you to pretend that knock on the head has changed your personality. You get a second chance." I stood up. "I used the word *unforgivable*, but other people are nicer than me. You might find they're prepared to accept your apologies, if you really mean them."

"I've got nothing to apologize for," he said.

"Just everything you did and everything you said." I shook my head. "You must be such an unhappy person to behave the way you do. Why don't you try doing things differently for a change? See how it goes."

He didn't answer me. I stood up and went to the door, then stopped. "You know, I was wrong. There was one person who was genuinely upset you were in here. Beth loves you. Even when I had to tell her you had done some terrible things, she still felt the same way. She's your sister and she cares about you, even knowing what the real you is like. It might not even change her mind if she knew what you'd done with her mother, but I'm not going to test her and I suggest you don't either."

He put a hand up to cover his eyes, struggling not to cry.

"You don't deserve to have a sister like her at the moment," I said. "But one day, you might."

He gave a proper sob. I felt a glow of satisfaction that evaporated as I remembered one more thing I needed to mention. I stopped at the door.

"By the way—if your dad says anything to you about me, just play along with it, OK?"

"What sort of thing?" Seb looked at me, red-eyed.

"He thinks I'm your girlfriend."

"What?"

"Long story. Anyway, for the avoidance of doubt, we just broke up."

I left without waiting for a fond good-bye. I'd said what I could. It was up to him to decide what to do. I didn't know if he could change, even if he wanted to.

I really hoped he would try.

23

I couldn't see a thing. I blinked, and it made no difference.

"Mum?"

"Is the door closed behind you?"

"Completely."

"Are you sure?"

I know how to close a door. "Yes," I said sweetly. "All closed."

There was a rattle and the door to the darkroom opened. Red light spilled out into the little space where I stood.

"Come in, quickly."

I did as I was told, fitting myself into the very small space beside Mum. As darkrooms go, it wasn't the most lavish or spacious arrangement. Jack had made it in one of the sheds behind Sandhayes. The windowless outer room had storage space for prints, but nothing else. It was basically just where you waited to be allowed into the darkroom itself, so you didn't let any daylight in. The darkroom wasn't much bigger than the outer room. Mum didn't mind puttering around in the dim,

cluttered space, but I always felt as if I was going to knock something over or brush against a drying print or spill some chem-
icals or cause some sort of disaster. Mum sent most of her
pictures away to be printed, but she liked to experiment with
different techniques, for fun, and she was always happy in the
red glow of the darkroom lamp.

"How is it going?"

"Fine." She checked the time. "I have about five more minutes before I have to go to work. It's going to be busy. Satur-
days are always hectic and the tourists will be heading home
tomorrow, so they'll shop today."

"I'm glad you're going back to the gallery."

"Me too."

"Nick must have been very persuasive."

She looked sideways at me. "What are you getting at?"

"Well, he got you to come out of your room."

"I meant to talk to you about that. I can't believe you told
him I was hiding."

"You were. So what did he say?"

"Nothing." In the red light I couldn't see if she was blushing or not.

"Nothing," I repeated.

"Just that he wanted me to come back to work and he
thought I was doing a good enough job."

"I see."

"Stop, Jess."

"I didn't say anything. It's your guilty conscience that makes
you think I'm implying something."

"Too complicated for me," Mum said, shaking her head.
"There. I'm done."

"Speaking of guilty consciences . . ."

"Go on?" She was tidying up and I watched her hands, waiting to see if they stilled.

"About Dan."

She didn't miss a beat. "What about him?"

"I keep getting the impression that you've been sneaking around with him."

"Sneaking around." She looked at me, her expression ironic. "Does that sound like me?"

"No, but—"

"No. Your impression is wrong."

"Have you see him? Alone?"

"Once or twice. We talk." She was washing her hands, the water running loudly into the sink. "We have a lot to talk about. I like spending time with him. But not in the way you're thinking."

"What way is that?"

"Romantically. That's all over." She sounded definite.

"I don't think it's over for him."

A one-shouldered shrug. "You can't control other people's feelings. You know that."

I did. "But you were madly in love."

"Once upon a time. It was very intense and short-lived. That sort of thing doesn't last forever."

And yet I couldn't imagine ever thinking about Will without the sharp twist of regret that we couldn't be together.

"Have you told Dan that's how you feel?"

"What I've told him is none of your business." Mum dried her hands and pointed to the door. "Come on. Let's get out of here."

"But if he thinks you might be interested—" I walked backward so I could watch her expression.

"He doesn't. He knows exactly how I feel, believe me. I know you're just doing your best to look after me, but you can stop with the moral panic. I haven't done anything wrong, and neither has Dan. We were friends before we were involved with one another, and we're friends now. That's all."

I felt reassured. I didn't think Mum would ever lie to me. And if she tried, she could never be that convincing.

Outside the shed, there was a battered garden bench. I sat down on it, and after another look at her watch Mum joined me. It was a beautiful morning, cold and clear, and the dew made every cobweb look like strings of pearls.

"What about Dad?"

"What about him?" Her tone was much less encouraging.

"You know he wants you back."

"Ugh." She rolled her eyes. "As if."

"OK," I said. "Good."

"Is that everything?" Mum ticked it off on her fingers. "Nick, Dan, your father. Anyone else?"

"You tell me."

"I hope not," she said seriously. "That's enough for anyone."

"And you thought we were going to have a quiet life down here."

"I should have known *you* wouldn't. Can we stop with the near-death experiences, by the way? Two is too many."

"I'll do my best," I promised.

"In other news of remarkable resurrections, your coat came back from the cleaner's while you were in hospital."

"Seriously? How is it?"

"Good as new." She corrected herself. "Good as vintage, anyway. It's hanging up in my room. I forgot to say."

"Brilliant." I stretched. "I love your leather jacket but it stinks of smoke."

"To high heaven," Mum agreed. "And it's covered in scratches. I'm never lending you anything again."

"It saved my skin."

"Did you ever find out who stole your coat in the first place?"

"I didn't bother." I was almost certain it had been Claudia, or Immy, or both of them, showing off so everyone would remember seeing them at the disco. There was no point in asking them about it now. We'd moved on. I'd seen enough that week to think seeking revenge was a bad idea. "I've got it back now. No harm done."

She checked the time again, clicked her tongue and stood up. "I'd better go. I don't want to be late."

"Mum, can I ask you something?"

She sat back down because she was that sort of mother. "Of course."

"Will said he had a picture you took in his locker at school. Which one is it?"

She tilted her head to one side, considering. "Why?"

"I don't know. I just—I didn't know he had one. I suppose I want to see it to know what makes him happy."

Mum nodded. "Because you care about him."

"He just seems so far away at school. I want to know what he looks at when he thinks of home."

"Wait there." She got up and went into the shed, reappearing a minute later with a cardboard folder. "This is the one."

I opened the folder and caught my breath from sheer surprise. It was a picture from the summer, a close-up of me. I was looking past the camera rather than at it, and I'd never seen myself look quite like that—happy and sad and full of love and longing at the same time. I didn't get the shiver of self-consciousness that usually came with seeing a photograph of myself. It was less a picture of me than of what I was feeling. Apparently, I had been feeling all the feelings in the world.

"I've never seen this before. Why have I never seen this before?"

"You don't usually like seeing pictures of yourself."

"How did Will know about it?"

"I got it printed with lots of others I took in the summer. I had the prints all spread out on the kitchen table, and you know how slippery they are. Some of them fell off the edge. Will helped me pick them up." She smiled, remembering. "He picked this one up and he just stopped. He kept looking at it. In the end I asked him if he'd like to keep it, and he said he'd thought I was never going to ask."

"I don't remember you taking my picture at all."

"You didn't know I'd taken it."

"What was I doing?"

"You were in the garden. That's evening light." She tilted the picture to look at it, with a technical eye rather than a mother's. "Not bad."

"What was I looking at?"

"Do you need to ask?" She smiled. "The reason you didn't notice me was because you only had eyes for Will."

I handed it back to her. "Thank you."

She put it on the bench beside her. "You know, Jess, if you want to be with Will, you should be."

"You are literally the only person who doesn't think it's a terrible idea."

"And you two are literally the only people who count in all this." Mum put her arm around my shoulders. "Forget about Will's parents, and your dad, and anyone else who has a view. If you want to be with each other, be together."

"What if we're together and something happens to his mum and he ends up regretting it?"

"What if you miss your chance to be together and regret that more? I know you think you've got forever to be together, but look at me and Dan. That's the only lesson you should take from us, but it's a big one. Sometimes now is all you get." She stood up. "And by a lovely coincidence, now is when I need to leave."

"Thank you," I said again, meaning it. She nodded and walked away through the long grass, leaving tracks in the dew. I pulled my knees up to my chest, shut my eyes, and lifted my face to the sun. I sat for a little while, thinking about life, and how good it was to be a part of it, and how I had had enough drama for a while, up to and including almost dying a couple of times.

A bird was cheeping nearby, short joyful sounds that cut the air into slivers of gold. Even as I listened, it spilled over into a flurry of complaint, a waterfall of sound. I opened my eyes to see Diogenes shoot past my feet, followed gamely by Aristotle. Ari was twice Di's size and sounded like a charging rhino as he disappeared into the undergrowth. I watched the grasses wave and settle into stillness after the cats had passed, peace reasserting itself.

"All by yourself?"

Will was standing in front of me, his hands in his pockets.

My heart dissolved into a cloud of butterflies that battered against my chest wall, trying to get out. "I didn't know you were there."

"You were distracted." He looked around. "Where's Ella? Has she gone back to London yet?"

"Not until tonight. She's with Hugo and I'm staying out of the way."

Will grinned. "You didn't get to see that much of her, did you?"

"I think she enjoyed her trip. That's the main thing." I hugged my knees. "Also, I've never seen Hugo so goofy over someone. I have hours of teasing saved up for when she goes back."

"Don't be too hard on Hugo. He really likes her."

"Spoilsport." I looked up at him. "Are you going to stand there all day or do you want to sit down?"

"I was just waiting to be invited. You might have wanted to be alone."

"No. On my own but not wanting to be, particularly."

He settled beside me, stretching his legs out. "This is the kind of thing I miss at school."

"Just sitting?"

"Exactly." He didn't say anything else and we sat in silence for a minute or two while words tumbled over one another in my brain. He wasn't even looking at me and I couldn't seem to form a sentence.

What I ended up saying was the opposite of romantic. "Your dad saved my life."

"I know."

"I'm not sure I said thank you properly."

"Don't worry about it. It's his job."

"That's what he said." I squeezed my hands between my knees, on edge. "And thank you for not giving up on finding me. If you hadn't worked out where I was, I probably wouldn't be here."

"I should have just looked in all the most dangerous places in Port Sentinel. Generally, that's where you'll be."

"I didn't know talking to Harry was going to be dangerous."

"If you *had* known, you'd still have done it. Your trouble is that you're not afraid of anything." He looked at me sideways. "Actually, that's not true. There's one thing that makes you absolutely terrified."

"What's that?"

"Being with me."

"You don't scare me." I played with the laces on my trainers, trying to decide what to say. The truth seemed like the best option. "What scares me is how risky this is. The chances of it all going wrong are too high."

"I disagree."

"I can't make you happy. I thought I could, but I can't, and I don't want to be the reason you're sad."

He raised one eyebrow. "You're not that bad."

I nudged him with my toe. "Sad because of being sent away."

"Oh. What if I told you I don't mind? The only thing I miss when I'm away is you."

"That's not true."

A gleam from the silver-gray eyes. "How do you know that?"

"You must miss your home. Your mum."

"I worry about her," Will said, choosing his words with care. "But I don't miss being there. It's not easy, with her. Sometimes I need to get away from her." He winced. "That makes me sound like a terrible person."

"No, it doesn't." I was thinking of Karen in her room, spinning bitterness and lies like a spider. I'd felt trapped after five minutes.

"You must have noticed that I basically live here at Sandhayes. It's not just because you're here, or because I like Tilly's cooking. I can't stand being in the house. If Dad's not there, Mum's fretting about where he is. If he is there, they fight, or Dad fights with me." He looked at me again. "I wouldn't mind being away at all if I could take you with me."

"I thought I was ruining your life."

"Only by refusing to be a part of it." He reached out and ran his fingers down the back of my neck. "Which is just stubborn and wrong."

"I was trying to do the right thing." It was hard to think, when he was touching me. It was hard to breathe, even.

"Breaking up with me made you miserable. It made me miserable too. That doesn't seem right."

There were so many reasons to think it was a bad idea, though, for all that I liked him and he liked me. It wasn't that simple. It would never be that simple, with Will. And I'd struggled to keep my life together when we'd broken up after only a few weeks. People kept telling me I should avoid danger, but I couldn't think of much that was riskier than trusting him with my heart.

Then again, taking risks was sort of my thing.

I unfolded myself and leaned toward him. "If we get back together, I don't want to try to hide it any more."

"If we get back together I'll try to forget you lied to me."

Brought up short, I leaned all the way back. "I didn't!"

"You did. You said it was just a holiday fling. *A meaningless holiday fling* was the exact phrase, I think."

"I wanted you to forget about me."

"I could never do that." The gray eyes were steady on mine. "Jess, I've got twenty-six hours until I have to leave for school. I'll need to sleep and eat, but I calculate that leaves seventeen hours, give or take a few minutes. I'd like to spend them kissing you. How does that sound?"

"Ambitious," I managed to say. "What about saying goodbye to people?"

"I'll write." He drew me toward him.

"What about packing?"

"That'll take two minutes." His mouth curved in the almost-smile that made me shiver.

"What about homework?"

"Now you're being silly." He slid a hand round the back of my neck and buried his fingers in my hair.

"What about—"

And then Will's mouth was on mine and every thought in my head whirled away like fallen leaves.

Sometimes now is all you get. It's OK, though.

Sometimes now is all you need.

Acknowledgments

I am tremendously grateful to the following people, without whom Jess would not exist:

The lovely Lauren Buckland, a wonderful editor, cat-lover, and friend, who gets every cultural reference, no matter how obscure. She encouraged me to make *Bet Your Life* even darker than the first draft was, and made it so much better in the process.

Sophie Nelson, super copy editor. Among many other corrections, she made all my days and dates match up—no mean feat.

Publicists Lisa Mahoney, Alex Taylor, and Harriet Venn have done a great job of looking after me.

Ariella Feiner, who is so much more than an agent. Always incisive and supportive, she's an ideal reader and my best asset. Her colleagues at United Agents are just as important in introducing Jess to readers around the world.

Emma Young, who I don't see often enough, brightens my

day every time I hear from her. She's a truly gifted editor and writer, and this book is dedicated to her.

Finally, my thanks to my lovely family, all of whom support me and encourage me in many different ways. The one who helped most in writing this book is undoubtedly NOT Fred, my cat, who likes to sleep on my hands when I'm typing—but I love him anyway.